T0050038

AND JUSTICE FOR MALL

Also by E.J. Copperman

Jersey Girl Legal mysteries

INHERIT THE SHOES *
JUDGMENT AT SANTA MONICA *
WITNESS FOR THE PERSECUTION *
AND JUSTICE FOR MALL *

Haunted Guesthouse mysteries

NIGHT OF THE LIVING DEED
AN UNINVITED GHOST
OLD HAUNTS
CHANCE OF A GHOST
THE THRILL OF THE HAUNT
INSPECTOR SPECTER
GHOST IN THE WIND
SPOUSE ON HAUNTED HILL
THE HOSTESS WITH THE GHOSTESS
BONES BEHIND THE WHEEL

Asperger's mysteries (with Jeff Cohen)

THE QUESTION OF THE MISSING HEAD
THE QUESTION OF THE UNFAMILIAR HUSBAND
THE QUESTION OF THE FELONIOUS FRIEND
THE QUESTION OF THE ABSENTEE FATHER
THE QUESTION OF THE DEAD MISTRESS

Mysterious Detective mysteries

WRITTEN OFF
EDITED OUT

Agent to the Paws mysteries

DOG DISH OF DOOM
BIRD, BATH, AND BEYOND

* *available from Severn House*

AND JUSTICE FOR MALL

E.J. Copperman

SEVERN
HOUSE

First world edition published in Great Britain and the USA in 2022
by Severn House, an imprint of Canongate Books Ltd,
14 High Street, Edinburgh EH1 1TE.

Trade paperback edition first published in Great Britain and the USA in 2024
by Severn House, an imprint of Canongate Books Ltd.

severnhouse.com

Copyright © E.J. Copperman, 2022

All rights reserved including the right of reproduction in whole or in part in any
form. The right of E.J. Copperman to be identified as the author of this work has
been asserted in accordance with the Copyright, Designs & Patents Act 1988.

British Library Cataloguing-in-Publication Data
A CIP catalogue record for this title is available from the British Library.

ISBN-13: 978-0-7278-5077-5 (cased)
ISBN-13: 978-1-4483-0809-5 (trade paper)
ISBN-13: 978-1-4483-0808-8 (e-book)

This is a work of fiction. Names, characters, places and incidents
are either the product of the author's imagination or are used fictitiously.
Except where actual historical events and characters are being described
for the storyline of this novel, all situations in this publication are
fictitious and any resemblance to actual persons, living or dead,
business establishments, events or locales is purely coincidental.

Typeset by Palimpsest Book Production Ltd.,
Falkirk, Stirlingshire, Scotland.

To Jessica Oppenheim, my wife,
who is the bravest and best person I know.

PART 1: YOUNG

ONE

'Sandra, can you explain what Communism is?'
I remember being eleven years old. They talk about kids
(girls, to be honest) going through an 'awkward phase',
which usually means the change from childhood into puberty,
and is often a way for disapproving adults to comment on a
young girl's body. Heaven forfend you gain a few pounds
around age eleven; you'll be remembered that way by your
classmates and your family for the rest of your life, and possibly
beyond.

That was not my experience. I had begun the physical changes
to be expected and had noticed some new thoughts, like about
how good Jeremy Crichton looked in his Yankees T-shirt, but
that was true of everyone. I didn't have a *crush*-crush on Jeremy,
exactly, but Sarah Panico did and wanted everyone to know it.
I didn't know why that bothered me.

Otherwise, we did what we were told young women (suddenly
we were young women) were *supposed* to do, which is of course
not at all the case for an entire gender, or even an entire sixth-
grade class in Westfield, New Jersey.

I'd heard all the usual crude nicknames – which I will not
repeat here – regarding my bodily development or lack thereof
at that moment (the comments went both ways, which should
give you some idea of how I looked at eleven). And I'd gotten
shoved around a little because, hey, it was Jersey and that's what
happens. It eventually made me a tougher prosecutor and now a
better family attorney/defense attorney. That's complicated.

But at this one moment in my life, in Ms Carbone's class
(which was called Social Studies despite having nothing to
do with socializing), I reached what you might have called a
turning point.

I looked up and felt the same rush in my stomach as I did
anytime I was called upon in class. Being right was *so* important.
'Communism is a form of government based on the idea of

communal living. Everything is owned by the people, meaning
everything is owned by everyone, and there is no need for a
capitalist system that bases its reward system on the amount of
money a person has.'

Ms Carbone seemed to wince a little, which I didn't understand.
Had I gotten the answer wrong? Was that really Socialism I'd
described? Was that why they called the class Social Studies?

'That is technically correct, Sandra,' she said. 'I'm not sure
that was the answer we were looking for, though.'

What? Something was correct but not the right answer? But
before I could ask how that was possible, Sarah Panico's hand
had risen and Ms Carbone was pointing at her. 'Sarah?' she said
with a sunny smile.

'Communism,' the little kiss-ass said, 'is a system of government favored by evil regimes that bans religion and restricts the
people's freedom.'

'Very good, Sarah,' Ms Carbone said. She gave Panico a warm
smile and a nod. Those types stick together.

I rose my hand again. 'That's not true, Ms Carbone,' I protested.
'Some Communist governments have attempted to do those
things, but that's not part of the definition of the system itself.'

'I believe Sarah had the correct answer,' Ms Carbone said,
because she'd been brought up in the 1950s. 'Let's move on.'

If I'd been in high school, or (believe me) college, I would
have continued the fight for truth, justice and not enabling Sarah
Panico. But I was eleven and among the most average girls in
the world and that meant I didn't want to make a fuss.

'Yes, ma'am,' I said.

When I told my mother about it that night – which was a
blatant mistake and I should have known better – she praised me
profusely. For not making a fuss.

My father gave me a look that said we'd talk later, but that
was the night he had the heart attack.

'I want to hire you,' said Riley Schoenberg.

'How did you get in here?' I asked her.

Riley, all of eleven years old, had walked into my office at
Seaton, Taylor, Evans and Wentworth without knocking and
sat down in my client chair. Her feet did not dangle and she

didn't twirl her hair with her finger. It was too short. I was already intimidated.

I was, it should be noted, working on a motion in a divorce proceeding and was preparing to meet my client, a woman named Olivia Partridge, in less than an hour. Olivia's husband had not cheated on her, which was refreshing in the family law business, but he had confiscated most of her money and moved to Acapulco, which somewhat complicated matters. I was working on my understanding of California's laws regarding bank accounts, as this one was in Olivia's name and not her husband's. But he was in another country, which meant I had to circumvent that little detail as well.

So the fact that I was now talking to an eleven-year-old girl who had never even heard of my appointment calendar was in itself something of an anomaly. It was also a pretty substantial inconvenience.

'That doesn't matter,' Riley (whose name I did not yet know) answered.

'Yeah, it kind of does. This is a law firm, I'm an attorney, and little girls don't generally barge into my office because we have receptionists and security officers, so I'd like to know who to blame for the interruption. I'll say it again: How did you get in here?'

'Your receptionist was looking at a handsome man with very blue eyes who was asking about seeing a divorce lawyer, and the security guard in the back smiled at me when I waved.' Riley didn't seem to be congratulating herself for her clever entrance, and I certainly wasn't, but I did sort of admire her drive. And I'd have to talk to Gus the security officer and Celia McKenzie, our main receptionist. 'Now like I said, I want to hire you. What do you charge?'

'If you or your parents want to make an appointment with me about something, I'm sure my assistant can help you,' I offered.

'My mom is dead and my dad is in jail for killing her,' Riley said. 'I want to hire you to get him out of prison because he didn't do it. So what do you charge?'

TWO

'So how did you get the young lady out of your office?' Patrick McNabb asked me.

We were driving in Patrick's new all-electric Rolls-Royce (a prototype car, he told me) from my office, where Patrick had picked me up, to a property Patrick wanted me to see. We had been together for some months now and had agreed recently that we'd move in together, but I refused to just move my things into Patrick's enormous mansion, largely because all of my possessions would have taken up a small corner in one room. Also because I was afraid I'd need Google Maps to get from whichever bedroom I was in to the kitchen.

The place was large, is what I'm saying.

Patrick being Patrick, he'd dived into researching any available properties in the Los Angeles area, meaning that he'd gotten my best friend Angie, who was now Patrick's executive assistant, to research them. He'd contacted the real-estate agent listing one of them and now we were on our way for a tour. Patrick had promised me this house, the first we'd ever gone to visit, was not too big. I was about to find out what the Patrick version of 'not too big' might mean.

'I agreed to look into her father's case,' I answered.

Patrick glanced at me briefly because he was driving. He could have taken a long look at me because we were driving in Los Angeles traffic, which consists more of sitting still than actually moving. 'Really,' he said. 'I didn't think your firm catered much to walk-in business.'

'We usually don't,' I admitted. 'But each attorney gets to use her own discretion on such things as pro bono cases.'

Patrick smiled a little. 'You're doing this for free? I'm proud of you.'

Patronizing though that was, I knew Patrick was coming from a place of love and respect. 'She's an eleven-year-old girl,' I told him. 'I didn't see any way to tell her I wouldn't look into her father's conviction for killing her mother.'

'*Did* her father kill her mother?' he asked. He was watching the GPS on the screen. We must have been getting closer to the house we were scheduled to tour.

'I don't have any idea yet,' I answered. 'I barely got the file from the LAPD and the records bureau. I'll dive into it, starting tonight but mostly tomorrow. But the odds are that the dad probably killed the mom.'

Patrick is a very talented actor, but I'd begun to catch the tells he has when he's less than riveted by the conversation. He cares about my work but he was clearly preoccupied with the search for a home to call our own. So I knew what it meant when he twitched his mouth a bit before asking, 'Why do you say that?'

I was about to answer that most murders are not mysteries and that they generally happen within families, that domestic violence is far less often reported than it should be, and that the cops tend to find out who killed someone before they arrest anybody. But instead my voice caught, I ducked under the dashboard as best I could and I hissed at Patrick, 'Speed up! We've got to get out of here!'

Clearly he did not understand what I was saying because I felt the car actually slow rather than speed up and my stomach clenched; I felt nauseated. 'Patrick!' I said slightly louder. 'It's Emily Webster! Get us out of here!'

Patrick laughed and that was the most chilling sound I'd ever heard. 'Don't be silly,' he said. 'Emmie's going to be showing us the house.'

OK, *second* most chilling.

'Are you nuts?' I sat up in the car seat and saw that Patrick had parked the car in front of a very big, very modern house, which was not nearly as alarming as the sight of Emily Webster walking toward the car with what I'm sure she thought was a warm smile on her face. 'She tried to have us killed! Multiple times!'

'She's very sorry about that,' Patrick said. He'd actually been engaged to Emily Webster for a brief time before he and I started dating. And Patrick has, let's say, blind spots when dealing with the women he's thought he loved. I believe he loves me now, but I made him wait a lot longer than any of the other girls to get to that point. It's a strategy.

So was running away. 'There's still time,' I said. 'Hit the gas.'

Patrick laughed and turned off the engine. He opened his door and got out of the car. 'You are a one, Sandy,' he said. 'You are definitely a one.'

Before I could jump into the driver's seat, hot-wire the car and take off for parts unknown in an electric Rolls-Royce, Emily Webster was right next to my door. 'Sandy,' she said. 'So good to see you again.'

It was becoming obvious that I was the crazy person in this scenario because the other two players didn't seem to notice the complete insanity of the situation. 'I'm surprised,' I said to Webster. 'I wasn't aware you were out on your own recognizance.'

'I'm awaiting trial, but that should happen in a month or two. I imagine they'll contact you to testify.' The Stepford Wives smile on Emily's face didn't falter at all. 'But I'm still able to show you this fabulous property. Come on in.'

Not getting out of the car no longer seemed an option, but I was hyperaware of the surroundings. If Emily was following her previous modus operandi, someone would be inside the house with a machine gun or a bomb. It was like touring a house with Natasha Fatale. 'Maybe we should just look at the outside,' I suggested.

Both Emily and Patrick laughed as if I had said something funny. Patrick walked to my side of the car, opened my door and extended his arm for me to get out. So I did because that's how stupid I am. 'Come on, love,' he said to me. 'Emmie's just the real-estate agent on this house and I think you're really going to like it.'

I stood on the sidewalk next to the gated driveway. (This was Patrick's idea of less ostentatious.) Webster hovered around to my side and pushed a button on a remote that made the iron gates open.

'How did you even retain your real-estate license?' I asked her.

'I haven't been convicted of anything,' she reminded me.

'That's because I'm not a prosecutor anymore,' I said under my breath.

'What?'

'I think that wouldn't happen in Jersey,' I said.

Webster decided she'd puff up in 1960s TV housewife fashion and ignore the rude remark. 'Let's go in and see this wonderful house!' she gushed.

Patrick smiled his tolerant smile, since I was clearly the one being difficult, and gestured that I should walk through the gate first. It's a testament to how well I know him that I did not wonder whether he was in on the plot Webster had cooked up to kill me. The poor man; he was probably on the hit list himself and didn't see it coming.

Oddly, there was no attempt on anyone's life. I wasn't exactly disappointed, but I do confess to wondering if Patrick and I had become that much less important in the crazy lady's estimation.

The less baroque home Patrick had been promising me turned out to have six bedrooms, seven baths (how many people did they think would live here?), a kitchen that the most senior chef in a Paris restaurant wished he could have, *another* kitchen, smaller, on the lower floor (don't you dare call it a basement!), and two full-size palm trees growing in its atrium. The house had an atrium with palm trees. Live palm trees. In the atrium.

'It's kind of . . . big,' I said finally.

'Yes!' Webster said, as ever misinterpreting what I meant.

But Patrick, who had clearly either been here before or seen the listing online (no doubt after Angie had found it; I made a mental note to ream Angie out when I got back to the apartment we were still sharing in Burbank), had been paying less attention to the place itself and more to my reaction. What he was seeing was clearly not what he'd hoped to see.

'You don't like it,' he said. A bit of the Cockney end of his accent was audible, and that's unusual. Patrick can do a remarkable unspecified American accent and several regional ones when he's acting. He learned to do them when he first came to the US for a small role that got him noticed by TV producers, who gave him a medium-sized role on a series that became a starring role on the same series, and so began Patrick McNabb's career. Then he was getting divorced and was charged with murder, and that's the story our grandchildren will hear (if it lasts that long) about how we met. It's a story told elsewhere if you're interested.

'I didn't say that,' I told him. It's a time-honored way to say, *yes, you're right*, without actually sounding like an old stick-in-the-mud.

Patrick looked concerned. 'Tell me what's bothering you.'

I didn't want to have a frank conversation with Patrick in front of his ex-fiancée and our mutual attempted murderer. Call me crazy. 'We can talk about it later. I don't hate the house, but it's really not my idea.'

To his credit, Patrick did get that and he nodded. 'We can talk about it at my house,' he said.

'I'm going back to the apartment tonight,' I reminded him. 'I have stuff there I need for work tomorrow.'

Webster was watching us with an inscrutable expression on her face, and that wasn't making this scene any easier. 'I have a few other properties I can show you,' she said. To Patrick. 'Remember, we went through this the last time and I found you the home you're enjoying now, didn't I?'

The palm trees were intimidating me. The atrium was intimidating me. Emily was *definitely* intimidating me. This house was, well, not going to be my home, ever.

'I think maybe we'll do some more looking on our own,' I answered her, despite not having been addressed at all. 'We'll call you in a couple of days.'

'I'm sure I have something you'll like, and I have access to listings that won't show up on Zillow,' Webster said.

'Maybe we should let Emmy handle this until we find the right house,' Patrick mused. I felt my throat dry out just a bit. We had to use a homicidal maniac to find a house my boyfriend and I could agree upon?

My phone buzzed and there was a text from my boss, or at least the partner I deal with most often, Holiday Wentworth. Holly had become something of a work friend but if she was texting it was serious.

Did you take on the Jack Schoenberg case?

How could Holly have found that out? I hadn't told her, but only because there hadn't been time in my afternoon after Riley left. But if there was one thing this interruption was doing, it was providing me with an opportunity to exit the real-estate situation I had found myself in. Good old Holly.

'I have to take this,' I said, despite knowing that a text would probably have handled the immediate question Holly had asked.

Without waiting for a reply, I walked to the other end of the atrium, which took a while because the room was the size of a baseball diamond. I told my phone to call Holly, which it did.

'What are you doing taking that murder case?' Holly asked as soon as she picked up. I miss the old days, when people had to wait until you spoke to know you were on the other end of a phone call. But it's this century and there's no going back.

Holly's question caught me off guard. Why wouldn't she want me to take on Riley's case? 'I'm the head of the criminal justice division,' I said. 'You made me take that title. Are you saying I can't accept a case without permission?'

She let out a low whistle. 'Wow. We just a little bit testy today?'

'Sorry.' I lowered my voice even more to make me less audible to everyone but Holly. 'Patrick is making me look at houses.'

'I thought you wanted to move in with him,' she said.

'I do, but he wants to move into Xanadu and I'd like a nice little place with a picket fence Anyway, what's wrong with me taking the Schoenberg appeal? The convicted man's daughter came and asked me to help her dad get out of jail.'

There was a light sigh from the other phone. 'I know. You're the third attorney she's asked in our firm alone, and we only have two criminal lawyers.'

'You mean she asked Jon before me?' Jon Irvin was my only staff attorney in the criminal justice division of Seaton, Taylor, and even he spent most of his time working on divorces and custody cases. Which, to be frank, is mostly what I do and what I had wanted to do when I moved to Los Angeles from New Jersey.

'This is no time to worry about not being the first choice of an eleven-year-old,' Holly pointed out. 'Everybody is turning this case down, and for a very good reason: the guy did the murder.'

Coming from Holly, who is a very good lawyer and an excellent judge of character (case in point: she hired me), was not encouraging. 'I just told her I'd look at the files,' I said. 'I didn't commit. How do you know he's guilty? I can't imagine you looked into a criminal matter.' Holly *never* took anything but the highest-profile family law cases we had, and she brought in business, which is why her name is in the firm's logo and mine is . . . going to be on the firm's home page the next time they do a website redesign.

'No, I didn't,' Holly said. 'But I was following the case when it was happening, not long before you got here, and I know the lead detective who worked it socially.'

'You're saying he worked it socially?'

'I'm saying I know *her* socially.' There was a grin in Holly's voice.

'So it's not Lieutenant Trench, unless I've missed a great deal of news,' I said.

'No. Believe it or not there are other detectives in the homicide and robbery division of the LAPD. I know Lieutenant Valdez, she's *very* good and she said she had the case cold. The jury saw it the same way.'

'When you say she's *very* good . . .' I began.

'How much do you like your job?' Holly asked.

I hadn't actually thought about it before. 'Quite a bit,' I admitted.

'Then don't finish that sentence.'

I nodded as if Holly could see me. 'I don't see any harm in looking over the police reports and the court records,' I said. 'If I'm as convinced as you that the guy killed his wife, I'll stop there. But I promised the little girl I'd look into it, and I will.'

Holly has gotten to know me well enough in the past two years that she could have expected nothing other than that response. 'OK,' she said. 'But I'm willing to bet the girl made you take the case pro bono, so I don't want you missing time on paying work when you're doing this, OK?'

'The way you say that makes me feel like I should have charged a preteen our usual hourly rate,' I said.

'Riley Schoenberg inherited roughly four-point-seven million dollars when her mother died,' Holly said. 'Her mother Helene was the inventor of ImagiNails.'

'ImagiNails?' I said. 'She worked in construction?'

'Google it,' Holly said, and hung up.

I looked back over my shoulder and saw Patrick standing there with the still eerily grinning Emily Webster.

'So. Something smaller, then?' she said.

THREE

'There's a very simple solution,' Angie said. 'Don't move
out.'

We were in our living room, which led into our kitchen,
where there was a pile of empanadas and arepas and one cachapa
from the Venezuelan restaurant we'd discovered on Grub Hub.
And we'd already eaten. It was kind of amazing in its own way,
especially given how Angie never gained so much as an ounce.
The two hours a day she spent exercising, in addition to her
full-time job as Patrick's executive assistant and her (very)
part-time job as apprentice of sorts to Nate Garrigan, the investigator who works with me from time to time, had clearly been
paying off. I admired it as one does a noble deed performed by
someone else.

And I will admit, it was awfully easy to be there with Angie,
no makeup, no shoes, no bra if I'm being honest, and just relaxing.
I loved Patrick passionately but I was never fully relaxed when
in his house. He has such a larger-than-life presence and an
energy level that hummingbirds would envy. It's just short of
exhausting to keep up with him. Relaxing? You never know
what's going to happen next. That's intriguing and exciting but
it's not relaxing.

'You're just saying that because if I move out you'll have to
find another roommate,' I told my best friend. I did feel bad
about 'abandoning' Angie after she'd actually moved to LA just
to save my life, but that was a while ago and she *could* have
gone back to Jersey if she'd really wanted to. I guess being the
executive assistant (I am bound by law to use the whole term)
to a major television star was somehow more attractive a life
than running three Dairy Queen franchises in central New Jersey.
Imagine.

'Or move into a smaller place I can afford,' she said. 'But you
know I don't want to do either of those things. All my stuff is
here.'

'There are people who will help you move your stuff,' I said. 'They're called . . . what's the word? Movers. That's it. They're called movers.'

'Mock me in my time of need. Go ahead.' Angie got down on the floor and started doing sit-ups. After empanadas. I'm asking you.

'Hey, you're Patrick's most exalted assistant,' I began.

'Executive.' She wasn't even breathing hard.

'Fine. You must have been in on that great big barn he showed me today and you definitely knew I was going to find it – at best – incredibly excessive.'

'What's your point?' She switched to push-ups because I guess sit-ups weren't showy enough.

'Why didn't you say something to Patrick so I could have avoided seeing our old pal Emily Webster and touring Madison Square Garden? And by the way, what *about* all of a sudden Webster being Patrick's realtor again?'

'You want me to tell Patrick you're going to hate the house he picked out? That's *your* job, pal.' Angie lay on her back and started doing bicycle legs, her favorite ridiculous exercise. I'd started doing some workouts I watched online from a company called Body Project and was worn out after the least strenuous videos. This is one of the differences between Angie and myself. 'As for your buddy Emmie, my understanding is that she was the agent attached to the house, not to Patrick. At least, not like she *used* to be attached to Patrick.'

Wink, wink; nudge, nudge.

'You could have warned me. I practically called in the National Guard when I saw her standing on the sidewalk in front of the estate.'

'That kind of thing is good for you. Gets the blood flowing.'

'Yeah. Generally out of my body.'

Angie stood up without so much as a grunt and picked up two twenty-pound dumbbells (weights, mind you; not some unusually stupid toddlers who were just lying around) from the floor. She started doing curls and lifts. This was going to get on my nerves, despite my seeing it every single day we'd lived together. It wasn't Angie's intention to make me feel physically inadequate. She just did that naturally.

'So what are you going to do about this girl and her dad the murderer?' she asked me.

'That's it; keep an open mind. What do you mean, what am I going to do? I'm going to look through all the information I can get on the case and then decide how to proceed. If there were errors made in the original trial or there's evidence that didn't get entered and might clear Riley's dad, I'll go ahead. If it's clear that he definitely did it – and everyone seems to think that's what happened – I'll try and break it to her gently.'

Angie was watching her bicep expand and contract very closely.

'You won't do that,' she said.

'Yes I will. I just told you I will.'

'I'm saying.' She switched to the other bicep. 'You think that you'd just calmly tell Riley her dad killed her mom and move on to the next divorce, but I know you and you won't do that. You'll see some loophole somewhere or get Nate involved and the next thing I know I'll be tracking down one of the mom's ex-boyfriends or something.'

I put my head back on a couch cushion. It felt good so I closed my eyes, too. That felt better. With any luck at all I'd be asleep and out of this conversation in a couple of minutes. 'I can only do so much,' I told Angie. 'If there's nothing to base it on, I can't go ahead with a request for a new trial.'

'Uh-huh.' She either wasn't convinced or her left bicep was the most fascinating thing on the planet. I was betting on the former because I didn't find Angie's arm all that amazing. There are men who would. Some women, too.

'Believe what you want. The law is the law.' Yes, eyes closed was definitely the way to go.

'I thought you got everything emailed to you,' Angie said. I heard the weight being placed on the floor. She was about to start high knees. Angie's workouts weren't as organized as the ones from the Body Project, but they were more predictable. 'Why aren't you looking at all that stuff now?'

'I'm off the clock,' I told her. 'I'm actually asleep now.' Just to prove my point, I stopped moving entirely and let the sofa engulf me. Better and better.

Her feet started rising off the floor and coming back down again; I could picture her doing that sort of stylized slow march, but she'd twist her torso into each knee raise and 'work the obliques.' Maybe it was time to move out if I could follow Angie's workouts without actually opening my eyes.

'You're afraid you won't be able to find something for an appeal and that's why you're putting it off.' Patrick wouldn't be goading me, either. He could get into my head in ways Angie couldn't, but she was still the champion at figuring out my psyche. We've known each other too long.

I started to fake snore.

'You're not fooling anybody,' she said. Her voice was still annoyingly devoid of any sign that she was exerting herself. 'You know I'm right.'

'*Fine.*' I forced myself to open my eyes and sit up from my comfy couch just to prove Angie wrong. 'I'll look at it right now.' I pulled my laptop out from a drawer in our coffee table (who was going to get the coffee table when I moved out?) and turned it on. The laptop was issued to me by Seaton, Taylor and was bought as part of a bulk purchase, so it was going to take a few minutes to boot up. This is the price a corporation pays for not paying the price a regular person pays. I was willing to guess the corporation was perfectly happy with the trade-off.

'Don't do it for me,' Angie said, but there was an edge of amusement in her voice. She moved on to jumping jacks. I'm sure our downstairs neighbors loved every moment of it.

'I'm not.' I was watching the blank screen on the laptop as if it actually contained any information at all and instead got the reflection of myself with no makeup, not enough sleep and a little bit of empanada on the corner of my mouth. I wiped that off with a napkin but the image I was looking at wasn't improved by very much. And the damn laptop just took its sweet time starting. I began to think it was intentionally mocking me. 'I'm doing it for Riley.'

'I totally believe you,' Angie said. We're both Jersey girls, so I knew she didn't mean that.

Just before I would have dozed off, the screen came to life, and my operating system shortly (by relative standards) after that. I made a mental note to buy myself a personal laptop that would probably add twenty per cent to my leisure time. Because

I remembered leisure time. That was when I used to go down the shore and lie on the beach. Except that was 3,000 miles ago. I began by looking up ImagiNails because that was what Holly had suggested I do. And it turned out, after several web pages and three YouTube home manicure videos, that it was a company specializing in synthetic finger- (and toe-!) nails with a twist: they bonded with the original, natural nails and actually grew, but they were stronger than the organic ones.

Riley Schoenberg's mother, Helene Nestor, had gotten out of college with a degree in organic chemistry but didn't want to become a doctor, at least not a medical one. The ImagiNails website and Facebook page were both very proud to note that she did eventually earn a PhD at Stamford University in physics, which I believed was a whole other branch of science, but I was a political science major who had gone to law school so I'm probably not the person to ask. Still, Helene had not gotten her doctorate until she'd already made her first ten million dollars.

Helene (sorry, *Doctor* Helene) had developed the formula for ImagiNails in her spare time while working as a receptionist for a commercial fishing concern in San Pedro, California fifteen years earlier. Once she'd proved that it could work and had been preliminarily approved by various federal agencies, she and three investors started the business locally out of a storefront in Long Beach. The business quickly relocated to Santa Monica when Helene and her partners realized the one-time-only use of the product required it to have a more upscale price (that is, more expensive) and therefore should be located in a ritzier neighborhood.

In Santa Monica it took off and almost immediately ImagiNails was being offered in salons all over Southern California. The storefront shop eventually closed so the company could concentrate on serving its customers, who in turn provided the product to rich women (and some men) on the west coast and eventually internationally.

Helene married Jack Schoenberg right before merging ImagiNails with her three initial investors and a conglomerate for more than seventy million dollars. They had Riley two years later but stayed out of the public eye, which I could understand. (Since I'd gotten Patrick to state in public that he wanted me to move in with him, there had been almost daily tabloid stories about McNabb's new 'gal pal' (seriously) and I was already longing for my good old anonymity.)

And then two years ago, when Riley was nine, just as the company was about to go public, Helene had been shot in the head in the family's home in San Marino and Jack had been arrested, charged and convicted of the crime. And that got me up to speed but didn't tell me anything about the trial, which was what I most needed to focus upon.

The court's records bureau had sent me the entire transcript of Jack Schoenberg's trial, which naturally was enormous. It was too much for me to read tonight, so I started with the initial police report, filed by Detective Lieutenant Luciana Valdez the night of the shooting. It was one-sided (the police had decided Jack had done the killing so the report, even though focused only on facts, would naturally lean in that direction because facts are actually open to interpretation) but much shorter, and that was a very desirable quality as my brain started to send me urgent sleep emails.

Lieutenant Valdez had been assigned the case after the initial four uniformed officers from San Marino had called in the crime. They don't get a lot of murders in that neighborhood and the victim was a wildly rich person, so guess where the jurisdiction was suddenly assigned. The LAPD took charge particularly after it was determined by the medical examiner that Helene had been shot in another location then placed in the 'music room', an especially secure area of the house, in an easy chair and left to be discovered. Why stage the killing without leaving the room?

And yes, there had been bloodstains found in Jack Schoenberg's bedroom and a handgun in a chest of drawers he kept there. They'd been cleaned and scrubbed, but the bedroom rug had failed the light test you've seen on *CSI* (even though it doesn't really work like that) and suspicion quickly fell on Riley's father and Helene's husband.

Lieutenant Valdez had taken that evidence, coupled with the layout of the music room and the fact that it had been locked after the shooting, that Jack had the only key other than the one found in Helene's pocket, and pieced together some statements from friends indicating the couple's marriage had not fallen into the *idyllic* category. I didn't worry too much about that because no relationship is perfect. Some of us can't even find a place to live that we can both agree upon. Because one wants to live in Versailles and the other is from New Jersey.

I read some press clippings about the trial. There are always reporters hanging around courthouses, which they should, and they will converge upon a murder case (especially one involving rich people) like Springsteen fans at the skirt of the stage. (All Springsteen references are offered with no trademark infringement intended.)

There wasn't much there and, again, I was too tired to read the trial transcript tonight, even as Angie settled in for an evening of streaming on our flatscreen TV in the living area. I put on my headphones and listened to some Vivaldi so I could read and think without words coming into my ears.

The *Los Angeles Times* reporter, T'Aisha Kendall, seemed especially good at her job, not editorializing in her coverage while not being so lawyer-y that the story would be dry and technical. I started reading her articles after other news outlets had turned out to offer either rehashes of Kendall's stories or flat-out opinion pieces disguised as news.

From what I could tell, the trial had not been especially sensational despite the murder and money at its center. The assistant district attorney, Albert Fleischer, had leaned into the inheritance Jack Schoenberg had received from his wife's estate and the idea that there had been friction – but no allegations of adultery – in his marriage to Helene.

Jack's attorney was named Cagney Weldon IV. No, I'm not making that up; people had passed that name along three times. In a row. And based on the newspaper and online photographs, I decided he was the human embodiment of tasseled white golf shoes.

Weldon had based his defense on the idea that Jack had no prior history of violence, did not actually own a firearm (although there were some in the house, either belonging to Helene or kept by the staff for protection) and had never been known to threaten his wife or anyone else. Jack appeared to be the very picture of a husband whose wife outshone him in every aspect of life. Except perhaps parenting, to which he had devoted himself for nine years.

But there was one article that made only a passing reference to a decision the judge, Lamont DeForge, had made that caught my eye. In discussing the early proceedings, Kendall wrote that a reference to 'the transom over the music room door' was struck from the record because Judge DeForge ruled that there was no reason to admit Jack Schoenberg's claim that someone could have crawled through. The transom window was, apparently, only two feet by two feet, and no human capable of entering the room through it would presumably be large enough to hold a gun and shoot Helene Schoenberg in the head, then climb back up without a ladder or any visible way to achieve that altitude. It was, simply, physically improbable at best.

And that was when I knew.

I called Holly back, noting that it was now close to ten p.m. and I was probably overstepping my position in the firm a bit. But Holly didn't sound sleepy when she answered on the second ring. 'You didn't actually relax tonight, did you?' she said. I could hear the smirk on her face.

But I was prepared to match her smirk for smirk. 'No I didn't,' I answered.

'You worked on the case for that little girl, didn't you?'

'Yes I did,' I admitted.

'And you found that she has no legal basis for an appeal, right?' Holly sounded almost triumphant. She knew me so well.

'No,' I said. 'It's not an appeal we're after. There were mistakes made. I'll bet you I get a new trial.'

FOUR

Riley Schoenberg did not look pleased. 'Of course there's a reason for an appeal,' she said. 'My dad didn't kill my mom. Duh.' She was sitting in my office – with an actual appointment this time – looking like an eleven-year-old girl who thought all adults were complete and total idiots and was out to prove her point one adult at a time. Her feet made it to the floor but she had to lean forward a little in the chair. Riley wasn't going to have a career in women's basketball. Although, with her mind, she'd probably make a really good prosecutor someday. There are trade-offs.

'That's not how appeals work,' I said. 'And we're not filing for an appeal. That would have had to happen within sixty days of the original conviction. Why didn't your dad's lawyer do that then?'

Riley's lips rolled over a bit with her distaste for her father's defense attorney. 'He was a guy who did, like, company law or something, and he only did the case because he knew my mom from when someone bought her company. He didn't know what he was doing. As soon as I could, I started looking for a new lawyer, but nobody wanted the case until . . .'

'. . . until you conned me into it,' I said.

'Something like that.' She never broke eye contact.

'So let's talk about getting a new trial, not an appeal,' I reminded her.

She didn't roll her eyes, but only because she was probably saving that for later. 'It doesn't work that they put the wrong man in jail?'

'No.' I was trying very hard not to sound like someone who thought kids were too stupid to understand. The fact is that most grownups don't really get the idea of an appeal either. 'In order to get a judge to agree to a new trial, I have to prove that mistakes were made at the original trial that made the verdict there improper and erroneous. It's called a significant error of law. The first step is not to prove that your dad is innocent; it's to prove that something at his trial was wrong and that makes it necessary for him to have a new trial.'

Riley didn't strike me as a spoiled rich kid. It was possible that her mother, who had made all the money, had been a down-to-earth type because it had happened to her so quickly. I had yet to meet her father, but I had put in a request for a visit with Jack Schoenberg at the state prison in Lancaster, which I had never visited before, and was waiting to hear back.

'OK, so what was the big mistake?' She had grasped the concept much more quickly than most adults probably – no, definitely – would have. I've explained it many times and gotten more puzzled looks than a high-school calculus teacher.

I was looking at the file on my monitor. 'Your dad's defense was a suggestion that someone had entered through the transom window in the door to the music room and the judge refused to admit that idea into the record.'

Riley didn't move a facial muscle. She just stared at me. Then she seemed to reanimate. 'That's *it?*' she said. I was pleased the door to my office was closed, because the shriek might have sent people in the outer office diving under furniture for safety. 'You think somebody climbed in through that little window over the door? My dog couldn't fit through that little window over the door. And I don't even have a dog.'

I held my hands palms out and shook my head. 'No. I don't believe that someone got into the room and killed your mom that way. It doesn't matter that it couldn't have happened that way. The fact is, your dad wanted to enter that explanation as his defense and the judge refused to admit it. In our system, the defendant is always allowed to present a defense and you can't stop them for any reason, even if that defense is physically impossible. The judge didn't allow your dad's defense, and that's enough to get us a new trial. You have to trust me.'

Riley sat back, raising her feet an inch or two off the floor in front of her. 'That's crazy,' she said.

'Maybe, but it's the system and you're paying me to work the system.'

'I'm not paying you,' she reminded me.

'Yeah, I wish I'd known about your finances before I offered that.'

Riley smiled an innocent smile. 'It helps to be eleven.'

'In any event, our next move is to write a brief petitioning the court for a new trial based on the errors made in the original trial. I'll do that in the next couple of days and send it to the appellate court. First I want to meet with your dad and make sure all this is OK with him.'

'He's not your client. I'm your client.' Suddenly Riley *was* avoiding eye contact.

I regarded her closely. 'Did you not tell your father that you were looking for a new lawyer?' I asked. 'Has he never heard of me?'

'*I* hadn't even heard of you a couple of days ago,' Riley said, feet back on the floor. But she was watching them instead of my face. She thought I was going to be mad at her.

I let out a long breath and then spoke with a quiet, calm voice. I thought. 'OK. So my first order of business will be to see your dad and clear this with him or we can't proceed.'

'But he's not—'

'The client? Maybe not technically but I can't defend him against his wishes. And if there's a reason you didn't tell him you were doing all this, I'd better hear about it right now. Later is going to be too late.'

Riley was a very strong, intelligent, determined young woman. She clearly wasn't afraid of me and she knew what she wanted me to do. So the fact that she was staring at my diploma from Rutgers Law (Newark, not Camden) was telling. She didn't care that I might get upset with her; she was concerned that I wouldn't continue with her father's case and that was scaring her.

'Riley,' I said.

'My father has kind of changed his story since the trial,' she said. 'He's not talking about someone coming through that little window anymore, OK? So I guess you can't use that to get a new trial.'

I relaxed a little. 'Yes I can,' I told her. 'It doesn't matter if he won't use that defense again. The point is that he wanted to and the judge wouldn't let him. That's enough. So don't worry about that.'

Riley set her jaw, took a breath (not a deep breath) and looked right into my eyes. 'I'm not worried about that,' she said.

She didn't look any less tense. I suddenly wasn't, either. 'So what are you worried about?'

'He changed his story after the trial.'

'You said that and I told you. It doesn't matter.' What didn't she understand or, more to the point, what didn't *I* understand?

'Now he's saying he did it,' Riley said.

I leaned back in my chair and heard it squeak. 'Well, that's certainly a change,' I said.

FIVE

Detective Lieutenant K.C. Trench was my go-to cop. We had developed a rather tenuous regard for each other, mostly based on the idea that I thought Trench was a really good detective and he didn't hate me as much as he hated some other lawyers. Mutual respect is rarely as mutual as it seems.

So it was somewhat disappointing that Trench was not the investigator on the Jack Schoenberg case. Or the Helene Schoenberg case, depending on how you looked at it. I considered my case to be for Jack; Trench would think he was advocating for Helene. Homicide cops have a really interesting thought process about the dead.

Still, I dropped by Trench's office the next day just to pay a friendly visit. Trench, a very tightly wrapped, neat (some would say anal-retentive, but not me) man, looked over at me with the very warm smile you'd expect if someone were looking at a door-to-door salesperson. Do they still have those?

'To what do I owe the inconvenience?' he asked as soon as I walked in and closed the door behind me. 'I'm not aware of your name being listed as the defense attorney on any case I have closed.'

'It's not,' I assured him. 'I'm here to visit.'

'This is the Los Angeles Police Department, Ms Moss. It is not a tourist attraction. And you are, finally, not a tourist.' Trench rarely lets me forget that I moved to Southern California fairly recently because I thought I wanted to be done with criminal law. I certainly wanted to be done with the county prosecutor I'd been dating and the drug dealers and petty criminals I'd been sending to jail, often because they couldn't afford an attorney other than a criminally overworked public defender. 'So perhaps you can tell me why you really decided to drop by and then I can get on with my work.'

'OK.' I sat without being invited to because Trench and I are such good buddies. He didn't draw his service weapon and kill me so I figured it was OK with him. 'I'm here about the murder of Helene Schoenberg about three years ago.'

Trench's eyes narrowed. At first I thought it was a rare display of an actual emotion, which I took to be anger, but Trench had been brought up on Vulcan and really wasn't capable of such things. No, he was trying to remember the case and he didn't need a computer to help him. The computer was between his ears. His expression convinced me even more than usual that Trench was a prototype device developed by the LAPD to be the most efficient police officer in history.

'The case was closed,' he said finally. His memory banks were obviously still in working order. Maybe his hard drive needed a little cleaning out but the few seconds of lag time in his delivery were inconsequential. 'Her husband was convicted of the crime with very little trouble, as I recall.'

I resisted the urge to applaud and shout, 'bravo!' because I was thinking about my client sitting in a cell after two years despite his being (according to his daughter) innocent of the crime. Instead I looked over at Trench and held his gaze so he could see I wasn't being flip. 'I'm in the process of filing for a new trial,' I said. 'There were serious issues with the first trial and I believe any judge in the county will agree with me that injustices were done.'

'I admire your optimism, counselor, but I believe I should inform you that I was not the primary investigator on that case,' Trench said, his voice as usual authoritative without being belligerent. He must have practiced that. 'In fact, I didn't work that case at all, or did you think I was the only homicide detective in the county of Los Angeles? After all, we have over two hundred murders in the average year.'

'You're good but you're not *that* good,' I admitted. Trench didn't look insulted. He didn't look anything. 'I knew you weren't involved with that investigation.'

'Then I must once again ask exactly why you have decided to interrupt the work that the good people of Los Angeles are paying me to do.' Trench sat straight up in his chair. I have seen him lean back but only when he was trying to be snide about how relaxed he really wasn't.

'The lead detective on the case was a Lieutenant Luciana Valdez,' I said. 'Tell me about her.'

Trench let his eyebrows rise approximately a quarter-inch. I almost fled the room with that display of fury. '*Tell* you about her?' he said, his voice sending icicles across the room. 'You think that I should tell inside stories about a fellow member of the Los Angeles Police Department? To a *defense* attorney? What exactly would be my motivation to do that?'

I couldn't mention the idea of friendship because Trench might actually have laughed and I would have had to look out the window for any stray flying pigs. Luckily I'd dealt with him before. 'Because it's the most efficient way to keep the criminal justice system operating the way it's supposed to,' I said. 'You tell me your opinion – confidentially, of course – of the kind of detective Lieutenant Valdez might be. I therefore can base my evaluation of her handling of the Schoenberg case partially on your comments because I trust your judgment. No one's time is wasted and everyone has done their job as the system is set up for them to do it. Now what part of that doesn't make sense?'

He didn't react facially, of course. One doesn't expect miracles. But I did let myself believe I saw a glimmer of approval in Trench's eye. I hadn't reacted the way he expected but instead played to his sensibility. But I did not anticipate him immediately telling me everything I had asked him to tell me; that would be too much. And I was right.

'The part that doesn't make sense is you not going to see Lieutenant Valdez yourself and making your own evaluations,' Trench said. 'I do not function as your advance staff, Ms Moss.'

Like I said, not unexpected. 'I fully intend to go see Lieutenant Valdez immediately after I leave here,' I said. 'But I value your instincts and I'm not asking for any personal information. I'm not asking you to violate any trusts. I'm simply requesting that you, as a colleague of hers, give me your most general evaluation of Lieutenant Valdez's work as a homicide detective, much in the same way I would ask a plumber of my acquaintance what he might think of another plumber if I needed one.'

'A plumber.' Trench seemed to roll that around on his tongue for a moment. 'Why would you ask one plumber for an opinion and not simply hire the one you trusted?'

'My plumber lives in New Jersey. We're off the point, Lieutenant. Can you give me a thumbnail profile of Lieutenant Luciana Valdez? I don't think the request is out of line.'

Trench briefly closed his eyes. I mean briefly. More than a blink, less than a second. 'In my professional opinion,' he said, 'Lieutenant Luciana Valdez is a member of the Los Angeles Police Department, assigned to the Robbery Homicide Division much as I am.'

I waited. 'That's it?' I asked.

'I have no information that Lieutenant Valdez has ever been reprimanded, investigated or placed on suspension. I don't know of her ever having been accused of any misdoing. She is, as far as I know, a competent detective and police officer.'

So we were casting Trench in the role of LAPD computer hard drive. He'd only respond with verifiable facts. Fine. 'Have you ever worked on a case with her?' I asked.

'On a few occasions, yes.'

'And did you observe anything about her style of investigation that was distinctive in any way?' If someone's going to present themselves as a hostile witness, you might as well cross-examine them with that in mind.

Trench looked like he had on the occasions I'd seen him testify in court. He stared straight ahead but not at me, just over my right shoulder. He was presenting absolutely nothing that could be considered prejudicial. He'd answer the question in the most minimalist fashion he could.

'I did not notice her having a particular *style*,' he said.

'See, now I don't believe you.'

He shifted his gaze to my face.

'You're a good detective, Lieutenant. You know you have a way that you conduct an investigation that's your own. Every detective does. So I'm asking a rudimentary assessment of the way that Lieutenant Valdez conducts hers. What did you observe?'

'Answering you will be—'

I finished the sentence for him. 'The easiest and fastest way to get me to leave.'

'Very well. Lieutenant Valdez is efficient. She is observant and she asks the right questions. She is thorough. She does not have preconceived notions about the case. She presents relevant evidence and she does so with impartiality.'

There was clearly a 'but' hanging there. I knew better than to ask Trench what it was, but I knew he had opinions. The best tactic was to ask around them. 'How does her method differ from yours?' Trench knew I'd seen him in the midst of an investigation so I'd be familiar with the way he gathered his facts.

He took a moment, no doubt to consider how to present his opinion without divulging any actual, you know, opinion. 'She becomes emotionally involved in the cases she investigates,' he said. That definitely was a change from the way Trench did things. 'She will empathize with the victim and that drives her work. I am driven more by the search for the truth under any circumstances. And now, Ms Moss, I would like to continue to do the work the people of Los Angeles have so generously hired me to do for them.' He casually waved a hand at the office door.

I stood but didn't leave immediately. 'Are you saying that Lieutenant Valdez is an emotional woman?' I asked. I didn't know Trench to be especially sexist, but one does have to rule out certain societal preconditioning.

He didn't look up from his computer monitor. 'No Ms Moss, I am not. I could name you five male homicide detectives considerably more emotionally demonstrative than Lieutenant Valdez.'

'But you won't,' I guessed.

'You are absolutely correct.'

'First time today,' I said.

SIX

What the hell; I was already in the building. Detective Lieutenant Luciana Valdez did not have an office like Trench's. In fact, she didn't have an office. She worked out of one of the larger cubicles in a bullpen at the Division of Robbery and Homicide and was pretending not to mind. She had agreed to talk to me when the name Schoenberg had been mentioned and, once I sat down in her guest chair and took in the splendor of her government-issued surroundings, it became clear why that had opened the (proverbial) door to me so quickly.

'So Riley finally found herself a lawyer,' she said. The tone was not unfriendly but definitely leaned toward amused.

'I believe I've found significant errors in the trial, and I will be filing for a hearing on a new trial,' I told her. 'I'm here because I'd like to know why you concluded so quickly that Jack Schoenberg killed his wife. Was he the only suspect?'

Valdez had already opened the case file on her desktop computer and consulted it briefly, but I got the impression she didn't really need to do that. 'He wasn't the only suspect initially, but there were solid alibis for everyone else and, before you ask, no, that's not the reason we arrested him. Schoenberg had motive, he had opportunity, and he had possession of the weapon that was used to kill his wife. And now in prison he has admitted to the crime, so I'm not sure why you're letting an eleven-year-old girl talk you into such a futile pursuit. You might get your new trial – I'm not sure what your grounds will be, but let's say you do – but you'll lose that one, too. He'll plead guilty if you bring him into court and that'll be it.'

'Anything he's said while in custody is irrelevant,' I pointed out. 'If he didn't do the crime, him bragging about it to the prison population isn't going to make a bit of difference in court.' OK, so that wasn't true, but I'd never dealt with Valdez before and we were like a couple of prizefighters trying to determine each other's strengths and weaknesses. I was feeling her out.

'You haven't met him yet?' She was doing the same to me but there was also some knowledge she had that I didn't. Was Jack Schoenberg a raving lunatic? Had he found religion in prison? Was he a pathological liar? Did I ask too many questions that I didn't know the answers to?

'No. I've gotten an appointment for tomorrow.'

'You'll see when you meet him. He's going to tell you he killed Helene and he's going to be very, very convincing. When he first decided to confess after the trial, he got in touch with me, because he thought you had to confess to your arresting officer. The fact that he'd been sentenced to life without parole didn't seem to be relevant to him.'

I thought about that. What would make a man start confessing to a crime while he was serving the time he'd been sentenced to after his conviction? Was Jack Schoenberg covering for someone else? Who did he have to protect . . . other than his daughter?

'I'll make my own evaluation when I see him, and maybe send in a psychiatrist if I think it's necessary,' I told Valdez. 'The question was, why did you think he was the guy? As I understand it, the room where Helene Schoenberg's body was found had been locked. That in itself is some indication that she might have committed suicide.'

I knew that wasn't the case; I just want to let you know that in advance. Helene did not kill herself, and the correct term is 'died of suicide'. But I was talking to a cop and you have to sound like a cop when you do that or they won't respect you. Except Trench, who talks like an Oxford English professor.

'The gun was discovered outside the room, so unless she killed herself and then got up to deposit the weapon in her husband's sock drawer, I think suicide can be ruled out. And the proper term is "died of suicide".' Valdez clearly wasn't your average police officer either, or I wasn't up on the current lingo. I'd have to get a Cop/English-English/Cop dictionary and carry it around with me. 'So the fact that he was in possession of the murder weapon an hour after the discovery of the body was one reason.'

'You know perfectly well anyone could have planted that gun in his sock drawer,' I said. 'That's circumstantial at best.'

Valdez shrugged. 'I don't prosecute the cases. I just arrest people and send the report to the attorney general's office. They decide to indict or not and guess what? A jury of his peers found the guy guilty based on all this circumstantial evidence you're talking about. But the fact that the doors were locked also pointed to Schoenberg. He had the only key to the music room door and it was in his sock drawer when we searched the house.'

'The only key you know of,' I said. But I'll admit it: I was feeling a little shakier than when I'd arrived at police headquarters this morning.

'One last thing,' she said, and my stomach tightened just a bit. I didn't need one last thing, and she was sounding awfully Lieutenant Columbo about it. 'Friends say Helene Schoenberg was in the process of filing for divorce and cutting Jack out of her will when she died.'

'That's two last things,' I said. It wasn't much but it was all I had. 'Did her lawyer tell you that?'

'He refused to answer the question, citing confidentiality, and insisted we look only at the will that was filed.'

'So you don't know that for sure,' I said.

'I know he had motive, opportunity and means. And he says he did it. So I'm wondering why you're so hellbent on getting him another trial so he can get convicted again.' Valdez was even decent enough not to smirk when she said that.

'The trial had errors,' I said. 'I can't let that verdict stand.' What I really meant was, *his daughter asked me and what else could I do?* But that didn't seem terribly persuasive.

'Then Godspeed, Sandy Moss,' she said. I felt like I was the main Viking at a Viking funeral. 'And say hi to Holly Wentworth for me.'

It was none of my business.

SEVEN

'This is much smaller,' Patrick said.

Indeed, the house we were standing next to – 'we' being me, Patrick and the inescapable Emily Webster – was not as cavernous as the first family compound we'd toured, but it was hardly modest. It had a stone wall around it with a gate that required a keycard to open. I understood that, because Patrick was a very famous actor and some people get a little crazy when he's around. There are also death threats on occasion when he's done nothing at all, but a character he plays manages to displease the viewers. I say go attack the writer who told him to do that.

(In the interest of basic decency, no, don't go attack the writer. I've met a few television writers and some of them are decent human beings.)

So I got the necessity of some security measures in any home we were going to occupy. Given some of the cases I'd been involved in, and how they'd played out regarding my own person, a little security wouldn't be an awful thing.

But this place had six bedrooms. It had a pool house. It had a game room, a screening room and a smoking room, despite the fact that neither Patrick nor I smoked. It had three extra rooms that Patrick said could house his film memorabilia collection. I thought Patrick's film memorabilia collection, which added to the probability of a break-in the way I saw it, should be at the Academy Museum of Motion Pictures on Wilshire Boulevard. Or in the Smithsonian. Or someplace else where I was not living. Patrick had other ideas.

'It's smaller than San Simeon but still about the same size as the Taj Mahal,' I noted. I had no idea of the size of either of those places, but I was willing to bet Patrick didn't either. 'This is less a house and more a palace. Patrick, I don't want to live in a palace. People from New Jersey shouldn't live in palaces.'

'It's not a palace.' Emily, ever helpful (to Patrick), was

weighing in. Her voice sounded like every annoying neighbor in every cheesy sitcom, but without the Staten Island accent. 'It's a very livable home. It has enough room for the two of you to raise a family if you want to.'

That was so many miles ahead of where we were now that I'd need an airplane to get there. And from this place I'd get a private jet. I was used to flying coach.

I chose to ignore Emily, which I'd made a policy, and focus on Patrick. Sometimes I have to remind myself of why I love him. It's not that he does anything wrong; it's that he's so not what I'd always pictured, and that had more to do with my vision of myself than anything to do with Patrick.

'I grew up in a two-family house,' I told him. 'We had tenants upstairs and I was used to it. Now, I'm glad I don't have to live with tenants upstairs anymore. I've worked really hard to get there and so have you, Patrick. This is just a little too big a leap for me. Does that make sense to you?'

'Of course, love.' That was his answer most of the time, and it was among the reasons I'd been trying to remember. 'But could you just tell me what size leap we can make?'

We were standing in an empty entrance hall – Emily called it a 'foyer', with the French pronunciation – looking at the twenty-foot ceilings and skylights, the open staircase up to a balcony (a *balcony!*) and the guaranteed-Italian marble floor. Smaller than Delaware, maybe not Rhode Island. And they were staring at me wondering why I wouldn't be dazzled.

That was the thing – I *was* dazzled. But not in the way they were. Maybe Patrick and Emily were the better couple after all.

But then I remembered she'd tried to have us both killed and I thought that was a bad thing. She was the grown-up version of Sarah Panico and didn't deserve Patrick. I did. Just not in this house.

'Let me put it this way,' I said. 'I want to live somewhere that I can talk and not hear an echo.'

That was when I was reassured. Patrick nodded with under-standing and Emily looked at me as if I had just told her I wanted to live in a penal colony because they grow their own brussels sprouts.

'All right,' he said. 'We'll do some looking in a more comfortable neighborhood, won't we.' That was not a question.

'Like where?' Emily said.

I felt like saying, 'Zillow', but Patrick had apparently promised her she'd be the broker on our new home and I wasn't going to have *that* argument in front of her. 'I'll text you with some possibilities,' I said, which meant, 'Zillow.'

As we were walking to the car, and I was noticing the castle-like parapets on the upper floors, I said to Patrick, 'Do you mind not being in such a fancy house?'

He smiled his Patrick half-smile and shook his head. 'No place for a Dunwoody,' he said. 'I grew up in a building with six other families, love. Two would have been an unfathomable luxury.'

'But lately you've been in such big places,' I noted.

Emily smiled broadly at Patrick as she got into her Tesla, then nodded curtly in my direction and pulled away. We (that is, Patrick) drove back to Patrick's house and parked in what he calls the driveway, which is actually an approach that can be seen from the Hollywood hills.

'I was proving to myself that I was a big star,' Patrick said. 'I probably don't need to do that anymore.'

'You don't need to prove it to me,' I said. 'I don't care if you're a big star as long as you're Patrick.'

He kissed me for a long time and I felt like I was in the back of my mother's minivan in tenth grade, but better. (Why my mother needed a minivan is one of the great mysteries of our age and is never to be questioned when she is present. It's all transmission fluid under the bridge.)

When I opened my eyes, Angie was staring through the window with an expression of grand amusement on her face. 'What's the matter?' she asked. 'You couldn't wait to get inside?'

'What are you doing here?' I asked, while trying not to blush and no doubt failing.

'I work here.' Technically she had an office at Dunwoody Pictures, Patrick's production company, but she often worked from his house, organizing every aspect of his life that I wasn't connected to because she's my best friend and you have to have some boundaries.

Patrick's face went all business when he saw Angie because he knew she'd be telling him about all the things for which he was currently late. We got out of the car as Angie took a couple of steps back from the driver's side door to let me by. 'What's our situation?' Patrick said.

Angie went through the list of appointments, phone calls, emails and text messages Patrick had been ignoring, so I thought it was an appropriate moment to check through my own. I was halfway through the texts that had come through (all divorce-case related) when I found one on my cell phone from Riley Schoenberg. That was odd because I'd only given Riley my office number. Someone at Seaton, Taylor must have passed on the number and I'd have to give them heck later (I'm not great at giving people hell except in court).

My dad won't see you, it read. *He says he's guilty and should stay in jail.*

We'll see about that, I sent back.

EIGHT

ancaster, California was a town dominated by the state prison it houses. That hadn't always been true, the locals at a coffee shop told me, but it had been for decades now and the people in town really weren't very disturbed by it. They said. There was no reason not to believe them.

It had taken me over an hour to drive there from my apartment in Burbank, but going north and east away from Los Angeles is always an easier drive than trying to get close to the downtown area or any district near it. I had put on a Spotify playlist of some Nineties bands and tried to focus on the resistance I was certain to get from Jack Schoenberg once I was cleared for an attorney visit inside the prison.

Such encounters are not held in the same open areas as family visits, like you often see in movies. There are separate, private areas where lawyers can meet with their clients. But the first hurdle I had to vault once I arrived was that Jack Schoenberg had not listed me as his attorney, so my name was not on the approved list.

'I was hired by his family,' I told the corrections officer at the window. That was true but I did not feel the need to identify exactly which family member was my paying client. 'I'm just here for a conference.'

'You're not on the list,' she pointed out for the third time.

'And yet I was approved for the visit,' I countered, and showed her the email I'd received from the Department of Corrections (what exactly is it they correct?) confirming that fact.

She let out a long breath that sounded suspiciously like a groan. 'Let me check.'

Standing next to a window in any bureaucratic setting is something other than a joyful experience. Doing so inside a prison is something just a little bit more disturbing. We tend to not think of prisons unless we know someone who is being kept in, or works in, one. This is just as true of defense lawyers as anyone else. So the six minutes (by my watch) that I waited at this particular window seemed just a little bit more like three days than it might have at, say, the motor vehicle agency. Imagine.

After an eternity or two, the officer came back and let out another sigh just to show how hard she'd worked. 'Schoenberg agreed to see you,' she said. 'Mostly because he wants to say to your face how he won't see you.'

'Whatever works,' I said.

I signed the proper paperwork, submitted to the necessary searches, surrendered my phone, my keys and my purse but not my (searched) briefcase, and was led through a series of corridors to a door with no signage on it. The officer who had guided me through the labyrinth took out a keycard and opened the door.

Inside was exactly what you'd expect: blank walls (other than the odd notice taped up and left to yellow forever), a table and two chairs. There were no windows. You notice right away how there are no windows.

Seated at the table, no handcuffs but in the requisite prison jumpsuit (yes, orange) was Jack Schoenberg.

He was a man in early middle age, of medium height and just starting to go grey. His face could be described as generically handsome, in that it didn't have any particular character but the features were pleasing to the eye in a bland sort of way.

He held up his finger as soon as I sat down, as if he were preparing to make a point. I had anticipated this, being an astute observer of the human condition and also because the corrections officer had told me he wanted to tell me to go away. So I'd prepared a countermeasure.

Before Jack could say a word I started with, 'I'm here because your daughter sent me.'

Oddly his finger stayed standing up. It was incongruous with his face, which suddenly looked less assured than it had been a minute earlier. 'Riles sent you?' he said.

'Yes she did, and she gave me a retainer with the explicit instruction that I get you a new trial,' I answered him. 'Now, I don't want to hear whatever nonsense you've been telling the other inmates or the guards around here. I want you to tell me exactly what happened on the night that your wife died.'

Jack looked at his finger, as if he'd forgotten he had pointed it in the air, and with a note of embarrassment he lowered it and put his left hand over the closed fist he'd made, perhaps negating the silly gesture. 'I killed her,' he said with as little conviction (if you'll pardon the expression) as I had heard in a confession since the one a low-level weed dealer had given me when I was an assistant county prosecutor, insisting that his cousin Pothead Cantonini, who had been arrested with more than a pound of weed on him, had never touched an illegal drug in his life.

We have since legalized marijuana in the state of New Jersey, but I think Pothead might still be in jail.

'I'm going to assume that's something you're saying to impress your peers here in state prison,' I said. 'You have no history of violence and California's divorce law would have afforded you plenty of money if you'd really needed out of your marriage. There is no change in her will on file, no matter what anyone told you. There hasn't been so much as a rumor that either of you was engaging in an affair. So you don't have a motive. Let's start there. OK, you say you killed your wife and your daughter says – just as emphatically, if not more so – that you didn't. So tell me. Why did you do it?'

'I hated her. Isn't that enough?' Jack's eyes were vague and unfocused to the point that I wondered if Pothead Cantonini had been transferred to California for reasons I couldn't even begin to imagine and had revitalized his business inside the prison walls.

'No,' I said, 'it's not enough. I don't even think it's true. I think for some reason that you don't want people to hear your defense. You held that someone crawled through the transom over the door to the music room and shot Helene, then left the same way. If you think that's what happened, why have you suddenly changed your story?'

Jack looked from side to side and then seemed to scan the ceiling, perhaps for cameras or microphones. 'There's no surveillance that can pick up what you're saying,' I assured him. 'I'm your attorney and this is privileged communication. So you can say anything you like and I can't be made to tell anyone what you said without your consent. Feel free.'

His voice dropped to something very close to a hiss. 'They think I'm crazy,' he said at me. 'They think I'm incapable of caring for my daughter. It's easier if I just say I'm guilty and they keep me here, because I couldn't bear it if they said I wasn't good enough to be her father. Do you have children, Ms Moss?'

I shook my head.

'Then you only think you can understand. That girl is the best thing I ever did. She's all of me and all of Helene. I'm her family now and I've got to think of her ahead of myself. If they sever my ties with her she'll end up with someone who just wants the money she inherited. She's staying with Helene's sister Alicia now, and that's bad enough. I can't not be her dad anymore. So I have to stay here for the rest . . .' His voice caught and then he regained control over it. 'Rest of my life and be considered sane but dangerous.'

'No you don't,' I told him after I'd digested what he said. 'You don't have to stay here and you don't have to be considered dangerous. You can be back in your home with Riley again. But in order to do that, you have to stop saying you were guilty and let me get you a new trial. Then you have to answer every single question I have for you – honestly – and I will do everything humanly possible to get you out of this prison. Do you think you can do that?'

Jack Schoenberg bit his bottom lip. I understood; he didn't want to be offered hope because he wouldn't be able to withstand it if that hope was dashed, like so many had been until now. He couldn't be that vulnerable. He couldn't risk the idea of being replaced as Riley's father (which wouldn't happen legally without his consent anyway).

'I don't know you,' he said finally.

'I understand that,' I assured him. 'But you have one indicator that should be enough.'

'I do?' His eyes were telling me that maybe hope could be welcomed again but I'd have to earn it.

'Yeah. Riley trusts me.'

Jack sat back in his chair as if I'd punched him lightly on the shoulder. A little air came out through his mouth. He swallowed. All the clichés of having been stunned, in one brief moment. I wished I'd brought Patrick with me because he'd know if Jack was being honest or was a remarkably bad actor.

'I guess that'll have to be enough,' he said finally.

I nodded. 'All right. Then let's get to work.'

NINE

'You're on your own with this one,' Jon Irvin said. Jon had assisted me with two previous murder trials, acting as second chair and filling in when I couldn't be in court. He's a terrific strategic thinker and a better courtroom lawyer than I tended to give him credit for.

I hadn't come to Jon's office to ask him to be my second chair; I could get one of the associates in the firm to do that and spare Jon the worry. I knew Jon had enough to take care of already, and one of the times I'd asked him for help he'd gotten shot, so I'm a little (ugh) gun-shy?

Let's say 'reluctant' instead.

'I expect to be on my own,' I told him. 'But I can still come in here and ask for your perspective, can't I?'

Jon has a nice easy, open smile, which he used at that moment. It was genuine. 'Of course you can. You know that. But this isn't an appeal; it's a petition for a new trial. What are you using as your basis?'

I told him. 'Well, that's a clear denial to hear his defense.'

Jon nodded to himself. 'But it's a nutty defense. If you get the wrong judge, one who doesn't interpret the law strictly, you might have a battle on your hands.'

'I only know a few of the criminal judges in Los Angeles County,' I reminded him. 'You have a little bit more experience with them. Who should I avoid?'

He gave me a few names and I noted them on my iPad, which I was holding in my lap. 'Tell me something,' I said to Jon. 'If you were the judge, would you grant me a new trial on this?'

Jon doesn't do anything without thinking about it first. He probably spends time each morning deciding which underwear to put on, which is something I used to think only women did. But Patrick . . . well, that's for the tell-all book I'm never going to write. The point is, Jon thought about my question carefully and practically.

'I think I would,' he said, 'but only because the law is so clear on the subject. Nobody is going to think someone got in through such a tiny space and managed to get out again without at least one accomplice. And there's no person over the age of eight who might fit through that transom.'

'Should I believe Jack Schoenberg when he tells me he only changed his claim about being guilty because he was afraid sticking to his crazy defense would result in his losing custody of Riley?'

Jon answered surprisingly quickly. 'No.'

I waited. Then I waited some more. 'That's it? "No"?'

'OK. I think your client wants you to believe that because he thinks it proves how much he loves his daughter.' Jon doesn't do the lacing-your-hands-behind-your-head thing when he leans back in his chair, probably because he thinks that would make him look like a suave douchebag. And he'd be right. So he doesn't do that. But he *does* lean back in his chair. 'So right off the top I wonder how much he *really* loves his daughter. But he also wants you to believe something that's not true, and you know as well as I do that's never a good thing with a client, especially one on the criminal side.'

'Yeah, in divorces I just assume everyone's lying and try and split the truth down the middle,' I admitted.

'Not a bad strategy.' Jon got up and walked around his office a little. He's done that regularly since the whole shooting thing and he doesn't even need the cane for support anymore. It was hanging on a coat-rack in the far corner of the room, perhaps as a reminder of how far he had come. 'Why would Jack Schoenberg lie and say he was guilty if he wasn't guilty?'

'Maybe he is guilty,' I suggested.

Jon nodded. 'Naturally it's possible. We've both defended enough guilty people in our time.'

'Not me,' I said. 'I've done three murder trials and all my clients were innocent.'

'All of us besides *you*,' Jon allowed. 'But you knew when you were a prosecutor which defendants were definitely guilty and which ones might not have done the crime.'

'Even the ones who didn't do that crime probably did another,' I said.

'Stop talking like a prosecutor and don't change the subject,' Jon said. He walked to the coat-rack and back, as if to prove to the cane that he didn't need it. 'Riley thinks her father is not guilty and she's the one who isn't paying us to work his case.' Jon can sneak in a little friendly dig when necessary. I wasn't charging the millionaire eleven-year-old, which was probably a source of some amusement among other members of the firm. 'We have to operate under the assumption that he didn't kill Helene until and maybe even after we find evidence that he did. It was a couple of years ago already. Is it worth getting Nate Garrigan involved?'

I felt myself scrunch up my face. 'I dunno,' I said. 'The firm isn't going to be thrilled with the idea of spending money on an investigator for a pro bono case unless it's absolutely necessary.'

I looked at the copy of the police report on Helene's death that was stored on my iPad. It wasn't telling me anything I didn't already know. 'I don't want to go back on my word if I don't have to,' I said. 'Millions or no millions, she's still a kid. It makes me feel like I'm taking advantage of her. Anyway, it's a cold case, and I don't have any reason yet to think there's evidence that wasn't presented in the original trial. I don't need Nate yet. If I do, I can always ask Angie to talk to him. She works with Nate twice a week.'

'I think you need to talk to your client again,' Jon said.

'Riley?' Like I didn't know who my client was. 'Why?'

'To see why *she's* lying.'

I met Riley Schoenberg at a very fancy bakery in Santa Monica, a town where I'd once defended Patrick's half-sister Cynthia Sutton from a homicide charge, but that's another story. The bakery was desperate to show off how whimsical and yet artistic it was, so I was eating a cupcake that was decorated like a Salvador Dali painting. Riley, whom I'd offered to pick up in the Hyundai but who had laughed and said she'd taken an Uber, was drinking from a glass of sparkling water.

I felt like her child. Not the impression you want to give your client.

'You knew your father would cave in once I used your name,' I said. 'You said he'd never agree to filing for a new trial. Why did you lie to me?' I believe in being very straightforward in my dealings with clients, and mostly everyone else.

Riley didn't miss a beat; she took a sip from the sparkling water and didn't even smile a little bit. 'I figured you needed some incentive,' she said. 'You aren't getting paid, so I thought a challenge would get you going.'

Was this really a thirty-two-year-old disguised as a sixth grader? 'Riley,' I said, 'I'm your lawyer. You can't lie to me, not even a little bit. So can we agree that you'll be a hundred per cent honest with me from here on in?'

She seemed to consider the question very carefully; her eyes got serious and her lips puffed out just a little in thought. She nodded her head. 'No,' she said.

'No?' That response is a perfect indicator of exactly how much Riley's answer had taken me by surprise. 'I'll tell you this now: If you're planning on lying to me, you can find yourself another attorney.' I closed the cover on my iPad, on which I'd been doing a crossword puzzle, just to lend an air of finality to my threat. 'So make up your mind. Why would you want to lie to me while I'm trying to get your father out of prison?'

'Sometimes it helps to lie to adults,' she said as if instructing me. 'It speeds things up. Everything with grownups seems to take tons of time. Besides, lying can get me what I want.'

I figured I'd change tactics. 'What do you want?' I asked.

'I want my dad back.'

'And I'm committed to helping that happen,' I reminded her. 'But I can't do my job efficiently – and that means successfully – if I don't have the truth in every aspect of this case. You lie to me and we're done. Clear?'

She rolled her eyes just a bit because she was an eleven-year-old girl. 'Fine. I won't lie to you. Can I leave things out?'

'No. You can't leave things out, you can't *bend* the truth, you can't lie to me and you can't try to manipulate me. We have to be a team, and if a team doesn't pull together they pretty much always lose. Those are my rules, and any violation of them will result in my leaving. So get used to it.'

'*OK.*' I was so exasperating.

Glad we had that out of the way, I moved on. 'Your dad told me he had said he was guilty because he thought that he'd lose custody of you if people thought he was mentally ill, and that the defense he was offering would make people think that.'

'What? The idea that him staying in jail forever instead of trying to get out is better for me? Who thinks that?' She stopped sipping the sparkling water and was, I think unconsciously, eyeing my cupcake, which I had stopped eating because it was screaming *SUGAR* at me with each bite. That wasn't a surprise exactly, but it was a concern. I lived in a city with every movie star in the world, and that gets a little intimidating.

I pushed the cupcake toward Riley, who did not resist it; she dug in. 'I don't think he's crazy,' I said. 'I think he's lying.'

'I guess it runs in the family.' This through a fog of green and white fondant.

'Don't be a wise guy,' I said. 'Why would he lie to me? Because he wants something from me, like the reason you lied?'

Riley shrugged. 'I dunno. I've barely spoken to my dad in two years.'

I reopened the iPad and actually opened a file to take notes because that was something I hadn't been expecting and those are always significant. 'You haven't?' It's not that I was questioning her memory of speaking to her father; it was that I wanted a fuller explanation. I'm not actually stupid; I just sound it sometimes.

'No. I mean, I've gone to have a visit with him a couple of times, but he never shows up.' She scowled. 'I guess he'd rather hang with the guys in the prison than his daughter.'

'I think maybe he's ashamed to face you,' I suggested.

She shook her head slowly. 'I'm not not-paying you to analyze my family,' she said. 'What are you doing to get a new trial?'

'Easy, young lady.' Because there's no better phrase to get a preteen girl to listen to you than *young lady*. It was surprising she stayed seated, but the cupcake was keeping her occupied. 'My doing your case pro bono doesn't give you license to treat me any way you want. I'm submitting a brief and the proper forms petitioning for a new trial within the next three days. I want to make sure we're not missing anything so yes, this will take a little time. I've got to get it right the first time.'

'Do you want me to read it for you?' my eleven-year-old client asked.

'No. I want you to focus on telling me all the truth.'

Eye-roll. 'I'm focused. I'm focused.'

I sipped from a cup of coffee because even though I was the one who bought the multicolored cupcake I was, at least chronologically, the adult. 'So. You're certain that your father didn't shoot your mother, for any reason, even one you might not have known about.'

The eye-roll was supplanted by a glare of some fury. 'Nobody was cheating on anybody else, if that's what you're asking,' Riley said.

'It's not, actually. I'm asking whether it's possible there was *any* reason he might have been angry enough to hurt your mom? Maybe he didn't plan on killing her.'

'No.' Fury was replaced by determination. 'My father did not kill my mother. Period.'

'OK, then,' I said. 'Who do you think did?'

Her eyes narrowed. 'You think he killed her, don't you?'

'I don't think anything. I've barely started looking into it. I'm curious about what *you* think.'

Riley looked wary. 'Do we have to know who really killed her to get a new trial?' she asked.

'No. This is for after we get the new trial. We don't even have to know it then. We don't need to present the real killer to get your dad acquitted, but it always helps to have an idea. Who do you think it might have been?'

For the first time Riley seemed to consider the question and not the intent behind it. You see that in hostile witnesses, especially after the third or fourth time you ask what is essentially the same question. They forget about why you might ask such a thing and give an answer that is usually less guarded than they might have offered the first time.

'I don't know much about her business other than what I found out after she died,' Riley said. 'But there was this one guy who—' She was distracted mid-sentence by that ubiquitous attention hog of teens, preteens and everybody else, her cell phone, which made a noise like a gong you hear in Chinese instrumental music. She picked it up and looked at it, then blanched a little as her eyes widened.

'What's wrong?' I asked. I was afraid she might be having

some kind of medical problem, and I'm not anybody's mother, so this was not my area of expertise. I mean, I used to *be* an eleven-year-old girl, but it's not like I've tried to remember every sensation I had at the time. It was a while ago.

When Riley answered, which was after a considerable moment, she did so breathlessly. 'It's my mom,' she said.

Never say I'm too quick on the uptake. 'What about your mom?'

'I'm saying, I'm getting a text from my mom.'

TEN

'Clearly someone has gotten hold of Helene Schoenberg's cell phone and, for some twisted reason, is trying to convince her daughter that she's still alive, or communicating from the grave,' Lieutenant Valdez said. 'But please, explain to me how this has anything at all to do with me. I closed that case two years ago.'

I sat down despite not being invited to do so, because who has that kind of time? 'And what happened to her phone when her body was discovered?' I asked.

She didn't have to refer to notes. 'It was confiscated as evidence and examined in great detail by forensics. Her husband knew her password and volunteered it, which was foolish on his part because there were some angry texts going back and forth between the two of them. So we got to see everything that phone had to offer.'

'And what happened to it after that?' I tend to ask questions of authority figures and witnesses as if they were testifying on the stand.

'It was returned to the family.'

Well that was certainly vague. 'Who in the family?' I asked. 'Her husband was in jail for allegedly murdering her, and her daughter tells me she never saw it. So who in the family got Helene Schoenberg's cell phone?'

'Her sister, Alicia Nestor.'

I had vaguely known that Alicia was housing Riley but didn't know if they had been close or communicated at all. 'Why didn't you give the phone to Riley?'

'She's underage. We had to give it to an adult. Helene's mother is dead and her father is suffering from dementia. So we surrendered it to Ms Nestor with the instructions that she should pass it on to the daughter when she felt it was appropriate.'

'So the sister is texting Riley in her dead mother's name?' I said. 'I mean, it's not a crime that I'm aware of, but holy crow.'

'It actually is a misdemeanor to make calls or use an electronic device to annoy or harass another person,' Valdez pointed out, making me feel inferior for not having known that, especially since I work largely in divorce law and it must have come up at one time or another. 'But I'm not the cop you talk to about misdemeanors.'

'But you're smiling,' I told Valdez, 'so it's clear there's something you want to lord over me. What is it?'

She didn't even deny wanting to prove how much more than me she knew. 'The phone was taken off all existing mobile accounts and is not connected anywhere in the United States,' Valdez said. 'As far as I know, you can't use it in another country, either.'

'But someone could have transferred the number to another phone and used that one,' I said. 'Do you know if that's happened?'

Valdez gave me a look that indicated I had used up the amount of her time my taxes had paid for. 'No, because the case is *closed*. The guy's in prison. Let's move on.'

I returned a look that I hoped indicated I was an attorney and not a gadfly off the street. 'Do I have to tell Lieutenant Trench on you?' I asked.

She grinned. 'You feel free. I'd love to see how that goes.'

I felt like I wouldn't love it much so I dropped that. 'Lieutenant, you and I have gotten off on the wrong foot and I regret that. But my client is an eleven-year-old girl and she's getting possibly dangerous messages from someone claiming to be her mother who was murdered two years ago. I think we can agree something needs to be done about that, don't you?'

'You're right. Something does need to be done. I suggest you go do it.' Valdez was a tough case. Now, however, she was being callous about a preteen and that didn't play for me.

'Seriously?'

'Yes, seriously. If you want to file a complaint on behalf of your client with the bureau that handles such harassment, I'd be glad to direct you to that office. In fact, it can even be done online. But I'm a homicide detective and this is not a homicide.' Valdez shuffled files on her desk, which was not nearly as spotless as Trench's, and pretended to be done with me.

'It's homicide-adjacent,' I said.

Valdez's shoulders hunched and relaxed as she let out the most theatrical sigh since Lin-Manuel Miranda stopped playing Hamilton. (It's brilliant; you should see it.) 'What did the text say?' she asked.

I checked the notes app on my phone. I'd actually taken down the text exactly so I'd remember it, but it helped that Valdez wanted to know. Any flicker of interest on her part was welcome, not for Jack Schoenberg's case necessarily, but to help Riley going forward. And I was playing the long game.

'It says, *Long time no see, honey. Did you think I was gone? Never leaving you. Let's meet somewhere. Alone.*'

Valdez's mouth twitched at the word *alone*. 'That ain't cool,' she said.

'No. It ain't. Riley said it doesn't sound at all like her mother, who never called her "honey". And she wasn't crazy about the *never leaving you* part, either.'

She started clacking away at her keyboard. 'OK. Let me see what I can dig up on that cell phone. This might take a while.' Then she stopped and looked stunned at what she saw on her screen. 'Or maybe not.'

I didn't feel comfortable enough with Valdez to walk behind her desk for a view of her computer monitor. For that matter, I wouldn't have done so with Trench either, unless he'd specifically invited me to do so. I'd be afraid he'd consider it an unforgivable breach of protocol. 'What?' I asked. 'How bad is it?'

'I honestly don't know. Helene Nestor's phone seems to be registered to Helene Nestor.'

I felt my eyes narrow. 'Isn't it basically routine to close the account and reassign the number after a year or so when someone dies?' I asked.

'Basically routine,' Valdez repeated, looking at the screen and moving the mouse on her pad around. 'So that leaves us with one possible plan.'

Well, someone had to say it: 'What's that, Lieutenant?'

'We've got to let the girl set up the meeting and see who shows up.'

ELEVEN

'How is *that* supposed to work?' Patrick asked. 'Isn't it rather dangerous to set that little girl out somewhere to meet the person pretending to be her dead mother?'

'I'm sure the cops will be watching the whole time,' Angie said from the Hyundai's back seat. 'They want to catch whoever comes to meet Riley and question them. This could be great for Sandy's case, right Sand?'

I was driving and therefore distracted. Before GPS, how did anyone navigate the streets of Los Angeles and its outer suburbs? In New York you had a grid. In New Jersey you had highways on which cars could actually drive at speeds above thirty miles per hour. In fact, New Jersey's legal speed limit is ten miles above New Jersey's legal speed limit. 'I don't know about great, necessarily,' I said. 'But there's something more going on than a person trying to spook Riley. Especially if they've ever met Riley. Stephen King would run cowering from Riley. Where is this place, anyway?'

'You'll know it when you see it,' Angie said. We were without the usual Emily on this trip because we weren't planning on touring the house in question; we'd just look at the outside for this one visit to determine whether it was more suitable than the two theme parks Patrick had suggested before. This one was Angie's find and I felt like she had my interests at heart ahead of her boss's. 'It's very teal.'

Not that I mind teal but that had an ominous ring to it. '*Very* teal?'

'Trust me,' Angie said. But I'd already noted Patrick's mouth twitch at the left corner.

There are many things with which I trust Angie, not the least of which is my life. But her taste runs to the spectacular, whereas mine lives more in the slightly-above-functional area. So I had agreed to this fact-finding mission based on my confidence in my best friend but not exactly expecting to find the house of my dreams.

'Still.' Patrick hadn't forgotten what the conversation was actually about. 'Even with the police nearby, this plan sounds quite risky. Are you going to be there, Sandy?'

'That was a very tricky negotiation,' I said. 'Lieutenant Valdez says I'm not but I've decided I am, and I figure as long as one of us is being reasonable, there's no point in arguing. I'll have to get my information on the setup from Riley.'

'We're here,' Angie said, pointing at a spot off the street. 'That one.'

We were in fact there, but you can say that wherever you are. You're always 'here', wherever you go. Still, I decided Angie was looking out for my interests and besides, I've probably said that a thousand times myself, so who made me the grammar police?

I didn't have to ask Angie which house she meant. It was, in fact, teal, but not in the hey-I-live-at-the-shore way that other such places might have been. This was, if such a thing is possible (and it seemed that it was) a restrained teal, almost understated but still that flirting-with-aqua hue that announced its proximity to lovely weather and nice views. Angie, if first impressions meant anything, had chosen well.

'Nice,' I said almost instinctively.

'You like it?' Patrick was ready to sign a check.

I had to be careful. Patrick really wanted us to live together and I did too, although I felt bad about stranding Angie in our apartment with all the rent to pay. I hadn't fallen madly in love with this place yet, but even if I did, I'd have to go slow. Patrick would agree to any house I said I liked (because it really didn't matter that much to him); he just wanted me to be happy. But I had to worry about his needs in a home too. Was it possible to have the level of security a famous TV star would need? Was it grand enough for us (him) to host parties for his industry friends? Patrick's ego is fed by the status he's achieved in the entertainment business. He's entitled to that. Did the house reflect that sufficiently? But if I showed too much enthusiasm, he'd pretend to love any house I pointed at, no matter what he really thought.

'I don't know yet,' I said as we got out of the car. 'I've only seen one side of it, and the outside at that. And don't forget, Patrick: It matters whether *you* like it too.'

'Of course.' That's Patrick for *whatever you want is fine with me.* I had to tread lightly.

I walked a little to the front of the house so I could take it in. It wasn't completely modest, which was nice for Patrick, but it lacked the explosive grandeur of the places we'd already seen. It was expertly painted, with careful accents and small touches on each shutter (yes, it had shutters) that made you think it was special without feeling pretentious.

'How old is it?' I asked Angie.

She didn't look at her phone; she'd memorized every detail. 'It was built in 1939 when the studio system was at its peak and people who weren't in the highest levels there were still doing well enough to buy houses. It's been owned by a cinematographer, a costume designer, a studio accountant, a chef at a studio commissary and – for the past twenty-five years – a home contractor who kept it up impeccably herself.'

'Interesting,' I said, when what I wanted to say was *wow!* 'Why don't we take a look inside?'

'We can't,' Angie said. 'You need a realtor to do that. I don't have the code to open the lock box.'

'I can call Emmie,' Patrick offered. 'Angie?' When Patrick says, 'I can call,' he means, 'Angie can call.'

'Not yet,' I said, mostly because the last person I wanted to see right now was Emily Webster. Besides, keeping her out of the deal – and out of our lives – would no doubt piss her off to the max, never a terrible aim. Hold a grudge? Just because she tried to have me killed? Would I be so petty?

Yeah, I would.

'Let's take a look around first,' I said. Angie caught my eye and nodded, understanding my reasoning.

There was no gate. The house was set back from the sidewalk and there were no buildings immediately to either side, but this was not a gated community and it was not a mansion like Patrick might have found himself accustomed to in the past few years. This was a house.

To be fair, it was a pretty large house. There were clearly three rooms across on the second floor, one with a little balcony to stand on and survey the neighborhood. The ground floor had more windows than the upper one, and it was clear that the house went back farther than might have been assumed at first glance. The entrance was not overly formal, but it was sheltered from the rain that I'm told we get in Southern California on occasion. (Mostly it's hot, at least to someone from the East Coast or, as they say out here, 'Back East'.)

Once we started walking around the house, the depth and breadth of the place became more clear. What was meant to look like a modest little home on a pretty upscale street was actually something on a considerably larger scale, with a pool and the necessary pool house behind the building itself. There was no tennis court, which I considered a plus. Patrick did not play tennis but I liked to watch it on television. I could do that inside.

But what got me more than anything else was the view behind the place. I hadn't realized, because the grade had been so gentle, how high a hill we'd been climbing when we drove up here from Patrick's office. From the back windows (and glass doors) of the house came a view that you absolutely had to be a television star to afford. Luckily I had one in tow. The Hollywood hills and the city of Los Angeles were almost literally at our feet.

'That's pretty impressive,' Patrick said.

'I would say so,' I agreed.

'So you like it?' Patrick, who has an actor's ego and a definite point of view about pretty much everything, can be like a puppy dog when he deals with people he wants to please. And I was currently in that enviable position.

But we're always honest with each other. Almost always. Very close to always. 'I don't want you to immediately start setting up a real-estate closing,' I told him. 'You need to be as on board as I might be, and I'm not sure about me yet because we still haven't even seen the inside. Let's take this slowly, Patrick.'

He stopped gazing at the rooftops of whatever section of LA that was (I did fine in social studies, despite Ms Carbone, but I still can't deal competently with the geography of the city I live in) to look at my face and read my intentions.

'Of course, love,' he said. 'We can't buy a house on a whim.'

'You have before,' Angie, who is never far away, noted.

'Not this time. I'm not buying it just for myself.'

That was the moment my phone buzzed and the caller was indicated as Riley Schoenberg. That was significant enough for me to disengage from the possible purchase of a new home (we really did have to get inside; the place could have been totally without walls for all I knew) and pick up.

'What's going on, Riley?' I asked. Remember when people used to say, 'Hello?'

'A man just called and said he was going to kill me.' She wasn't breathing heavily. She wasn't sobbing. She was just reporting the news. Like it happened every day in Riley's world, and for all I knew it did.

I was her attorney, and for the moment her most significant adult who wasn't behind bars. My voice must have betrayed the jolt because Patrick and Angie both turned to look at me, but I was trying my hardest to keep it even and calm. 'Was it the same number as the text?' I asked.

'No. I never saw the number before. I wouldn't have picked up, but I figured maybe it was someone who knew about the text and that could be helpful. But instead he just said, "You're Jack's daughter and I'm gonna make you die," and then he hung up.'

OK, so it was probably an enemy of her father and not her own. 'I'm going to call Lieutenant Valdez and then I'll come and get you and we'll go talk to her,' I said.

'But there's more,' Riley said before I could go on.

More? 'You just said that was all the man told you,' I reminded her. 'What more?'

'He also said he was going to kill you,' Riley answered. 'He mentioned you specifically.'

That figured. I looked over at Patrick. 'Have you been talking to Emily again?' I asked.

He looked baffled.

TWELVE

To my surprise, Detective Lieutenant K.C. Trench was standing (because sitting would cause a crease in his trousers) in Lieutenant Valdez's cubicle when Riley and I arrived, having dropped off Patrick and Angie back at Dunwoody Productions over both their protests. It can be really useful to be the driver.

'I asked Lieutenant Trench to sit – that is, to join this meeting – because I knew he has some history with you and death threats,' Valdez told me a little too gleefully. 'I think his perspective can be helpful, don't you?'

After just a few days I didn't know what I thought about Valdez yet, but this little ploy certainly wasn't getting her a thank-you note with a fruit basket. I could only imagine that Trench wasn't thrilled with the idea of getting involved in a case to which he wasn't assigned, and his dealings with me on those rare (I think it's important to point out that they were rare) occasions when I had been threatened were not, I knew, among his favorite moments on the LAPD.

'I always think the lieutenant's perspective is helpful,' I said in what I hoped was a diplomatic tone. Riley, seated next to me and slumping in her chair, looked like she'd been called to the principal's office and knew she was guilty of the crime. I thought she might bolt or maybe hit someone, probably me.

'I take it the mobile phone in question has been surrendered and examined,' Trench said. He wanted to get to the facts and out of the way of the two women in his presence who seemed to be having some kind of competition, although I doubt he could tell for what, largely because I was one of those women and I didn't know either.

'It's being examined now,' Valdez told him. She turned toward Riley. 'There was a slight amount of difficulty getting it surrendered.'

'It's my phone,' Riley said, as if that explained it. 'My whole life is in that phone.'

These kids today, am I right?

'It will be returned to you as soon as the officers can determine who might have made that call,' I told her.

'That's not entirely accurate,' Valdez said, thus further cementing my close working relationship with my client. 'The phone is being analyzed now and you *will* get it back, Riley. But we don't know if anyone in the lab will be able to trace that call, and I don't know how long it will take to make the determination.'

Riley looked truly disturbed for the first time I'd ever seen. 'You mean I might not get my phone back soon?'

'Let's hope you do.' Trench wasn't looking impatiently at his watch because he wasn't a bad actor in a bad play with a bad director. 'For the moment, I think we should concentrate on the threats that were made to you. Have you told us absolutely everything the person on the phone said?'

'What do you mean, "let's hope"? Usually that means no.' Riley was an unusually intelligent eleven-year-old girl.

Trench ignored her comment because he was an unusually intelligent police detective. Arguing with an eleven-year-old girl is a pointless exercise; you never win and often come away feeling foolish for having tried. 'Was there anything the person on the phone said that you haven't mentioned yet?' he asked. 'Even something that doesn't seem important?'

'He didn't talk a lot,' she answered, voice exasperated for having to answer the same question more than once. 'I answered and he said, "You're Jack's daughter. I'm coming for you and I'm gonna kill you *and* Ms Sandra H. Moss, that lawyer you hired. Jack's not getting out of jail." And then he hung up.'

'You're sure it was a man's voice?' Valdez probably just wanted to remind us that she was involved in the case as well.

Riley looked a little shaken. 'Pretty sure,' she said. 'He sort of whispered, like a mean whisper.'

'And you definitely didn't recognize the voice?' Valdez asked.

That was worthy of an eye-roll. 'Yeah. I know just who it is but I don't feel like telling you. Is that what you think?'

As the adult representing Riley, I felt it was necessary to change the mood in the room. 'Nobody thinks that,' I told her. I was seated next to Riley so I was the only grownup who could look her directly in the eye without seeming like I was trying to establish my authority over her. Looking down on someone is a powerful thing. 'But the lieutenants need to cover every possibility so they can stop thinking about what they know *isn't* true. It's one of the ways they find out what is.'

Her face betrayed no irony. 'When you eliminate the impossible, whatever remains, no matter how improbable, must be the truth,' she said. This was a scary girl.

'Point taken,' I said. I looked up at Trench. 'You're on your own.'

'Thank you,' he answered, then focused on Riley. 'Do you know many of your father's friends or associates?' he asked.

'I've seen people come by the house, but most of the business ones were my mother's employees or the people who deal with her money,' Riley told him. 'They weren't exactly friends.'

'The text message,' Valdez jumped in. 'The one that pretended it was coming from your mother. Do you have any ideas who might have sent that? Because it might have been the same person who called and threatened you.'

Riley clearly was connecting more with Trench than Valdez, which was not what I would have predicted. Trench is something of a machine; he doesn't exude emotion at all. Valdez, a woman, might have been more in tune with Riley's feelings, but Riley wasn't your off-the-rack kind of girl. Her face looked attentive, like a pupil learning from a really interesting teacher, when Trench spoke. When she had to deal with Valdez, she just seemed annoyed.

'Isn't that sort-of your job?' she said. 'Aren't you the cop who put my dad in jail?' That explained a few things; it never occurred to me that Riley, who was nine at the time of her father's trial, would remember that. 'And when can I get my phone back?'

'It's true that I arrested your father,' Valdez said. She leaned forward in her chair. Trench, still pretty much at attention as he was most of the time, was observing. Mostly he was observing Riley, although he did seem to have some interest in Valdez's technique with the witness. 'But I didn't do it because I didn't like him. It wasn't personal.'

'Funny. To me it was personal. Can I get my phone back?' Riley wasn't chewing gum, but in a bad movie she would have been.

'Young lady.' That was Trench. I instinctively moved my chair back a few inches to be out of the line of fire from Riley. 'A police officer follows the evidence. That is what we do. If the evidence in a crime indicates that one person is the most likely to have committed that crime, we make an arrest, but not before we have exhausted every possibility.'

Riley nodded, which was the last thing I expected. 'But sometimes you get it wrong, don't you?' she said, and her voice was more little-girl than it had been since we'd arrived.

Trench, fingers intertwined behind his back, nodded. 'Unfortunately, it is always a possibility,' he said.

Valdez, no doubt feeling just a little betrayed, looked back and forth between the two of them. 'I didn't get it wrong,' she said, a little more forcefully than I thought was necessary with the prisoner's daughter in the room.

'Yes you did,' Riley said quietly. 'Now. My phone.'

Because the screenplay must have called for it, a uniformed officer showed up in the cubicle at that moment and talked to Valdez. He seemed to be purposely not looking at Trench, who might have been something of a legend in the LAPD. 'Lieutenant Valdez,' he said, just to be clear about which lieutenant he meant, 'Sergeant Johnson asked I give this back to you. He's done with his examination.'

He held out Riley's mobile phone.

Before Valdez could twitch, Riley had snatched it from the uniform's hand and was opening the evidence bag in which it had been delivered. But Trench held up his left hand in the universal gesture for 'stop' and, amazingly, Riley stopped.

'We can't have that out of the bag before we know its disposition,' he said.

'Its what?' The first time I'd known Riley not to have recognized a word. Leave it to Trench.

'Its status of the moment,' he answered. 'We don't know if it's being given to the lieutenant as evidence, which it would be if Sergeant Johnson has made a determination as to who might have called or texted you. If that's the case, we wouldn't want to contaminate the evidence by touching it. If it's ready for you to take it, I promise you will.'

Trench held out his hand and, to my amazement, Riley placed

the phone, still in its protective bag, in his palm. Perhaps great minds think alike. I know Valdez looked as stunned as I must have and was already holding up her index finger as if to admonish Riley, then tried to cover by checking her fingernail and putting her hand back down on her desk.

'Thank you,' Trench said. 'Officer, did Sergeant Johnson issue a written report when he handed you that evidence bag?' Trench never looked the uniform in his face; he was making a point of looking at Riley, possibly to soothe her anxiety over the phone.

'He told me to tell Lieutenant Valdez he would call in a moment and email her the report by the end of business today,' the cop said.

'Assume you have told me, Officer,' Valdez said. 'Thank you.' The cop turned and left, probably wondering what all the drama was about, or about where he'd order a sandwich for his break. You never knew with cops.

Riley turned her gaze to Valdez. 'Can I have my phone back?' What my mother would refer to as a 'broken record'.

Valdez sighed. 'Let me find out.' She picked up her phone and punched in an extension. 'Sergeant Johnson,' she said. Then she listened for a bit while we watched, which is uncomfortable for everybody. 'All right. I'll get your email? Thank you, Sergeant.'

She hung up and looked at Riley. 'You may have your phone back.'

Trench held out the bag and Riley pounced on it like a starving man on a Snickers bar, because if you watch the commercials you'll find out exactly how nutritious a Snickers bar is, and if you read the ingredients on the side of the wrapper, you'll get another story. Riley powered the phone up with something approaching real love.

Valdez, oblivious to the heartwarming reunion taking place in front of her desk, looked at Trench. 'Johnson says the only useful piece of information he gathered from the phone is that the call and the text probably did not come from the same device. The numbers were different. The first was definitely from the number assigned to Helene Nestor.'

Trench stroked his chin. 'The other might have been from a burner phone.' He turned toward me to direct his next bit of Trench-ism: 'Despite what people think, such things are traceable. They just take longer than a phone assigned to a specific user.'

As an officer of the court, particularly one who used to be a prosecutor, I actually didn't need that little tidbit. But there was no point in tweaking Trench if I wasn't going to get anything out of it. 'Thank you, Lieutenant,' I said with a sweet smile. 'How are you going to deal with the threats made toward my client and me?'

'Counselor,' Trench said, 'surely you of all people are aware that death threats are made in murder cases and high-profile cases a good percentage of the time. The Schoenberg case got a fair amount of press coverage and there are entire websites devoted to it, some of which I scanned immediately before coming downstairs for this meeting. People can sometimes obsess on such things but those threats are rarely material. I doubt in this case that you or Riley are in any real danger.'

'So you're not going to do anything?' You'd think Riley would have asked that, but she was engrossed in all the emails she had missed in the past forty-five minutes. It's hell being a kid in LA. So the question was mine.

'What would you have us do?' Valdez said. 'We can't assign an officer to follow you wherever you go. There's no point in monitoring your phones even if I thought we could. I'd just say be especially aware of your surroundings wherever either of you might be.' She clapped her hands once loudly so Riley would look up, which she did. 'Wherever you go.'

'Uh-huh,' Riley answered, and turned her attention back to her TikTok feed.

Having had some experience in this area, I decided to direct my next question to Trench, because he has some too. 'Do you think I need to call Judy?' Judy was a bodyguard from a very efficient firm whom I had hired twice before. Judy – and I never knew her last name – was frighteningly efficient.

'I can't make that decision, but if it were me I doubt I'd invite the expense and the inconvenience,' Trench answered. 'These threats are not striking me as terribly credible just now.'

Just now.

I nodded and stood up and – once I could get Riley's attention – gestured for her to do so too. She did, but never broke eye contact with her screen. I mean, I rely on my phone for a lot, but I don't devote all my time to it. Those things are so needy if you give them a chance.

On our way out I looked at Trench and thought about his suggestion that a man calling an eleven-year-old girl (and by extension me) with a death threat was not urgent.

'I knew that stuff about the burner phones,' I said as we left.

THIRTEEN

Riley looked like a completely different girl, and her appearance hadn't changed at all. She was mostly, from what I could see, uncomfortable. Alicia Nestor Jennings, Riley's aunt and sister of the deceased Helene Nestor, sat on her beige sofa in her tastefully furnished living room and her tastefully chic off-white suit, her iPad open on the tastefully . . . well, you get the idea . . . coffee table in front of her. Her legs were perfectly crossed. Truly, I wanted to take notes on how well Alicia had crossed her legs so I could improve my technique the next time it was called into play.

'I think reopening Jack's case is a terrible mistake,' Alicia said. 'Why dredge up all that pain for a man who's guilty?'

'He's *not* guilty,' Riley said, her voice impassive. Alicia completely ignored her.

'There were errors made at his trial that make a new one viable. We intend to go ahead with the process,' I said. 'In fact, the papers have already been filed.' Well, they would be once I got back to my office. I was trying to remember what my office looked like.

I had dropped Riley off at Alicia's condo the evening before when we left the headquarters of the LAPD. Following Trench's kind-of advice I had not contacted Judy and her bodyguard agency but I was – and I had insisted Riley be as well – especially aware of any people I saw anywhere in my vicinity. I hadn't actually gotten DNA from Patrick or Angie, but I was on the lookout in case they started to act suspiciously.

This morning I was picking Riley up and driving her to school. I had made sure that was an option because I wanted to meet the woman she was staying with and start to get a feel for the dynamic playing out in Riley's life. Also to see if Alicia might have killed her own sister, but that was secondary.

'As Riley's guardian, I feel like I should have been consulted before any such action was taken,' Alicia said.

This is where being a lawyer and doing your homework came into play. 'But you're not legally Riley's guardian,' I told her. 'Her father retains that role. You were given temporary custody of Riley by the court when he was convicted, but he can still make decisions of this kind. Riley is not of age to make major life decisions for herself, but she is allowed to use some of her money in any way she sees fit.' I didn't mention that Riley wasn't paying me a dime because Alicia seemed to be the sort who would think that diminished me. 'She retained my services and I will provide them.'

Alicia's smile might have killed a lesser woman. 'Of course,' she said. Frost formed in the air between us.

'How did you hear of your sister's passing?' I asked. People tend to respond badly to words like *murder* or *death*, but they seem to think *passing* makes it better. I didn't especially care if Alicia responded badly to a word I said, but I did want clear answers out of her and I thought an angry Alicia would probably order me to leave her home. You get such bad answers when the other person kicks you out.

'Why do you ask?' Great. Alicia liked to answer questions with questions. It's hard to get anywhere with a person like that, and I know because I grew up with my mother.

'I'm interested in how the news was disseminated,' I told her, because *I want to know if the two of you got along right before someone shot her* seemed a little too on-the-nose. 'I didn't know any of you then, and understanding the chain of communication can help get me up to speed.' Sure it was double-talk, but it was darn good double-talk.

'Of course,' Alicia repeated. I saw Riley mouthing the words along with her. 'I got a call from the police, actually. A Lieutenant Velez, I believe.'

'Valdez,' I corrected before Riley could. Best to keep the atmosphere in her home chilly but not hostile. (Warm would have been better, but a woman who spends that much time worrying about how her legs were crossed probably didn't encourage sleepovers and make waffles in the morning.)

'Of course.' Maybe it was her mantra. 'Yes. I was stunned. I mean, I knew things were . . . difficult between Helene and Jack, but in my wildest imaginations it never occurred to me that he would kill her.'

'He didn't,' Riley said.

'Of course, dear.' A variation, probably to create the illusion of affection for her niece. But I try not to be judgmental. Most of the time. Alicia turned her attention back to me because children are so inconvenient. 'I went right to the house and talked to Jack. They didn't arrest him for at least two weeks after that night.' Some women might have shuddered a bit at *that night*. Alicia didn't and at least I admired her honesty. She wasn't going to pretend to be shattered by the events of the night when she inherited a king's ransom.

'How close were you to your sister?' Get right to the heart of the matter, I always say. I sometimes say it. When I can't think of anything else.

'We were very close,' Alicia said. I saw Riley shake her head negatively and it's possible Alicia did too. 'We were inseparable as children.'

'What about lately?'

Alicia's eyelids dropped to half-staff. 'Lately my sister has been dead.'

'Lately before that,' I said, pretending to correct myself. 'The last few years before what happened.'

'We were fine.' Alicia was looking at a magazine on the coffee table. She was the kind of woman who actually had magazines on her coffee table, like it was the waiting room at a dentist's office. *Vogue*.

'That's not the same as inseparable,' I noted. Maybe it was time to prod the bear just a little and see what would happen.

'We weren't children anymore. Helene had started this massive company and married that man.' The sound of the word *man* indicated Alicia was not in favor of the entire sex. But then Alicia didn't seem to be in favor of very much at all.

'Alicia doesn't like my dad,' Riley said. Not *Aunt Alicia*, but I didn't know if that mattered.

'He killed your mother, Riley,' Alicia said.

Riley launched herself off the couch and even let her phone, which she'd been cradling like a kitten, drop onto the cushion.

'He *didn't!*' she shouted, and stomped out of the room. After picking up her phone. You have to have priorities.

Alicia actually chuckled a bit. 'Riley can be somewhat dramatic,' she said.

I nodded. 'You're certain Jack is guilty?' I asked.

'That's what the jury said, isn't it?'

I thought that was a pretty easy answer, and maybe an evasive one. 'Juries do sometimes make mistakes,' I said. 'I think they might have been influenced by some of the errors I believe were made in the trial.'

Alicia leaned forward and put one hand over the other, which had been closed into a loose fist. She leaned her chin on her hands. 'The only error that was made in that trial was that they didn't give that son of a bitch the death penalty,' she said. 'I would personally like to be there when he was given the lethal injection. Maybe if you manage to get him a new trial, I'll realize my wish.'

So clearly we were going to have a free and mutually open-minded discussion. I stood up. 'I've taken up enough of your time,' I said. It was one of those moments when your adrenal gland screams obscenities and invective and your mouth somehow makes squishy noises of subservience. Your adrenal gland hates your mouth for that, but your mouth is connected to your brain and doesn't especially care. Humans are complex machines. And believe it or not I wasn't a science major in college.

'It was a pleasure,' Alicia lied. 'Let me call Riley so you can take her to school.'

I held up a hand like a stop sign. 'No need,' I said. Then, in as conversational a tone as I could muster (my adrenal gland hadn't shut up yet), I turned toward the hallway and said, 'Riley.' She showed up almost immediately, backpack already on and sunglasses – necessary in Southern California for any number of reasons – poised on the bill of her Dodgers cap. I nodded in her direction and Riley headed directly for the front door.

'Have a good day, dear,' Alicia attempted without uncrossing her legs.

'Of course,' Riley said as we left.

FOURTEEN

Riley and I didn't talk much during the drive to her school, which took twenty-three minutes and was honestly within walking distance. This is LA, and anybody who says it's not clearly can't read road signs. In New Jersey we invented jug handles to deal with a lot of this stuff, but people don't like things they don't understand, which leads to out-of-state drivers trying to make left turns off of highways and other lovely things. But this was not about driving; it was about how Riley reacted to her aunt, which was not, shall we say, in the warmest and most positive manner. She was as sullen as I would have expected her to be in, say, three years, when she'd be fourteen.

I gave her a smile and she didn't completely scowl at me when I dropped her off and I immediately started avoiding an inner monologue about whether or not I ever wanted to have children. The idea of moving in with Patrick was scary enough.

My office offered sanctuary, and I dived into a few divorce cases, actual paying work, and one criminal charge, which was from a long-time client (three divorces), whose son had been caught with more than the legal limit of marijuana on him, leading to a charge of intent to distribute. Weed is legal in California, and there are dispensaries pretty much wherever you look, so the whole enterprise was something of an empty experience. It would, in my estimation, end in a plea bargain that would see him do no time in jail and eventually have the whole incident expunged from his record. It's nice to have well-to-do parents in America. And everywhere else.

My lunch 'break' was going to involve seeing the inside of the teal house with Patrick, Angie, and of course Emily Webster, whom Patrick simply couldn't avoid calling with the news that we'd found 'the right house', which I was not completely convinced we had. Patrick is loyal to a fault. Literally. So I had to drag myself out to go tour a house I actually found interesting with a woman who had pretty much taken out a hit on me not all that long ago.

My advice: when life gives you lemons, take them back to the farm stand and get oranges instead.

We all converged at the teal house at half-past noon, in three cars. Only Patrick and Angie had driven here together, because Angie is always organizing Patrick's life so she can't be far away for long periods of time. Angie is to Patrick what a secretary would be to normal people if the secretary was also an iPhone.

Luckily the house itself had not lost its appeal. (No that's not a legal joke.) It was still charming without being loud about it. The interior would make or break the deal in my mind. What I needed to know from Patrick was whether he had an opinion or just wanted to duplicate my own. So I had a plan.

Emily and I began by smiling insincerely at each other. She had once been Patrick's fiancée and thought that the reason she wasn't might be that I had sabotaged the romance intentionally. Which was only half true. I hadn't realized at the time that I was in love with Patrick, or that he might feel the same way about me. I just talked to him as a friend with advice, most of which boiled down to: *What are you doing getting married to a woman you barely know?*

'I think you've made a perfect choice,' she said after we reluctantly bumped elbows (I don't do the handshake thing anymore; call me a germophobe).

'I haven't made any choice yet,' I said. 'And neither has Patrick.' I paused to cast my winning smile at my boyfriend, who grinned his actor-taking-a-publicity-shot look back at me. 'I think a lot of it has to do with what the inside looks like, don't you think?'

'Ex*act*ly. That's where you live most of the time, isn't it? Why don't we go in?'

I couldn't think of any reasons, so we let Emily undo the lockbox. And after taking a good look around the street and seeing only one person in a gray hoodie, a black face mask and sunglasses walking on the far corner, I followed the other inside.

It seemed unfair that I was starting to forget I was the one who wanted to look at this place to begin with. Emily had that effect on me.

But the house soon took over my thoughts, and I forgot about my boyfriend's ex-fiancée and attempted assassin leading us on a tour. She was telling me facts and figures and what room each one was, as if I couldn't figure that out for myself, but I was hearing only about every seventh word because this house was asking me to buy it (or get Patrick to buy it, or, as we had planned, buy it jointly).

I won't go into excessive detail but I'll tell you this: for a large house (in my version of large), this home was incredibly charming. There were small touches like exposed brick in the kitchen, a real (not gas) fireplace in the living room, an atrium in the breakfast nook (the area in the kitchen where you can sit at a table and eat, and not just breakfast if you feel like it at other times of the day), real wood floors, a room where Patrick could have a home theater that was big enough for industry screenings, three baths with actual baths, and out through the back in what Emily – when I was listening – felt compelled to call a 'family room', glass doors showing off that view.

Sorry. I said I wouldn't go into excessive detail.

All you really need to know is that after being inside for four full minutes, I wanted to live in this house. I wanted to live with Patrick in this house. Maybe we could adopt Angie and she could live here too. There were five bedrooms, after all. It was big but it didn't feel like it was showing off. It was modest without being tiny. It was already what I wanted it to be and all we'd have to do was to move in furniture, which I imagine we'd have to buy because I had a couch from a Sears in New Jersey and Patrick's stuff was more attuned to the Guggenheim Museum in Manhattan than an actual dwelling for real people.

But there was that thing about making sure Patrick wasn't just going to be enthusiastic because I was, so I had to act like I was just so-so on the house. I caught myself smiling a couple of times and reined it in, particularly when Patrick was looking in my direction. Angie, knowing me longer than pretty much anybody, noticed and gave me a secret enthusiastic grin when she knew no one else was looking.

'It has *tons* of potential,' Emily was saying. 'Don't you think, Sandy?'

Potential? All I needed to do was stock the kitchen and roll out a couple of area rugs. I didn't see potential. I saw a home that was perfectly completed. So I could use that gap between our definitions. 'I suppose,' I said.

'Oh, you could do *anything* with it!' Emily had seen the first slight glimmer of hope for a sale and wasn't going to let go; I hadn't been negative enough. 'You could knock down these walls and make an open-plan space for entertaining!'

Knock down my walls? How dare she! 'I'd like to talk to Patrick about it privately, please,' I said.

Without asking for permission, at least more blatantly, I moved back through the spare bedroom toward the front window on the second floor, as far from Emily as I could get right now without actually booking a plane ticket. Patrick, having noted my tone and wanting to be supportive (which is wonderful of him but not helpful when I need his actual opinion), had followed me there. We spoke not in whispers but certainly in tones quiet enough so we wouldn't be overheard.

'You have reservations?' he asked.

'I'm not saying,' I said. 'I want *your* opinion.'

Patrick looked stumped, like he couldn't understand why his opinion on a place for him to live might be relevant. 'I want what you want,' he answered.

'And that's the problem, Patrick. We're going to be living . . . somewhere . . . together. It can't be because only one or the other of us wants to be there. I need to know what you really think about this house, and then I'll tell you my own opinion. Because you know I'm not going to buy a place just for you and you shouldn't do the same for me. You're always going to be the first to voice an opinion on every house we look at from now on.' Who was I kidding? This was the last house we were going to tour and I knew it. 'So. What do you think of this place?'

That was when I happened to venture a glance out the front window. And there, on the opposite corner from before, was the figure in the gray hoodie, the black face mask and the sunglasses. Just watching the house where we happened to be visiting right at this moment.

Patrick drew a deep breath, as if he were about to dive into deep waters. 'Well, I really like this house and I think we should buy it,' he said. 'What do you think?'

I continued to stare at the solitary figure, not even really moving, but keeping a very vigilant eye on the first floor directly below where I was standing.

'I'm not sure about the neighborhood,' I said.

FIFTEEN

'You're stalling,' Jon Irvin said.

We were at Hanoi Swan, a Vietnamese restaurant (in case you couldn't tell by the name) a couple of blocks from our office and no, Jon wasn't commenting on the time it had taken me to order lunch. I was having *pho*, despite its insistence that I should not pronounce the vowel at the end of its name. Jon was eating beef *saltado*, which didn't seem Vietnamese at all, but there it had been on the menu so I didn't judge.

'Stalling?' I said. 'What am I stalling about?' I knew exactly what I was stalling about and he was right. I was now stalling about answering why I was stalling.

'You know perfectly well.' At least we were in agreement on that. 'You're stalling about filing for a new trial for your young friend's father. What's holding you up? You nervous you won't get it and then it'll be all over and you'll have to tell the little girl you couldn't help her?' Jon knows me well enough to get up in my grille every once in a while. It doesn't make it less annoying, but at least I know he's doing it from a place of respect.

'I'm filing, I'm filing,' I droned. 'Later today. I swear.'

'I don't get it, Sandy.' Jon ate a little *saltado* and managed not to spill anything on his white shirt. Jon was a pro. 'You're dealing with I don't know how many divorces, a couple of child custody cases and that pot guy, but you're spending most of your time on the pro bono case that looks like a loser from all sides. I get that you want to help the girl, but are you driving yourself to disappointment?'

'Yeah, but at least my car is running like a top.' Not my best.

'Come on.' Jon knew it wasn't my best too.

I put down my spoon. 'OK, you're right. I'm worried that I'm going to fail Riley and that's making me delay. But I *will* get the filing out today.' (Spoiler alert: I did.)

There had been no sign of the mystery person (and I couldn't be clear on gender because I'd seen them from a pretty large distance) in the hoodie, mask and sunglasses since we'd left the teal house, which I'd told Emily Webster we would get back to her about. She'd told us there might be a bid on the house soon, but real-estate agents always tell you that. I'd promised Patrick we'd talk about it tonight and by then I was hoping I'd work out my paranoid fantasies and agree that this was the place for us.

'Look, I know I've said I wouldn't, but do you need help?' Jon asked. He really is a nice guy. He almost never bugged me about getting him shot. *Unintentionally* getting him shot.

'No, I know how to run the case,' I told him. 'I'm getting the request out today and then we'll see how it goes.'

'Good, because I'm swamped.' He put down the napkin to indicate he had finished eating, something I had done a while before. 'So what do you know about it?' Jon is great at analyzing the facts and procedures in a legal case, and we often go back and forth on the matters either one of us (mostly me) is handling at a time.

'You know everything I know,' I reminded him. I was a little puzzled about his question. What did he mean, what did I know? He knew I was going to request a new trial and the basis of my argument.

'I mean, what do you know about how Helene Nestor was killed and whether or not her husband did it?' Jon would have done a deep dive. I had immersed myself in the police report so far. He was right; that was what I should have done, but I'm rather plodding in my steps. Until the request was filed, I was unlikely to look beyond it to the arguments I might have to make in a second trial about how Jack Schoenberg wasn't the person who had shot his wife.

'What I know about is Jack's claim that someone came in through the transom and killed Helene and then left again,' I said. 'The police report is clear on how that would be pretty near impossible, how the gun was found in Jack's closet, and how there had been some reported tension in the marriage before she died.'

Jon waited. 'That's it?'

'Yeah, pretty much. I'm in a preliminary stage.' Yeah, it sounded as lame to me as it does to you.

I got the patented incredulous look from Jon.

'I'm getting the filing done today.'

The look.

'Really.'

Look.

'OK,' I said. 'Go on and say it out loud.'

Jon smiled his avuncular smile but it was tinged with a little
friendly advice. 'See? You know what I'm going to say. You are
a wonderful lawyer, Sandy, but you're a lousy investigator. And
this case, all this time later, requires a very good investigator. So
you do in fact know what I'm going to say.'

I pulled my phone out of my purse and called Angie. 'Tell
Nate I need him,' I said.

Nate Garrigan works out of his home. But when Seaton, Taylor
calls, he's more than happy to visit our offices, so the only surprise
when I found him sitting in mine upon getting back from lunch,
which was perhaps twenty minutes later, was the timing.

'How'd you beat me here?' I said as I put down my stuff and
sat at my desk. Nate was splayed out over the visitor's chair, leg
over one arm of the sturdy seat. He looked, as he often does,
like a cat when it has delivered an especially gross dead mouse
to your feet in hopes of praise and reward.

'I was already in the offices when Angie called,' he said. 'One
of the divorce cases needs somebody to take compromising
photographs.'

'I thought you didn't do that kind of thing,' I told him.

'I don't. I farmed it out. So what's up with you?'

I gave him the lowdown on the Schoenberg case and he stopped
me halfway through. 'I was reading about this one when it
happened,' he said. 'The guy's a nutjob. He thinks Plastic Man
got through a window over the door and then squished himself
back through after he put a couple of slugs into the guy's wife.'

'It's your compassion that brings clients back,' I said.

'I thought it was my winning smile.'

'That's a perk,' I answered. 'Nate, how much can you find out
on a case this cold?'

There was no hesitation. 'I won't know until I look, but I think
the evidence against the guy was circumstantial. Nobody saw
him shoot his wife. Nobody saw him with blood on his hands.'

'They found blood in his bedroom closet,' I pointed out, playing devil's advocate (or in this case prosecutor's advocate, which was roughly the same thing). 'And they found the gun in his sock drawer, also in his bedroom.'

'This guy's not the least bit creative in covering up his crime,' Nate pointed out.

'Which indicates to me that he didn't do it and someone else planted the evidence so the cops would think he did.'

'So it's going to be key to find out where your client was before his wife was found dead, and where he might have been driving from,' Nate said. 'What did he say when you asked him that?'

I hadn't asked him that. I'm a stupid lawyer. I should go into the cream cheese business, where I can't hurt anyone.

'Technically the client is his daughter Riley,' I said.

'So you didn't ask him. I get that.' He did?

'You don't think I should be drummed out of the legal profession?'

Nate chuckled. 'I didn't say *that*. But it's not the question anyone would think to ask on a first meeting in jail two years later.'

'Lieutenant Trench would think to ask it.'

'Too bad,' Nate said. 'He's not available to investigate for you and I am. What do you want me to do?'

'Finding the real killer would be a swell start,' I suggested.

'Let's build up to that and make it more satisfying. Suppose I check out the mansion and see the room for myself, then work backward. You go and ask the defendant where he was on the night of.'

I looked up at the bookshelf across the room in my office. Nobody in gray hoodie, black mask and sunglasses was perched there. But there was an autographed copy of *Greetings From Asbury Park, N.J.* by Bruce Springsteen (autographed by the bass player, but still) that my mother had gotten at the Stone Pony in the early 1970s. She was a young woman then. The album cover was framed.

'The estate is up for sale,' I told Nate.

'It'd still help to get a lay of the land.'

'I know a realtor,' I told him. Actually Patrick did, but it's always fun to tweak Emily Webster and not get her a very high-profile sale. That'd teach her to hire a guy to shoot at me.

Except what if she'd hired the person in the gray hoodie and sunglasses?

'Good. Send me the contact info.'

'Will do. Nate, this is a pro bono case.'

A short pause. 'Not for me, Sandy. Normal rates apply.'

'Understood.' Holly had given me a budget. It was tighter than I might normally have, but not so sparse that I couldn't afford Nate. Unless he decided to fly to Tokyo to check out a lead. 'Besides asking Jack about where he was that night, is there anything else I can do to help you?'

'See if you can find out where Plastic Man was the same night,' he said.

SIXTEEN

I decided to bring Riley with me to meet with her father in prison. Before you call Child Services, a few things:

1. He was her father.
2. She'd been there before.
3. She asked if she could come along.
4. It was likely he'd be more forthcoming with some answers (and not others) if she were there.
5. She was his daughter.

Sure, it was a calculated move, but I'd gotten the feeling at our first meeting that Jack hadn't trusted me as much as I needed him to, and bringing Riley might grease those wheels a bit. It would also help that his daughter would see how hard the lawyer she'd hired (conned into working for free, and no, I'm not going to stop complaining about that) was trying to get her dad out of prison.

Besides, she was good company on the drive.

'So what did you think of Alicia?' she asked me. She'd refrained from asking after we'd met at Alicia's apartment, so it came as something of a surprise that she'd bring up the subject now.

'She seems to care about your welfare,' I said carefully. 'I'm not sure she approves of you hiring me.'

'She doesn't want my dad out of jail,' Riley said. 'She gets paid for letting me live in her house. My mom's estate pays her a very nice salary for' (air quotes) '"taking care of me." But you didn't tell me what you think of her.'

'I think she's a certain type of California woman who lives for the exterior and doesn't care much about the interior,' I said. 'And that remark isn't really fair to women from California so I take it back.'

Riley clapped her hands and leaned back in the passenger seat. 'That's really good!' she shouted. 'I'll have to use that one!'

'Just don't attribute it to me. Now you tell me something. Before you got that text that we're setting up the meeting about, you were going to say there was a man who might have had some connection to your mother's murder. But you never told me who he is or what the connection might be.'

I didn't look directly at Riley because I was driving and, even though I'd been there before, I was relying heavily on the GPS for my directions. So I sat through the longish silence that I figured meant she was thinking back to that conversation.

'Oh yeah. His name is Jason Kemper. He was in on the beginning of ImagiNails, I guess, and kept bugging my mom about money she supposedly owed him. I was nine . . .' (A mere child, not like now.) 'So I didn't pay much attention.'

I told Siri to remind me to check on Jason Kemper and made Riley spell his name. 'Is there anyone else you can think of who might have been angry with your mom?' I asked her. It might not have been the most delicate way to talk to an eleven-year-old about her murdered mother, but it was the best I could think of at the time.

'I don't know,' she said. (Actually she said, 'I dunno,' but I'm trying to present her as the intelligent girl she was so I'm doing a little editing.) 'My parents didn't argue in front of me, if that's what you mean. The cops asked me that like a million times.'

'That wasn't what I was asking, but I'm glad you volunteered the information anyway,' I said. We were approaching the prison, so there wouldn't be time to butter Riley up too much more. Of course, we'd have the drive back, but I thought she was ready for tougher questions now. 'Did you see your mom or your dad with other adults? I mean, like people they might have been more than friendly with?'

Riley's voice dropped half an octave. 'You're asking me if one of my parents had an affair and was stupid enough to bring them around to see me?'

'Well, when you say it like that . . .'

'Look.' She was in mature-beyond-her-years mode. 'I don't know who killed my mom. If I knew that I would tell you and you would tell the cops and they would arrest that person and let my dad go. I didn't hire you to find out who killed my mom.

I hired you to get my father out of jail. Do you think you can do that?'

'If I didn't I wouldn't have taken the case,' I lied.

'Then you should be thinking about that.' Riley folded her arms across her chest. I didn't steal a glance but I was willing to bet she had a scowl on her face as well.

I pulled the car into the gated parking lot. There was an officer checking each car that drove in, naturally. I used my legal license as ID. Riley used her school ID, which looked to have been taken when she was about seven. They let us through anyway.

The usual prison rigamarole was in place and the two of us went through it. I'd done it before and understood its purposes. Riley had been here but not been successful in seeing her father before but simply accepted that this is how things were done in this alien environment. She had no basis for comparison. I'd seen prisons that were more and less rigid in their security than this one; she had never seen any other. Eventually we got to the visiting area and Jack Schoenberg was summoned and presented.

I'd seen him only a few days before so I didn't see any particular change in his physical appearance, but I was watching Riley and she reacted pretty dramatically. She gasped when he sat down and said without thinking, 'You got so *thin*! Are you OK?'

Jack gave her a lopsided grin, not wanting to indicate to his daughter that she'd been just a little bit rude. 'Just clean living, princess. I'm so glad to see you.'

Princess?

But suddenly Riley was acting very much like a 'princess' sort of girl, something I wouldn't have predicted in my first seven hundred guesses. 'I miss you, Daddy,' she said. 'Are you all right in there? I get so scared.'

I wanted to turn to this person and ask her who she was and what she had done with Riley Schoenberg, but that was not going to help my cause, which at the moment was getting better information from Jack. I figured to let their conversation go on for a few of the minutes I had allotted to me and then get to the business end of the visit later.

'Oh, it's not that bad,' Jack answered her. 'I don't bother anybody and they don't bother me.' The bruise on his left wrist might have told a different story, but bruises are so quiet about their origins.

'Have you seen Uncle Pete?'

This time I had to cut in. 'I'm sorry to interrupt,' I said to Riley, 'but did you just say you have an uncle here in prison?'

Riley's face flashed out of princess mode for a moment, but just when she was turned away from her father and toward me. 'He's not my *real* uncle,' she said in the same sweet voice she'd used to ask her father about his playmates in state prison. 'He's a friend of my mother.'

I looked at Jack. 'And he's in jail for . . .'

'Securities fraud,' Jack answered. 'He ought to be just about ready to get paroled, actually.' He turned toward Riley. 'No, I haven't seen him, princess. It's a big place.'

'Oh, that's too bad.' This masquerade was getting a little creepy. 'He's not hiding from you, is he?'

Jack laughed. 'Of course not, Riley. Peter's just . . . well, I guess they're keeping him in another cell block than mine. You know what that means, right?'

Seriously? Had he ever *met* his daughter before?

'I think so,' Riley's voice was small, like she was trying to be eight years old again. 'It's like different classes at school, right? You don't get to choose where your friends are.'

Jack nodded, the proud father of a precocious but not terribly streetwise child. 'That's exactly it,' he said. 'Maybe I'll see him before they let him go home.'

'I hope so,' she cooed. I felt like a substitute Riley had been switched out for the real one when we were walking through the metal detectors on the way in.

'I hate to intrude, but we don't have a lot of time. Jack, what can you tell me about the night this happened?' I was starting to feel like Riley was too young to discuss her mother's death, despite the fact that we'd been talking about it plainly in the car on the way here. On top of everything else, I was sure Patrick would tell me Riley was a gifted actor.

'I've already told you everything I know,' he said. 'They said she was shot in the music room, and the door was locked.' He turned toward his daughter. 'Sorry, princess.' For what I will never know. But Jack was talking to me again. 'I was the only one besides Helene who had a key, so they just assumed I'd killed her. Then they found the gun in my chest of drawers and clearly the cops figured I was stupid enough to have put it there when – if I *had* killed my wife – I would have known they'd be looking for it. That's really all I know, Ms Moss.'

'What about before she was shot?' I asked. 'What were you doing before that?'

Jack looked at Riley then back at me. Was he trying to communicate that he didn't want her involved in this conversation? 'I was visiting a friend,' he said.

I was already taking notes. Like *get Uncle Peter's last name.* That sort of thing. 'What's your friend's name? I didn't see them mentioned in the trial transcript. In fact, you never said where you were earlier that evening.'

'I wasn't asked.' The classic dodge.

'Your lawyer wasn't a great trial attorney but he wasn't stupid,' I said. 'You weren't asked because you didn't want to be asked. Now, what is your friend's name?'

'I'd rather not say.' Jack was looking back toward the guard, as if he was hoping he'd be taken back to his cell and away from his daughter, but mostly away from me.

'I honestly don't care what you'd rather not do,' I told him. 'I'm trying to get you out of here and back into your house to finish raising your daughter. So I'll remind you how this works: I ask questions and you answer every single one of them truthfully.' I pivoted and looked at Riley, who seemed about to admonish me for talking sharply to her 'daddy'. 'And you have to do the same thing: Every question answered, honestly. Got that?'

Riley didn't say anything, but Jack answered, 'Yes ma'am.'

So I faced him. 'What. Is. Your. Friend's. Name.'

'Lisa Conforto.' I didn't respond because I wanted him to understand that he hadn't given me enough information. It took a few seconds. 'She was a business associate of Helene's. Worked in the finance area.'

'And the two of you were . . . friends?' I asked.

Jack's eyes got cold in a hurry. 'Yes. We were *friends*. And that's all. I think the guard's coming for me.' He smiled insincerely at Riley and spoke very quickly. 'I'm so glad I got to see you, princess. I love you. See you soon!' Then he got up without being prompted and caught the attention of the guard standing about twenty feet away, who got the message and walked over to escort Jack away.

'Did that do you any good?' Riley asked.

'I have to talk to a lot of people,' I said, largely to myself.

SEVENTEEN

'Where the hell is my house?' Patrick said. He had almost no inflection in his voice at all.

I had never been to a 'table read' before, but we had a second visit planned to the teal house afterward and Patrick hadn't had time to drop me off before going back to work on the set of *Torn*. He'd offered to send for someone to 'bring my car round', but I could work from the set where they were reading and didn't mind waiting. I'd been listening in a dark corner while the cast, literally sitting around a table, had read their scripts without 'acting' at all. Patrick, playing 'Clarence', one of the personalities his character supposedly had on the show, was fretting over a move from 'Monty', another personality, to him, and personally I found it embarrassing. I knew the show had consultants on what the real disorder would look like, but they were still playing it somewhat simplistically, something Patrick had been trying to improve in his capacity as producer on the show (don't be too impressed; there were by my count eighteen producers working on *Torn*). But then I hadn't been paying that much attention.

Mostly I had been answering emails and setting up appointments with people I wanted to meet about Jack's trial. And before you ask, yes, the petition for a new trial had been filed the day before. I expected it would take a few days before I'd get a hearing date. So I was half-listening to a group of actors half-acting through a script that sounded half-written. But Patrick had said this was not at all atypical and that I shouldn't worry if it sounded like no one was trying.

Because it did.

'That's great, guys.' The director, a woman (for once!) named Pamela . . . something . . . applauded, as did the producer, a (very) young man named Brandon Halston, who looked like he'd graduated from a very expensive college approximately earlier that day. There were perhaps fifteen other people watching the 'performance', and they applauded too. 'Now let's all forget about it and go home to whomever we're sleeping with at the moment.' Can't say I was crazy about how that had been worded.

But like I said, I'd only been half-listening and I withheld my applause. I was in the far corner of the room and probably only Patrick remembered I was there, but if he stole a glance (and I was pretty sure he did), he would have seen me looking curious. That's what I was trying to project: curiosity.

Frankly, enthusiasm might have been beyond my acting skills, and Patrick knows me too well for me to pretend. He'd ask my opinion later and I'd have to tell him anyway.

I was googling Lisa Conforto and Peter Lucchesi (the 'Uncle Pete' that Riley had mentioned to Jack and then filled in a last name in the car on the way home) and coming up with some seriously skimpy information. Conforto was apparently a former mid-level executive at a venture capital firm, who had since worked for Helene, and Lucchesi was behind bars for something other than stock fraud, but it was unclear what. I'd have to check with the DA's office to find out.

Lucchesi had apparently started doing some consulting (which can mean anything) with ImagiNails, and that was how Helene – and by extension, Jack – knew him. How Jack and Conforto were acquainted was a matter of speculation. But my speculation and what Jack and Riley were telling me differed, so for the moment I would lean toward their judgment. They knew the parties much better than I did, seeing as I'd never seen Jack outside prison and I'd never seen Conforto at all (although there was a photograph of her on her company's website).

'What did you think?' Patrick asked when they'd adjourned for the day.

'It was exactly what you'd told me it would be,' I answered. 'What did *you* think?'

'I'll have to talk to the show runner about some of the transition stuff,' he said. 'It's not true to people with DID.' He meant Dissociative Identity Disorder. We'd discussed it enough times now that I'd remembered the acronym as well. 'This is one of the few things I can't ask Angie to do for me, alas. She'd be great at twisting their arms.'

It was true; Angie has very little shame and none of it is

directed toward her work, which is why Patrick has often told me she's the best assistant he's ever had, and that she will one day leave his employ to be a producer in her own right. I don't know about that last part. Angie is awfully fond of Patrick and committed to his career. She leaves the rest of him to me.

We got up to leave and I told Patrick about the latest in the Schoenberg case, which was to say that it was getting more and more confusing and frustrating the more I dug in. Patrick is a great listener (he says good actors always are) and seemed particularly worried about the planned meet, scheduled for the next day, between Riley and the mysterious text-sender who was pretending to be her dead mother.

'How sure is Lieutenant Trench that Riley can be kept safe?' he asked.

'Trench isn't on the case,' I reminded him. 'Lieutenant Valdez is, and she said that setting it up in a shopping mall makes it manageable because it's enclosed. The cops will be there early to set up surveillance, Valdez will have a direct line from Riley in her headphones and they'll basically descend upon her and take her away at the first sign of trouble.'

Patrick didn't look pleased as we left the theater and squinted into the inevitable bright sunlight. 'We did an episode of *Torn* where a young girl was a witness to the crime and the police set her up to meet a suspect,' he said. 'They didn't do it in a shopping mall, but in a bowling alley.'

'A bowling alley? Why?'

'Because we had the set already built from another show and we wanted to save money,' Patrick answered. 'But the suspect knew the girl was being watched by the police and managed to snatch her away despite having everyone watching. I don't like the setup Valdez is using. How well do you trust her?'

We got into Patrick's car. We'd each driven to the rehearsal in our separate vehicles but we wanted to go off together to the teal house, so Patrick (as he always does) said he'd 'have someone sent round' to pick up my car and bring it back to Patrick's house later. He has a network of people to take care of things for him that would put Sherlock Holmes's Baker Street Irregulars to shame.

'I don't know how well I trust Valdez yet, but Trench says

she's a good cop and that should be enough,' I told him. 'I plan on being nearby to monitor, and I have Nate looking at suspects, such as they are. I still can't figure how someone got into the music room and shot Helene without anyone seeing anything, then got out and planted evidence all over the place that would implicate Jack.'

Patrick drove silently for about a block. 'Maybe Jack really did kill his wife,' he said.

'It does me no good to think like that,' I said, shaking my head. 'I'm Jack's advocate. I operate on the assumption that he's not guilty and work from there. The prosecutor already did well enough to get him convicted once. My job is to prove it was done wrong and then mount as strong a defense as I can. The truth lies somewhere between what happened at the first trial and what I hope will happen at the second.'

'Are you certain there'll be a second trial?' Patrick asked.

'As much as I'm certain of anything. The rule they broke was a basic one and there are very few judges who would see it any other way.'

For reasons I'll never truly understand, I happened at that moment to glance at the side mirror through my passenger-side window. And I stopped talking.

It didn't take long for Patrick to notice. 'What's wrong?' he asked.

'There's someone behind us in a navy-blue SUV,' I said.

'That's not terribly unusual.'

'This person is wearing a hoodie, a black mask and sunglasses,' I told him. 'And not letting us out of their sight.'

I'd told Patrick about the person at the teal house. 'Are you sure? A lot of people wear hoodies and sunglasses.'

'I'm pretty sure.'

'Same hoodie? Same sunglasses?' Patrick was looking in his rear-view mirror. 'I see them.'

'No, last time the hoodie was gray. This time it's black.'

'Do you want to call the lieutenant?' he asked.

'And tell him what? That a casually dressed person is driving behind us? He'll lock us up for being embarrassing to all residents of Los Angeles.'

'I can try to lose them,' Patrick offered. 'I know these streets better than you do.'

'People who flew in this morning know these streets better than I do,' I said. 'And I'm really not interested in you trying to Steve McQueen all over downtown Los Angeles.'

'This isn't downtown Los Angeles.'

'What did I tell you?'

Patrick did pick up the pace a bit but the hoodie vigilante was keeping with us. I couldn't figure their angle; was the idea to find out where we were going, or to intimidate us? Because right now they were doing both quite effectively.

Finally Patrick nodded his head once, definitively. I knew what that meant; he had made up his mind about something. 'Patrick . . .' I began, worried.

'I know what I'm doing.' The scariest five words in the English language.

Then he told me to hang on, and before I could ask what the hell *that* meant, Patrick had veered the car across three lanes to stop near the curb on the side of whatever street this was. He stopped the car and put it in park.

'What are you *doing*?' I yelped. 'They'll catch us!'

'Exactly. And we will be able to ask what they're trying to accomplish and who they are.'

'What if they have a gun?'

Patrick didn't answer. He probably figured he could get out of such a situation with some gambit from a TV show he'd filmed, which would have had the advantage of having someone write down the scene with the stated purpose of getting Patrick out alive.

But we never found out. The hoodie vigilante just drove on without us, not even casting a glance in our direction.

I felt like waving at them.

We watched the car drive off – not into the sunset, not yet today – and then turned toward each other.

'Well, what now?' I said to Patrick.

He considered and then shrugged his shoulders. 'Let's go buy a house.'

EIGHTEEN

We didn't buy the house. Not right then, anyway. We both said we wanted to but it was disconcerting, let's say, to make such a decision right after having been driven off the road by a random person in sunglasses and a hooded sweatshirt. We told Emily, who had miraculously shown up just when we arrived at the teal house, that we would make an offer within twenty-four hours.

It was an inevitability; we both loved the house and saw things we wanted to do with it. That wasn't the issue. We were preoccupied with other things: Patrick had his series and its DID issues and I had Jack Schoenberg, Riley, and a strange doppelgänger with very drab fashion sense. It just seemed irresponsible to offer all kinds of money (largely Patrick's) on a house with all that going on.

So I found myself back at my desk sorting through a divorce file when Riley called to say she wasn't going to the meeting set up by Lieutenant Valdez for the next day.

'I just don't like the vibe,' she said after I expressed my astonishment. 'This weirdo texts me out of nowhere and pretends to be my mom. That's just creepy.'

'Yes,' I said, 'but going to the meeting is the best way to find out who the weirdo is and getting the police to stop them.'

There was a long pause. 'The police don't always catch the right person,' Riley said.

I didn't want the mystery texter out there possibly stalking Riley (and if the messages were to be believed, me), and I had a definite stalker I could point to in order to get a police sketch that would look like every police sketch ever drawn, putting at least one of us in danger and complicating matters. Besides, getting the straight story from this person could shed all sorts of light on the night Helene had died. My case was wispy at best right now. Any information I could get would be an improvement.

'I get that, Riley. Believe me, I do. But I'll be there at the mall and I'm going to be watching you like a hawk. Nobody is going to get near you without me knowing it. If there's anything the least bit hinky about what's going down, I'll end it. I promise.'

An even longer pause. 'Hinky?'

The only thing to do in that situation was to ignore it. I was trying to be a tough criminal attorney and sounded like an actor in a 1990s television cop show.

'Are you scared?' I asked, assuming Riley wouldn't admit to it but trying to communicate that it was OK to be worried about such a fraught situation.

'Yeah,' she said, and that was all.

OK, it was touchier than I'd thought. 'Here's what we're going to do,' I said. 'Before you even set foot in the place, you're going to dial my number on your phone. You're going to hold it in your right hand under the table. If there's *anything* you don't like about what's happening, you're going to hit send on that phone and not only will I show up but I'll have a bunch of heavily armed officers of the law and maybe a TV star who thinks he's a hero with me. Absolutely nothing bad is going to happen to you. Is that OK?'

'No,' Riley said. 'But it's probably the best I'm going to do. Will this help get my dad out of jail?'

Say what you want about Riley, she had a very focused mind. 'If things go well, maybe, but I'm not making any promises. Except that nothing bad is going to happen to you.'

'Bad stuff has already happened to me,' she said, and there was no rational way to argue with that.

'At the meeting tomorrow,' I specified. 'I can't promise your life will be permanently wonderful from now on.'

'OK,' she said and hung up.

I sat there for a moment. My preteenage client had just hung up on me after suggesting that perhaps I wasn't taking her feelings into account while trying to get a new trial for her father. Riley wasn't like any sixth grader I'd ever met. Maybe she was the girl I wished I'd been when Ms Carbone had asked me to define Communism and then told me I was wrong when I knew otherwise. Or maybe she was just a wiseass, the like of which I hadn't really run into since I'd left my home state. Either way she confounded me, and that was a little concerning at the moment.

Luckily I had little time for such ruminations because my phone rang and Nate Garrigan was on the other end. 'Come meet me,' he said.

'It's nice to hear from you too, Nate. We must do this more often.'

'I'm sitting here with Lisa Conforto,' Nate went on. 'I think you might want to talk to her.'

The name was familiar . . . 'Lisa Conforto? The one who Jack Schoenberg was with the night he supposedly killed his wife?'

'No, Lisa Conforto the most celebrated prima ballerina in all of El Paso,' Nate answered. Maybe I had met a wiseass or two in Los Angeles. 'I'm texting you the address.' And then he hung up, which seemed to be the pattern today. Mobile phones make things way too informal.

Sure enough an address came from Nate's mobile and I told Celia that I'd be out of the office for two hours. Celia is a professional but she's also a master gossip, so I had made it a practice never to tell her where I was going or who I might be meeting unless I actually wanted everyone – and I mean everyone – in the office to know my daily business. So I didn't tell her now. Celia nodded and I left. It wasn't like she couldn't reach me if she needed to.

I'd petitioned Judge Henry Drummond for the hearing regarding a new trial. The papers were in (although they weren't so much papers as Google files, but you get the drift) and there was nothing to do right now but wait. I didn't expect Judge Drummond to take long but it was far too soon for any such communication. So on the drive to Lisa Conforto's house, I played instrumental music (Strauss's 'Tales From the Vienna Woods') low and took mental stock. There was a lot to be done.

I instructed Siri to call the *Los Angeles Times* and asked for T'Aisha Kendall, only to be told she'd moved on and was now working as a producer on a television show in which a former municipal judge named Betsy held court – literally – for people who'd rather appear on TV than actually work out their differences through the legal system. The editor I spoke to at the *Times* gave me her cell number after I suggested I had been forced to wipe my contacts file, and I called T'Aisha, who surprisingly answered on the first ring.

'Who is this?' Like I said, way too informal.

I explained who I was and T'Aisha, apparently relieved that I was not a telemarketer calling about the non-existent extended warranty on her car, seemed to relax. 'I covered the Schoenberg trial but I don't know anything about an appeal,' she said. 'I got out of newspapers when this job came up.'

'But I'll bet you remember everything from that trial,' I said. 'How'd you like to write a book about Jack Schoenberg, including the inside story on his new trial – it's not an appeal – when that happens?'

Newspaper reporters, even more than journalists on radio or television, are a strange breed. It's not a job; it's a calling. Those who are called rarely give it up willingly, except for something approaching a living wage, which television is happy to offer. But the itch for a good story never really leaves them, and I was counting on that with T'Aisha.

I was not disappointed but her voice had a healthy skepticism attached to it. 'What's the catch?' she asked.

'There are a couple of catches,' I answered honestly. 'First, you have to sit down with me and tell me everything about that trial that's not in your articles. I need to get a sense of what was offered into evidence and why, and what kind of vibe was in the room, plus anything else you can remember. How's that?'

'I can do that. What's the other catch?'

'Jack hasn't consented to the book yet,' I said. 'In fact, we've never discussed it.'

The mobile phone was right next to T'Aisha's ear, so I might have actually heard the gears spinning in her head. 'I don't actually need his cooperation for the book but it would be nice. Do you have a publisher interested?'

'I literally thought of this two minutes ago,' I said.

'You're kind of a nut, aren't you?' she asked after a moment of thought.

'No. I'm just from Jersey.'

I could see her nod in my mind's eye, despite having no idea what she looked like. 'Of course. Well, I'm happy to share about the trial whether we get a book deal or not. How's Riley?' I hadn't mentioned Jack's daughter, so it was interesting to hear T'Aisha bring her up.

'She's actually my client,' I told her. 'She's convinced her father didn't kill Helene.'

'She's a real pistol,' T'Aisha said. We came up with a place (a bar near T'Aisha's offices on a backlot) and time (two days later after work) to meet, and disconnected the call.

I had time for one more before I'd arrive to meet Nate and Lisa Conforto. Siri was once again helpful in finding a phone number for Cagney Weldon IV, Jack Schoenberg's lawyer in what I was already mentally calling his first trial.

Mr Weldon refused to be in, but I left a message and was adamant in saying I would call back soon if I didn't hear from him. Sometimes you don't have to be annoying as long as you promise to be annoying. The phone rang two minutes later and Weldon was on the other line.

'What is this about?' he demanded. I'd been more politely greeted on the phone by bill collectors.

'Jack Schoenberg,' I said. 'I'm getting him a new trial.' I held back on the ammunition I figured I'd need.

Weldon laughed briefly. He was an abrupt man. Busy, you know. Other things to do. No time to put together a complete sentence with, like, verbs. 'How'd you get stuck with that?' he asked.

'His daughter asked me,' I said.

'How is Riley?' he asked.

'She's a pistol.' Because once someone refers to you that way, it should be your descriptor for the rest of your life.

He laughed again, more warmly. 'She is. So what do you need?'

'Why you let such a blatant error as not letting the defendant present his defense go without an appeal,' I said. That was the ammunition I'd held back; letting him know it was *his* mistake I was going to use. Well, his and the judge's, anyway.

Weldon's voice took on a sterner, more critical tone. 'Because my client gave me specific instructions not to file for an appeal,' he said. 'Don't you think I saw that at trial? I objected and when I was overruled I entered an exception with the judge.' Noting an exception is essentially a way of saying, 'I think you're wrong to overrule that objection.' It was the most inconsequential thing

Weldon could do, beyond doing nothing at all, which probably was his fallback position. 'I was laying the groundwork for an appeal right in the courtroom but Jack said no, he would go to jail, because he'd really killed his wife and deserved to be there. So no, Ms Moss, I did not file for an appeal. I wanted to, believe me.'

'Did you believe Jack when he said he'd killed Helene?' I asked.

'Of course not. The evidence they had was circumstantial and indicated not that Jack had murdered his wife, but that they couldn't show someone else who had. If DeForge wasn't such a stick-in-the-mud who wanted to run for governor, he would have presided over a much less biased trial.'

Maybe this Weldon guy wasn't so bad. You never know; occasionally guys with *IV* in their names aren't starched rich idiots. It's not the rule but it happens.

'Is there anything I need to know that I won't find in the transcripts and the police reports?' I asked him.

'The house where it happened hasn't sold yet,' he said. 'It took forever to get the title worked out after Helene died, and they're asking even more than the usual fortune, so it's still there and unoccupied. Even the furniture hasn't been removed. If I were you, I'd go there and see the layout. There's no way someone could do what Jack said they did, but the physical evidence indicated to me that he couldn't have gotten in there and shot her, either.'

'He had a key,' I said, bewildered.

'He also had a delusion about tiny people coming through a transom and shooting his wife, like he'd left it all for the elves that evening. But I knew he didn't kill her.'

'How?' I asked.

'The man had a broken right index finger and was in awful pain. He couldn't have pulled the trigger. Yeah, and the judge wouldn't let me introduce the medical records of that either because he said Schoenberg had a left hand as well.' More reason to get a new trial.

I thanked Weldon profusely for his help. He told me to forget it and, yes, hung up. But the file he had referred to did indeed show up in my email five minutes later.

By then I was walking up to the entrance of Lisa Conforto's house.

NINETEEN

She turned out to be a vaguely attractive woman, not a heart-breaker, dressed casually in all likelihood because she hadn't been expecting a visit from a private investigator when she'd put on clothes that morning. She sat on a mocha-colored sofa that was too deep and overstuffed, and across from her in an easy chair (as opposed to a difficult chair?), at least until he stood when I entered, was Nate Garrigan.

I had been led in by Ken Warshofsky, the most average-looking man in America and possibly the Western Hemisphere, who had introduced himself as Lisa's representative. Was that her agent? Her attorney? Her doppelgänger? It was hard to know. He stood next to the easy chair as if he wouldn't naturally bend at the waist to be seated. It was a wonder he didn't clasp his hands behind the small of his back in the 'at ease' position.

Nate, doing his gregarious act, came over and clasped my hand between both of his, greeting me fake-warmly and making a very big show out of how well he and I get along. We *do* get along well as colleagues, but he seemed to want Lisa and possibly Ken to believe we were at least good friends. For now, playing along was the best strategy available, so I took it.

'You look great, Sandy!' he began, which was as far from Nate's usual demeanor as he could get without putting on a tutu and dancing *Swan Lake*. 'Thanks for coming on such short notice!' Everything he said today seemed to have at least one exclamation mark attached to it. I'll spare you the extras I could hear in his voice.

'Not a problem,' I said. I turned my attention to the woman on the sofa. 'Are you Lisa Conforto?'

'Yes I am,' she said. Terse. She didn't want to be questioned. Her arms were clasped tightly across her chest. Her feet were flat on the floor. She was tense. This man had shown up at her door and asked her a bunch of stuff she'd rather not talk about, and now I was here and she didn't even know me and what the hell was I going to do? I understood her position, but Nate had obviously determined that she knew something of relevance, so I persisted.

'Mr Garrigan asked me to come because I'm the attorney representing Jack Schoenberg in his petition for a new trial,' I said. I looked at Nate to get some clarification and caught his eye.

He seemed to wake up; oh yeah, he *had* called me after all, hadn't he? He took a step forward. 'I was telling Sandy here about what you were telling me, Lisa,' he said. His voice was calm and almost tender. I was wondering if that was really Nate. 'I think it would be best if you told her, too. To help Jack.'

But Lisa wasn't buying Nate's tone any more than I was; she hadn't known him very long but she could spot an acting job when she saw one. She lived in the capital of make-believe. 'You know I don't want to talk about this,' she told Nate. 'I *told* you I don't want to talk about this. I especially don't want to talk about this in front of a judge.'

Since she wasn't interested in Nate's approach, I figured a woman-to-woman tactic might do the trick, but I wasn't optimistic. 'Of course you don't,' I said. 'And I'll do everything I can to keep you from having to testify in court. But if you have information that could help Jack get a new trial and then win it to get out of prison, that has to be worth the risk, don't you think?'

All this time Ken was standing silently near Lisa like – I have to say it – an especially protective dog guarding its mistress. His facial expression didn't seem capable of change and his posture was that of a man who'd had a particularly rigorous colonoscopy and was still getting over the effects. He said nothing, but his presence was at least a little baffling if not disquieting.

It didn't seem to have any effect on Lisa, who never so much as glanced at her 'representative'. 'Look, I'm sorry Jack's in jail but I'm not going to put myself at risk for him. I didn't know the guy all that well.' She gave me a 'we-girls-know' look. 'If you know what I mean.'

To be brutally honest, I had no idea what she meant. Was she implying that she and Jack had been lovers? Or that they *hadn't* been lovers? Or that they'd never actually met? Any of these scenarios was possible given her response.

'Why don't you tell me whether Jack was here the night that Helene was killed,' I said. 'We can go from there. Anything you want to keep confidential, we can talk about.' I wasn't committing myself to anything but I wanted to make it sound like I was. That thing about lawyers being tricky? It's not entirely unearned.

'He was here,' Lisa said. She did not elaborate.

'Ms Conforto will not incriminate herself under any circumstances, and anything said in this room today will be entirely confidential,' Ken said. Apparently he had roused himself from his trance and regained the power of speech.

'Are you Lisa's attorney?' I asked him.

His mouth twitched. Lisa did not bat an eyelash. She looked bored.

'No, I am not a member of the bar,' Ken said.

'Then you have no authority to speak on her behalf or to try to establish rules for this conversation,' I told him in what I hoped was an instructive tone of voice and not an admonishing one. That's what I hoped. 'So please don't impose any. I have no intention of trying to get you to incriminate yourself, Lisa, but Ken's suggestion that you could makes me wonder if he's trying to tell me that you are actually the person who killed Helene Nestor.'

That was, I should explain, a calculated move. I wanted to throw a little grenade into the conversation to get Lisa to react emotionally and Ken to shut up. It had the desired effect in both areas.

'What!' Lisa shouted. She did not get up off the sofa, so I assumed either that she had not studied a lot of bad acting or was simply too offended to do anything but look up at me and yell. 'You think *I* killed Helene? Why would I do that?'

Ken, as I noted, had shut up, and was back to doing an impression of his Madame Tussaud's exhibit.

'I don't think that,' I said. 'My point was that the suggestion you might incriminate yourself made it sound like that. So why don't you just tell me what happened and we can move on from there?'

If you confront someone with the suggestion that they committed a horrible crime and then tell them it was because *they* were being unreasonable, they tend to operate on the adrenaline rush but not direct it at you. I don't recommend it as an icebreaker at parties, but in legal cases it can have quite the effect.

Lisa blinked, physically and metaphorically. 'OK. All right.' She seemed to be talking to herself. 'Jack came here that night. He was upset with Helene and he wanted to talk it out with someone who knew both of them. I mean, he wasn't talking about divorce or anything, but she had been on him about not having a job, and that upset him. She had all that money and still she would give him a hard time because he didn't bring anything in. He was basically raising Riley on his own, you know, but that wasn't good enough for her.'

This was a somewhat different portrait of the marriage than I'd heard before from either Riley or Jack, and for that matter not what Lieutenant Valdez had suggested either. 'You knew Helene before you met Jack. Isn't that right?' I asked. Ask someone their backstory and you'll generally get much more than that.

Well, that's true *most* of the time. Lisa looked a trifle annoyed, as if I'd somehow prodded into a personal area that shouldn't have been breached. 'Yeah, I used to work for her at ImagiNails,' she said, and that was it.

'What kind of boss was she?' It's also true that people like to complain about their bosses. Except Angie, who adores Patrick and for good reason. And me, because Holly is wonderful and mostly leaves me alone. But Ken looked like he might have a story or two to tell, and maybe it would be a good idea to get Nate to talk to him privately when we were finished here.

'She was a boss.' Lisa did her best to sound indifferent, but the level of displeasure in her wouldn't allow a convincing tone to come out. Instead she sounded like someone who . . . might have been pleased, let's say, when her employer had been shot in the head and killed. 'She didn't yell or throw things. She wasn't a close friend or anything.'

Nate, keeping an eye on Ken for reasons I didn't entirely understand, sat on an ottoman next to me and asked Lisa, 'What was your job there?'

Lisa clearly had a stronger bond with Nate, who had gotten

there first and was male, than with me, who hadn't and wasn't. She smiled at him even as his gaze remained fixed on Ken. It was like Nate was expecting Ken to pull a gun and wanted to be ready to defend himself, me and Lisa, in that order.

'I worked in the financial division of the company,' she said, her voice much sunnier than it had been with me. I'd sit back and let Nate ask more of the questions, I decided. 'I wasn't in charge of it, but then Helene didn't believe in promoting women very much.'

Bingo.

'Why do you suppose that was?' Nate asked.

Ken, for some reason, felt it was necessary to step in at that point. 'Ms Conforto will not answer any questions about her relationship with the deceased.'

I let out a theatrical sigh that I like to think Patrick, now in his fifth season of series television, would have been proud of. 'Ken, do I have to remind you again that you are not an attorney and you don't get to set the boundaries for our conversation? In fact, I'm not completely certain why you're here at all.'

Ken drew himself to his full height, which – as you might have assumed – was average. 'I'm here because I am Lisa's husband,' he said.

It took me a moment. 'OK, that's a pretty good reason to be here,' I admitted.

TWENTY

To spare you the rest of our long and somewhat tedious (whenever Ken or I got involved) interview, Lisa had married Ken roughly a year earlier, or about one year after Helene Nestor had been murdered. They'd known each other at ImagiNails, where Ken was, well, an accountant who was working in Lisa's division. I did my best to avoid picturing that magic moment when their passion could no longer be contained. I imagined it had involved a good deal of paperwork.

Lisa told us (Nate) that she had never had a romantic relationship with Jack Schoenberg. They had bonded over a mutual irritation with Helene and had grown to be friends. He had come to her house the night of the murder – and Ken had been there as well, so he said he could confirm it – because Helene had essentially banished him for the evening. She was going to have an important board meeting, she'd told him, and that he was an embarrassment in such company.

Clearly they'd had an ideal marriage.

They'd conferred until about midnight, having discussed starting a business separate from ImagiNails that would supply craft services on movie sets, with disposable containers and platters more eco-friendly than the aluminum ones most often in use at the moment. Jack had some connections with manufacturers who could create such products, and Lisa understood the supply chain. As far as I could tell, Ken made snacks and nodded a lot.

But his guacamole was truly a thing of beauty. He said he'd made it the night Jack was there because the oven was broken and he couldn't make cheese puffs, so it was appropriate to make guacamole again while we discussed Jack. That was how Ken thought. It was best not to consider that too deeply.

'Why wouldn't all of this have been brought up in the first trial?' I asked Jon when I got back to my office to pick up some things on my way home. 'I've been through the entire transcript and there hasn't been so much as a mention of Lisa or Ken. I realize they asked Jack not to involve them, but that's above and beyond the call, don't you think? They're his alibi.'

Jon held up his hands as if defensively, palms facing me. 'Hang on. First of all, you have no evidence that they're telling the truth beyond them saying that they are, but they don't want you tell anybody. That's fishy in and of itself.'

'True. But even so, I could have them subpoenaed and they'd have to tell their story. If Jack was at their house until midnight . . .'

'. . . there's no guarantee he didn't kill Helene before he left and went there to use them as a cover.' Jon gestured toward the office door. 'Come on. For once let's both actually leave when we said we would.'

I nodded and picked up my iPad, my purse, and a pretty large file of T'Aisha Kendall's articles I wanted to discuss with her the day after next. Tomorrow would be devoted to watching Riley when the mysterious texter met her at the mall's food court (and working on some of my paying cases). We headed for the elevator and waited.

'The problem with this case,' I said aloud, giving voice to the thoughts I'd been having for days, 'is that I don't know what I want to happen. I don't know that Jack didn't kill his wife and therefore should be released from jail. I don't know that Riley is even telling me the truth when she says he didn't. I don't know if I want to defend his case in court.'

The elevator doors opened and Jon held the door for me, a chivalrous gesture I appreciate but think is outdated. I'm complex. We waited until the doors closed and then he turned toward me.

'You know perfectly well that what you want to happen is irrelevant,' he said. 'Everyone is entitled to a defense and the judge in Jack's trial didn't allow that. You're doing exactly what you should be doing.'

'Easy for you to say.' When the person talking to you is stating uncomfortable truths, the New Jersey way is to be snarky and defensive. We perform this as a service to the rest of the country. You're welcome.

'Good. You know I'm right.' Jon should have been born in

New Jersey. Instead I think he's from Minnesota. It's not true that nobody in Los Angeles is a native, but they're not easy to find. 'You prosecuted lots of people you probably knew weren't guilty because that was your job.'

'Most of them were guilty,' I said. 'Almost all of them were guilty.' We stopped talking because the elevator stopped at the seventh floor and the doors opened.

And in walked a person in a gray hoodie, black face mask and sunglasses. Inside an elevator.

My eyes must have widened to the size of hubcaps because Jon started to reach for his phone to call 911 and tell them I was having a stroke. I managed to shake my head briefly and then he looked at our new elevator-mate.

Even this close it wasn't easy to determine a gender. Whoever this person was, they hunched over as if having stomach pain and looked at the floor as the doors closed and we resumed our descent. Their hands were in the sweatshirt's pockets. The glasses were dark but not mirrored; they gave away nothing.

And all that person did was stand there. That was it. Not a threatening move, not a word of warning (or anything else), not a gesture of menace. Just stood there.

We rode in silence to the lobby. The doors opened and we all three stood there waiting to see who'd move first. Finally my arch nemesis (why not?) decided to take the first steps and walked away as if nothing had happened. Because technically nothing had.

Jon and I stepped out and I watched the hoodie person walk away and through the exit to the building. 'What was that all about?' he asked.

'I don't know, but I'm definitely calling my favorite cop.'

TWENTY-ONE

I f Lieutenant Trench could be somewhat formal and a wee bit condescending face-to-face, on the telephone he was borderline insufferable. I'm sure he thought the same of me.

'We've discussed this, Ms Moss,' he said. 'I'm not sure what actions you believe the Los Angeles Police Department should take against someone who had the audacity to share an elevator with you after work. Do you expect that I can look up past records of people who have ridden elevators and arrest the most likely suspects on charges of going downstairs under false pretenses?'

I was in my car, carefully assessing the area in every direction as I drove to Patrick's house, where he and Angie and I were to have dinner. Nobody seemed especially threatening at the moment but hoodies are ubiquitous. Everyone was a suspect.

'Someone is following me, stalking me, and you don't think that's a crime?' I asked. 'I could cite you literally millions of precedents.'

'Luckily this is not a court of law and I am not a judge,' Trench answered. 'I know you have been through some experiences before that have made you understandably anxious, particularly while you are working on criminal cases. And I am obliged to tell you that as a police officer I think you should take whatever legal steps you believe you need in order to feel safer. But I also feel it necessary to tell you that in my professional judgment you are overreacting.'

'So you refuse to do anything,' I said. Yes, for the record, I was being unreasonable. Trench was a homicide detective, and nobody involved in what I was doing had been the victim of a homicide or attempted homicide, not for two years at least. But I felt like someone was trying very hard to make a statement and it was not a wish that I have a lovely day. I was just a hair testy.

'I am not capable of doing anything more at this time, Ms Moss,' Trench said. 'I don't believe you have a credible threat on your hands. I can't send a cruiser to follow you around wherever you go, and no one, as far as I can tell, has committed any crime at all other than being in the same area as you on a number of occasions. So please tell me again why you called your friendly homicide detective today.'

There was a guy on the side of the road in a business suit carrying a sign that read, 'Please help. Homeless since LIVE-ACTION MULAN tanked.' It's a cruel city. Just to prove how cruel, I didn't stop and give him a dollar. Did he think that movie truly represented female empowerment? Please. (I didn't see it, but I'm guessing.)

'I called just to hear you say that I'm probably not in any danger,' I sighed. 'Thank you, Lieutenant.'

'Feel free to call anytime you feel the least bit anxious, Ms Moss.'

'You didn't really mean that, did you?'

'You are an astute judge of vocal tone.' At least before Trench hung up he said goodbye.

I made it to Patrick's house, which I had come to think of as his fortress, without incident. I swiped my card at the security gate and it let me in, which I thought was downright neighborly of it. Naturally, when I got into the house, Angie was already there. But Patrick was nowhere to be seen.

'He's in the you-know,' Angie told me. 'Which is good because there's something I have to tell you while Patrick's not in the room.'

I regarded her for a moment. 'You know we live in an apartment without him, right?'

'This won't wait, and besides, *some* of us haven't been staying at the apartment all that much lately, OK? Anyway, listen. Patrick knows you want to buy the teal house but he doesn't want it and he doesn't know how to tell you. He wants you to have what you want.'

That was a stunner; Patrick had seemed as enthusiastic about the teal house as I had thought I was, but it was characteristic of him that he'd suppress his preference in favor of mine. That was exactly what I'd been afraid of.

What bothered me was that he'd told Angie what he really wanted and hadn't felt comfortable enough to tell me.

But before I could even react, Patrick came bounding into the kitchen where we were standing, Angie with a bottle of red wine in her hand, and me holding out the glass for her to pour. We froze and stood there like a tableau. Patrick stopped and looked at us then broke out in laughter.

'Are you posing for a production still?'

We had to pretend it was a gag for his benefit, and Patrick seemed to buy that ruse, enough so that he let it go as a topic of conversation. I didn't let on about Angie's revelation and I went out of my way not to bring up the teal house when we sat down to dinner, no longer attended by Patrick's cook or butler, who had been snatched away, he said, by Jason Sudeikis 'now that the *Ted Lasso* money has kicked in.' Angie had, in fact, concocted a lasagna, something at which she excels because she is, after all, an Italian-American from central New Jersey.

What you have to understand is that there is virtually nothing Angie can't do if she decides it's worth doing. Why she hasn't cured cancer or solved climate change yet is a mystery. I asked her about it once and she said those things would require years in a laboratory (not to mention science classes), and she didn't want to be locked away for her best-looking years. One must have priorities.

The usual truths were exchanged about how delicious Angie's creation had turned out, and then Patrick, as he often did after a day of shooting, wanted to talk about anything except *Torn*. He loves his work but it's an exhausting day, even when all that's happening is a bland table read of the pages they're planning on filming. He needs to decompress in the evening and I'm glad to help because, frankly, I think *Torn* is not a worthy showcase for Patrick's talents. I'm a snob. Sue me. (I'm a lawyer and I'll win.)

'They're shooting mostly the scenes with the criminal tomorrow,' Patrick said. Yes, I know I just said he doesn't like to talk about work right after work, but give him a minute. And he does refer to the guest star of the week as the 'criminal', because his character(s) will be trying to catch that actor in the show, and it helps his process, or something. Actors are nuts, but some of them are very nice. 'So if you want me to come along when you're going to the meeting with Riley, I could be there.' See?

I had expected this offer because Patrick likes to be the knight on the white horse, when in fact he can just barely ride a horse and has never, to my knowledge, jousted. So I was ready with a response. 'It's at a mall food court, Patrick,' I reminded him. 'You're a very recognizable person. You're going to cause a fuss just by showing up; I've seen it happen. And the last thing we need tomorrow is a lot of attention in the place where the cops and I are keeping a close eye on Riley. So thanks for the offer, but why not run your lines for the next day or get Angie to help you take over another area of the entertainment industry?'

He smiled his 'modest' smile and crinkled his eyes at me, which was entirely unfair. He knows that expression was one of the first that got my notice (and probably that of many other women, but Patrick doesn't talk about that). 'That's what you really want me to do, love?'

I nodded. 'That's what I really want you to do. I appreciate you wanting to help, but you have to let me do this.'

We looked at each other for a long moment until Angie said, 'Hey guys, I'm right here.'

We all chuckled a bit and Patrick said, 'All right, Sandy. We'll play it your way. Patrick McNabb will be nowhere near that food court tomorrow.'

I reached over from my seat and kissed him casually, but he knew it meant something.

I dug back into my lasagna and looked at Angie. She was grinning. That was probably when I should have known something was up.

It must have been the red wine.

TWENTY-TWO

It was as ordinary a shopping mall as you could imagine, assuming you've spent any time at all in Southern California and know that nothing here is at all ordinary. The food court where Riley's meeting with the mysterious texter was being staged probably had hot dogs that I could afford. The stores surrounding it unquestionably were out of my price range. Maybe Patrick could have bought a purse here, but there's still that societal taboo about men carrying purses and against women having pockets in their clothes. It's a stumper.

I had picked Riley up at her Aunt Alicia's condo and driven her to the mall under the pretense of safety but really because I wanted to have an excuse to be in the building when the meeting was taking place. Lieutenant Valdez had not specifically called me up that morning and told me not to come, which I took as a sign that she secretly wanted me there and couldn't muster up the courage to ask me herself.

'Are you nervous?' I asked her. Until then Riley had simply been staring at her phone the way she always did.

'Of course I'm nervous,' she said, thus anointing me the stupidest woman in Los Angeles County. 'I'm going to meet someone who's pretending to be my dead mother for reasons I can't begin to think of and maybe called me up to say they're going to kill me. And you too, in case you forgot.' She continued to not look up from her phone.

'I didn't forget.'

She sighed heavily, once again simmering in the sheer idiocy of everything I might ever do or say. I was getting a preview of what it would be like if I ever had a daughter, and it was making me really sorry about things I probably said to my mother twenty years before. I mean, not so sorry that I'd call her up that night and apologize, because my mother would surely think I had lost my mind and attempt to start commitment proceedings.

'Look,' I told her, 'we can call this off right now if you're that scared. I'm sure Lieutenant Valdez can find another way to track down this person without putting you at risk.'

This actually prompted Riley to look up from her screen and, as far as my peripheral vision could tell, regard me with a sour look. 'I thought you said I wasn't going to *be* at risk,' she said.

'From everything I've been told the possibility is very remote,' I answered. 'But nothing is foolproof and there are never any guarantees. That's something I surely don't have to tell you.'

Back to the phone. 'Yeah.'

We were pulling up to the mall parking lot. If we were going to abort this operation, we'd have to do it within the next few minutes. 'So should I call the lieutenant and tell her we don't want to go ahead with this?'

Not a blink. 'No.' That was it.

'Riley.' I was turning the car right into the parking lot and heading for the entrance nearest the food court, where I would drop Riley off so she wouldn't be seen walking in with someone else. 'I'm just trying to look out for your best interests. You going in unsure of yourself won't help anybody. Don't do it if you don't want to.'

'Of *course* I don't want to!' she shouted. 'Who would want to meet someone that creepy? But I want my dad to get out of jail and this is the way to do it, so that's what I'm gonna do. Now will you please just stop the car so I can get out?'

We were easily six hundred yards from the entrance. 'What, here?' I asked.

'Yes! Here!' She thrust her hands up to the sides of her head to illustrate just how big an idiot she had to deal with in this car. 'I don't want anyone to see me with *you*!'

I stopped the car without parking it and Riley's hand was on the door handle the same second. She got out without saying another word and walked in the direction of her destination without ever looking back.

The only thing I could think of doing was driving closer to the entrance, finding a parking space that wouldn't require a shuttle to get me to the mall, and going inside to stand guard over my client while trying to look casual standing at the entrance to a Shake Shack.

Of course Riley had taken a head start on me, but she was on foot and I had the car. So it was a small surprise when I spotted her exiting a café with nothing more than a roll and a cup of coffee. I guessed she didn't want to be distracted by the food.

We were ten minutes early for the meeting. I ducked inside the Shake Shack and found a wall away from the entrance to lean against while I called Lieutenant Valdez.

'We're already there,' she said by way of greeting.

'So am I. How do I know if there's a threat?'

'What the hell are you doing here?' Valdez said. 'Is that you in the Shake Shack?'

She could see me? How much protection could I offer Riley if a cop could spot me from . . . wherever they were? How come I couldn't see her if she could see me? I got into the ordering line just to look more casual.

'No,' I answered. 'I'm not in the Shake Shack. Where are you?'

'In the Shake Shack.' She hung up.

My best guess was that Valdez was *not* in the Shake Shack, based largely on the fact that I could see the whole place from where I was and she was not evident, and that she wouldn't tell me if she was. I ordered some fries and a chocolate shake (I mean, they named the whole company after the shakes) and moved on because that's what you do at Shake Shack. But all that time my eyes were scanning the food court outside of this small store and looking for anyone who might be the mystery texter. But how could I tell who that might be? We didn't even know what gender the caller was, and Riley had heard their voice. We had no evidence the two messages had come from the same person, and a texter can be anybody.

So I just looked over the crowd of upscale shoppers stopping to buy some overpriced fast food. It wasn't exactly jammed, but this was a pretty ritzy mall and the people who don't actually live in Beverly Hills probably didn't want to maneuver their way inside and pay for valet parking (which I had not) just to get to stores with merchandise they couldn't afford. Silly peasants.

There were the predictable teenagers, far more stylishly dressed than I had ever been before I was at least . . . OK, more stylishly dressed than I had ever been in my life. So I'm not a fashion plate, but a big deal TV star loves me and . . . I'm sorry, what was I talking about?

Besides the teens were their moms (although they were certainly not shopping together). These women were pretending to be casual but their lockdown Zoom sweats had given way to expensive yoga pants and their jewelry indicated they weren't heading for a Pilates class. It was more like they were going to meet Marie Antionette before the unfortunate guillotine episode. (Not much point in meeting Marie after that, frankly.)

None of them appeared to be threatening, but there were two people almost at directly opposite ends of the food court who were causing the hair on the back of my neck to quiver, if not actually stand up.

The first was a man in his sixties, if I was correct in my estimation, dressed a little too nattily even for these surroundings. There were other men in business suits who had clearly come from their jobs, perhaps for lunch hour.

Not this guy. He was carrying an actual walking stick – not a cane, not something that would help him with balance – and an ensemble that might have been fashionable in the 1940s. It was pinstriped, dark blue with white, and double-breasted, possibly to cover the widening expanse of his waist, which wasn't huge but strained at the buttons. He was also wearing silk socks. I wondered at the fact that he wasn't wearing spats.

He didn't make a show of watching the table where Riley was seated, still warily eyeing everyone around her, eyes darting back and forth. But his casual stroll was just a little *too* casual, if you know what I mean. And even if you don't. He seemed interested in the food court's perimeter, probably (in my mind) trying to determine if there were police officers stationed there.

The other person, closer to the Panda Express (because this was a mall and it's the law), seemed laser-focused on the area where people were seated and eating and not on the places they had bought their food. She – and I was fairly sure it was a she but didn't want to be presumptuous – was dressed in jeans, denim trucker jacket and a T-shirt with no slogan or artwork on it. Navy blue. Baseball cap, no team insignia, pulled down close to her eyes. And a protective face mask, which was white. Just the kind of outfit to assure the security video would be inconclusive about facial recognition.

No matter how many times I surveyed the area, I saw no one of indeterminate gender in a hoodie, black mask and sunglasses. That was surprising, because I had just assumed my stalker was in some way attached to Riley's case (which was to say Jack's case, which was to say the case of Helene's murder), and not seeing them there was not exactly a disappointment but something more in the area of a surprise. I didn't know if it was a good or bad surprise.

By now I had eaten all the French fries and was already berating myself for having done so. The milk shake, while lovely, was only half gone because it was thick and sweet and my adult self has limits. In any event, it would be conspicuous to someone watching me (if there were anyone that bored) if I stayed and tried to nurse the shake. Better that I move to a new location, preferably less centrally located, where I might appear to be doing nothing.

There were two minutes, by my iPhone's estimate, before the exact time the meeting had been set. So I had a tiny bit of time to relocate. Spotting a rare open seat on a bench only sort of facing Riley's table, I saw a hard-to-find example of an unoccupied place to sit and a casual vantage point that wouldn't give me away. I decided to move.

While I walked to the bench, I noticed Riley carefully pushing the screen on her phone, hopefully to be ready to dial my number at the first sign of anything going awry. She was playing by the rules I had set and that was good.

I sat down and arranged myself so I wouldn't have to crane my neck to see Riley, but also wouldn't look like I was intent on watching her. It's not easy to project disinterest in something that has your heart pounding, and I'm sure I did a rather bad job of it.

What was somewhat more concerning was that the guy in the Edward G. Robinson suit chose that moment to sit next to me on the bench. That was all I needed. And now I had to wonder if he was indeed the mad texter.

But this close I couldn't just see the man. I could smell him and his skin had a very familiar scent. I stared at his eyes, which are among the few features a Hollywood makeup artist can't completely disguise.

'Patrick?' I said tentatively.

'Don't cause a stir, love,' he answered in a whisper. 'That's why I'm dressed like this. Nobody will recognize me and we can watch quite quietly together.'

'Are you out of your mind? You specifically told me you wouldn't come here.' I was trying not to raise my voice, but this was definitely not a circumstance I had anticipated and my skill set was just now beginning to reassert itself. 'You should get right back to your office and wait to hear from me.'

The woman in the jeans walked over to Riley's table and sat down. The mystery texter, and possibly caller.

'You didn't hire her, did you?' I asked Patrick.

'Never laid eyes on her before.'

'Good. I thought maybe you'd gotten Angie to play dress-up too.'

'Never,' Patrick said. 'It would ruin her dignity.' He didn't know Angie like I did.

Riley didn't look especially terrified, but she could probably hide that, and besides she was about twenty yards away so nuanced facial expressions were not going to register with me. Her hands did drop below the table, holding her phone just in case. I was hoping Valdez and her SWAT team were somewhat better equipped than I was and could anticipate any possible emergency.

My phone, which I had silenced, vibrated in my pocket. I ignored it. Riley had not visibly pushed a button on her device, so whatever divorce was approaching DEFCON 1 could wait. But I checked. A text from a CNN reporter, probably about Patrick and me. I ignored it.

Riley and the woman, who was wearing the face mask that I'd assumed was to hide half of her features, stood up casually and then things started to go nuts. I saw Riley working the screen on her phone and mine buzzed.

I looked at the most recent text, which was from Riley: *Help.* I said, 'Patrick.'

As the woman approached her from one side of the table, Riley tried to bolt away from the other side, but the mystery texter managed to grab Riley's forearm and hold her. Even from this distance I could hear Riley shouting, 'I'm *not going!*'

I leapt up and so did Patrick, which made his fake nose wobble and fall off. But before we could take two steps the mystery texter had removed what looked like a hand grenade out of her jacket pocket and gotten control of Riley from behind. Someone sitting near them screamed.

'Don't come close!' the mystery texter yelled out.

More heads turned.

The woman controlled Riley from behind, encircling her in a bear hug and grabbing the grenade in her left hand. And the pin in her right.

'I don't care if I die, but I'll take her with me!' she shouted. 'Where are you? Come on. I know there are cops here. Come on out!'

I saw Patrick lean on his back foot like he was going to launch himself forward. I grabbed his forearm before he could try anything remarkably foolish because he'd have forgotten nobody was writing for him in this situation. He gave me a quick look, caught himself and nodded. He relaxed his stance. We turned our attention back to the situation in front of us.

The bizarre scene in the center of the food court was developing slowly. Valdez had obviously given the word to her team to show themselves, but had not done so herself because I still didn't see where her observation post might be. The other members of the team, dressed in plainclothes but each carrying a weapon, stood in a circle around Riley and the mystery texter.

Riley, clearly distraught, said nothing. She could put on a good show but she was eleven and scared to death. I didn't know if I was breathing.

I could hear Valdez shouting from . . . somewhere. 'You don't have a clear escape route!' (Only Valdez would think that was an effective way of saying, 'We have you surrounded.') 'Put down the grenade and we can work this out.'

'I'll tell you how we're going to work this out,' the woman said, looking to the ceiling, as if Valdez's was the voice of some unknown deity. 'You're going to put down all those guns and let me walk out of here with Riley, or I'm going to blow us up and probably a good number of the people in this food court.'

In New Jersey, someone would have yelled something rude and then the crowd would have closed in on this madwoman, but this was California and people were more interested in doing three things, in order of priority: 1. Getting video of all this on their phones. 2. Understanding the poor woman's point of view and what drove her to this desperate act, and 3. Saving their sorry asses by hightailing it to the nearest door.

'Hold it!' the woman screamed. 'Nobody leaves until me and the girl are out the door!'

There were more screams. Under my breath I heard myself say, 'The girl and I.'

'That's not going to happen,' Valdez, or her disembodied voice, said. 'We have snipers who can take you down without endangering Riley at all.'

'Yeah, but my finger is in the pin of this grenade,' the maniac answered. 'You shoot me and my hand will spasm. Like I said, I'll die, but I'm taking the girl and a bunch of other people with me.'

Everyone sort of stared at each other. But Riley, eyes wide, was looking directly at me, wondering why I couldn't do something to get her out of this horrible situation. And I just stood there, rooted to the spot, because there absolutely wasn't anything that I could do. Nothing. I was as helpful to her as a Walkman I'd gotten when I was seven.

And I'd promised her I wouldn't let anything bad happen to her at this meeting.

Finally Valdez's voice came through whatever weird PA system she'd devised for this encounter. 'What guarantees do we have of Riley's safety if we let you walk away?'

I couldn't see the woman's face for the mask, but I could pretty much hear her grinning. 'None,' she said.

'That's not acceptable,' Valdez told her. 'I can't authorize any kind of a deal with you unless we know Riley is going to be all right. Let her go and you can walk.'

'With seventeen cops watching me everywhere I go? I don't think so. Besides, *Riley* here is the reason I came. I don't intend to walk away without her. She's my prize.'

OK, *that* was creepy.

None of the cops had lowered a weapon yet. The crazy woman

holding Riley was definitely aware of that. Her head was swiveling from one side to the other, and she was leading Riley in a circle, making the poor girl rotate with a grenade right next to her face.

'I promise no one will follow you,' Valdez said. 'But you don't get to take Riley.'

'My hand's getting awful tired,' the woman said. 'Wouldn't want it to slip.'

'We don't even know that's a real grenade,' Valdez tried.

'You want me to prove it to you? It'll get awful messy.'

Riley, looking more like a little girl than I'd ever seen her before, shut her eyes tight and shouted, 'SANDY!'

The crazy woman (terrorist, I'd decided) moved her head quickly toward Riley. 'Who's Sandy?'

That was significant, but I couldn't immediately figure out why. I was too busy recoiling in guilt. Patrick's hands were on my forearms and suddenly he was holding me close. People standing around us were probably wondering why that old man with the putty nose hanging off his face was holding that younger woman so tightly. They probably thought he was a perv.

'What do you want?' Valdez asked. Evidently now she was taking prompts from a police hostage negotiator and, frankly, it wasn't working that great.

'You have ten seconds and then I blow everybody up! Ten! Nine!'

Valdez let it get to three while people in the crowd were calculating how fast they could run away from Riley. 'All right,' her voice came washing down. 'Officers, lower your weapons.'

'What?!' Was that me? That was me. Nobody answered.

The cops circling the scene all holstered their guns, except for the one with the automatic weapon. (How'd he get in here without being noticed?) He just lowered it and placed it on the floor in front of him.

'Good,' my eternal enemy said. 'Now if everyone just stays calm, we'll all make it out of the mall safe and sound. Come on, Riley.' She pulled, but Riley was doing her best to stay immobile. 'Don't fight me, kid, or they'll be taking you home in buckets.' Riley choked a bit and moved in the direction the mystery texter led her, toward the escalator.

'There's got to be something I can do,' I said.

Patrick thought I'd been talking to him. 'There isn't, love. The police have to handle it.'

'I don't want the police to handle it. Look how they're doing so far.'

There was only one bold step I could take and it was a dangerous one, but I didn't see another move so I made this one. Before Patrick could react, I stepped forward and walked quickly toward the retreating mystery texter and Riley. 'Hey!' I shouted.

The woman holding the grenade actually stopped to look at me. 'What?'

I got within twenty feet of them and stood still, largely because I preferred that no one be blown to bits. 'I'm Sandy,' I said.

At least five seconds went by while she stared at me. 'So?'

I tried to memorize what I could see of her face. Bright blue eyes. Dark bangs just sneaking out of her baseball cap. Might have been a wig. The blue eyes might have been contact lenses. I couldn't see her nose or mouth. I was getting virtually zero information.

'I'm the one Riley was calling,' I said, just to see what reaction that would bring.

It got me a sarcastic tone of voice. 'So what? You want to come along with us?'

I felt Patrick starting to close in behind me, but he wasn't going to get this close.

'Yes,' I said.

Behind me, Patrick made a guttural sound in his throat.

But Grenade Gertie (because why not?) just laughed and said, 'Screw you, lady.'

Riley reached out as well as she could with her upper arms immobilized. 'Sandy, you promised,' she said. Her voice was raspy.

'I know.' I felt tears on my face. 'I'm sorry.'

'Come on, Riley,' the grenade-bearing lunatic said. 'I'll take you to see your mom.'

I *really* didn't like the sound of that. Riley didn't say anything more but she looked terrified.

Gertie pulled Riley onto the escalator and they disappeared from sight on their way down. Every single cop who had dropped a weapon picked it up again and ran for the overlook to the lower level. But none of them took a shot.

I didn't care to ask for permission anymore; I just walked over to where I could see, from opposite the Panda Express, and looked down at the base of the escalator.

Riley and Grenade Gertie had vanished into the crowd. Cops were hopping on the escalator while others ran for the stairs, but they weren't going to catch that awful woman and my client. Not in a crazed crowd, sure their lives were in danger.

I just stood there feeling useless. Patrick came over and put his arm around my shoulder. 'You did everything you could,' he said. 'You did more than you should have, honestly.'

I shook his arm off, but not because I was annoyed with Patrick. I was furious with myself. 'You warned me. She warned me. Everybody but Valdez warned me. I never should have let her be in that situation.'

'Sandy,' Patrick began.

But he was interrupted by my phone, which vibrated insistently in my pocket. This time it was a text from Holly Wentworth.

Jack Schoenberg and another inmate escaped from state prison three hours ago.

I sat down on the floor.

PART 2: GETTING OLDER EVERY MINUTE

TWENTY-THREE

'They had cops everywhere. Every entrance to the mall was covered. There's video surveillance from every possible angle.' Angie was sitting on my desk and I was pacing in front of it, unable to harness my nervous energy.

'And they've got nothing,' I answered her. 'They have no idea who that maniac was or where she's taken Riley.'

There had been a regrettable scene in which I had berated Valdez for letting Riley be abducted. It was regrettable because I hadn't actually cursed out the lieutenant, invoked the name of Trench and then drafted a letter reporting her incompetence to the chief of detectives in the Los Angeles Police Department. I regretted that.

Then Patrick and I had left. There was no point in having Valdez or her aides question us, because we'd seen the same thing everyone else had. At least twelve iPhone videos of the scene had already been posted to YouTube, which had taken nine of them down because Riley's face had not been blurred and she was a minor. They left the other three. YouTube has an interesting set of parameters.

Live news reports had begun only minutes after Grenade Gertie had dragged Riley off the scene. Even local stations couldn't get to the mall fast enough, and the twenty-four-hour networks were a good few steps behind them, despite all having Los Angeles affiliates. I didn't especially care that we weren't getting great press, but having Riley's actual face broadcast would, in fact, have been a help. They don't blur the faces of the kids on the milk cartons because they want those kids to be found. I didn't know where Gertie had taken my client, but I was willing to bet there were people somewhere between the mall and there.

I'd asked Patrick to drop me off at my office because I felt like I should be at the center of activity and I knew Trench wouldn't let me stay at police headquarters. I wasn't talking to Valdez.

And now it seemed I had to learn about jailbreaks. In my years as a prosecutor, I had never had to deal with one. They're not nearly as common as the movies would like you to believe, which is why they still make the news. I'd never even known an attorney whose client had escaped from detention. This was unwanted, unfamiliar territory for me.

As Jack Schoenberg's attorney of record, I had been notified by the Department of Corrections of the escape, but had been given scant details. From the incident report filed with the LAPD, I knew that Jack and his accomplice, Peter Lucchesi ('Uncle Pete') had been released from their cells for outdoor exercise, which the Department of Corrections referred to as 'leisure time', and on their way had overpowered the guards escorting them, stolen various access cards, and made it off the grounds by hitching a ride unseen on a truck bringing laundry supplies. They'd gotten out of the truck somewhere along its route and had, essentially, vanished into thin air.

At roughly the same time Grenade Gertie had begun implementing her plan to abduct Riley from the arranged meet at the food court. Coincidence? It seemed unlikely.

'What you need to do is call Nate,' Angie suggested. 'He can work on finding Jack and his uncle, and I can help him two days a week.'

'First of all, two half-days,' I answered. 'And Peter isn't Jack's uncle; he's some friend or business acquaintance or something who Riley calls Uncle Pete. But the real thing here is that I don't care where Jack and Peter are at all, unless Grenade Gertie is bringing Riley to them. It's all about finding Riley. That's all.'

Angie looked a little stunned for a moment. I rarely called her out on things because she's usually right about stuff, but this was a time I was feeling especially stressed, and if you can't lash out at your best friend, who *should* be your target? I knew that no matter what, Angie would always forgive me.

'OK,' she said. 'So we should get Nate looking for Riley.'

'Nate's been looking for Helene's killer and he's come up with nothing so far,' I pointed out.

'Oh, come on. You're not saying Nate doesn't know what he's doing.' Angie got up off my desk and sat in the client chair, which admittedly has much better padding. If I knew Angie (and I did), this was a hedge against doing sit-ups on my office floor, because that's what Angie does when she has excess energy, but she knew it wouldn't look especially professional in a law office. Not to mention she was wearing a skirt because she was on the clock as Patrick's assistant. Pardon me, *executive* assistant. He'd sent her here to keep an eye on me because I'd told him I wanted to be alone for a while. Patrick is always trying to help, but just letting me be isn't included in his skill set.

I let out a long breath. 'No, I'm not. Nate is very good at what he does. But I'm frustrated and scared and angry at myself and blaming Nate for not finding Riley in the past two hours is just an easy way to let all that out. I feel like I should find her myself, that it's my fault she's missing and so I should be the one to fix it.'

'The entire Los Angeles Police Department is looking for her,' Angie said. 'So are the FBI, the California State Troopers and – for all I know – the entire US Army. What good is going to be done by you getting yourself in a bunch of danger looking for a girl whose father shouldn't have killed her mother and then we wouldn't be having these problems?'

I walked around my desk and sat down on my lawyer chair. It was well broken in and felt like home. 'I'm not dealing with rational thoughts, Ang. I'm talking about how I feel.'

'When did I become your shrink?'

'I think in eleventh grade.'

We laughed a little, not with great mirth but out of camaraderie. They talk about how laughter breaks the tension. This didn't do that so much, but it reinforced our bond, which hadn't been in a whole lot of danger to begin with. 'What's the point of kidnapping Riley?' I wondered aloud.

'What do you mean?' Angie crossed her legs and I saw one of our paralegals paying great attention through the glass wall of my office. I reached up and closed the blinds. I'd talk to him later.

'I mean, what good does it do anybody? Hold her for ransom? Who's going to pay it? Her father was, at least until recently, in state prison, and certainly can't access any of his money now. Riley herself is a millionaire, but she's not going to pay her own ransom. Her Aunt Alicia isn't exactly the sentimental type. So I don't think this is about money.'

Angie was starting to catch on. 'Yeah. So if you want to get at Jack, if this is someone who thinks he killed his wife—'

'As you appear to believe . . .' I interjected.

'The jury's still out. If they're out to get him, why kidnap Riley? To make him worry?'

'Or to kill her,' I said quietly.

'They could have done that at the mall, and not just with a grenade. The cops were watching but did they look for snipers? Could they have found anybody with a knife who could simply bump into Riley and off her?' Angie was getting into her element. 'No. They didn't want her dead. At least not right away. So you're right: What's the point of kidnapping her?'

I picked up my head, which had been resting on my desk out of sheer apathy. When I spoke it was like a voice coming from another person and it was very quiet. 'To bring father and daughter back together,' I said.

TWENTY-FOUR

'Ms Moss, we have to stop meeting like this,' said Lieutenant Trench. I had called the lieutenant – who I knew would object to my asking him about either Riley's abduction or the prison break, because he'd been assigned to investigate neither of those – and had suggested a nice leisurely iced coffee on a bench in a park not at all close to police headquarters. I did not mention Riley, Jack, Peter or Valdez at all, and refused to tell him what the meeting might be about. But it wasn't like he didn't know.

I had guessed that Trench would want his iced coffee without milk or sugar. He hadn't taken as much as a sip yet, so it was hard to know if I'd calculated correctly. I was halfway through mine, with cream and sweetener, but then I hadn't had to guess about my own preferences.

'We've never met like this before,' I pointed out to him.

'That's true, and I am suggesting we not make it a habit. Ms Moss, what business of the courts brings you to me today?'

'Did I get you the wrong kind of coffee, Lieutenant?'

Trench doesn't roll his eyes; it would be too undignified. The eye-rolling I saw was implied. 'The coffee is fine, Ms Moss. Now please let me know why I have left my office in the middle of the day to sit on a bench with you.'

I wanted to be as sincere as I could with him. I'd known Trench a couple of years and had nothing but respect for him as a detective. So I thought through precisely why he'd been my first phone call after the insanity that had occurred today and I took great care in voicing it.

'I want to know how to find a missing person, and I thought you were the one person I knew who would have the best possible advice.'

Trench stared at me. Well, *stared* might be an overstatement. He looked at me for a long moment. Of course his expression betrayed nothing. I think Trench has various portraits of himself in his attic with facial expressions of amazement, annoyance, surprise, anxiety and, perhaps in a tight corner on a much smaller canvas, joy. I waited.

'Is this about the missing girl or her missing father?' he asked finally.

'I haven't decided yet.'

'Ms Moss, I can tell you with absolutely no uncertainty that the full resources of the Los Angeles Police Department are already mobilized in pursuit of both those individuals.' Perhaps just to appease me, Trench took a sip of his iced coffee. 'You have no reason to search for them yourself and would, in fact, most likely be a hindrance to those who are trained and employed to do just that. So I highly recommend that you go back to your office, pursue whatever legal remedies you can for a man who was convicted of killing his wife and will now be charged with escaping from prison, and wait for word from the professionals who are in the field, possibly locating both father and daughter as we speak.'

I could feel tears welling up in my eyes and that was the last thing I wanted Trench to see, possibly ever, so I turned my head away like an actress in a badly directed movie. 'You don't understand,' I said, voice already shaky. 'I *promised* her.'

Trench's voice was softer and more compassionate than I had ever heard it before, which wasn't much. 'I do understand,' he said. 'The people I most often advocate for are dead. I make a vow to each of them in my own mind to find them justice. Your problem is more immediate. But I maintain the best solution you have is to let the police and the Department of Corrections do their work.'

I shook my head, still looking away, because the tears were becoming more difficult to conceal. The idea that Riley might not still be alive was something I couldn't shake. Gertie had said she was taking Riley to 'see your mom'. I couldn't think of another explanation because it wasn't even a slim possibility that Helene was still alive. The medical examiner had been extremely thorough and clear on the subject.

'Please, Lieutenant. Let's just say that I'm asking from an academic interest. Let's not mention any names. I'm asking you as an expert witness. How do you track a missing person?'

I didn't look back and there was silence for what felt like an hour. I started to wonder if Trench had left quietly to avoid having to talk to me anymore. But then there was the sound of ice cubes rattling in a plastic cup and I realized he was taking another sip of the iced coffee.

'You start with where they might want to go,' he said quietly, after I'd lost a pound of water weight. 'You have to know your quarry very well. If the person being sought is not the victim but someone who has abducted another, you must understand their thinking. If the person is someone who has not been home in a long time and not by choice, that home might be the place you'd look first. But make no assumptions and do not try to prove a theory of your own. Let the facts take you where they might. You plot a logical course for each destination, keeping in mind that in all likelihood neither fugitive would want to be discovered and so would stay away from the most traveled paths. You talk to the people who know them best and you try to establish a pattern of behavior that can help you to anticipate the next move before it is made. And then you try to get there first.'

I finally found the courage to look back at Trench. He had barely moved a muscle and his iced coffee cup had been diminished by maybe a tenth of its contents. Before I could thank him, he stood up.

'But of course you know that the officers and agents who seek your two fugitives already know that and are doing exactly those things as we speak,' he said. 'They outnumber you by the hundreds and they have had years of training. So my advice stands: pursue legal avenues and leave the pursuit to the professionals. After all, Ms Moss, you wouldn't want me to start practicing law, would you?'

I shook my head. 'You'd be too good at it.'

Trench turned to walk away. 'Lieutenant,' I said.

He looked back at me.

'You forgot your iced coffee,' I pointed out.

Trench picked up the cup and placed it – gently, I thought – into a nearby trash can, then he turned back to walk toward his car. 'I don't drink iced coffee,' he said as he left.

*   *   *

Everything I've ever heard from law enforcement officials about kidnappings is that the first forty-eight hours are crucial. It had been four hours since Riley was taken. That left forty-four hours and I already felt like I was racing the clock.

Trench was right about a lot of what he'd said, which was not unusual. The cops, the FBI, and who knew how many other agencies *were* already doing all the stuff he'd suggested. It made no sense for me to duplicate the efforts of people who were wildly more numerous, better equipped, and trained far more thoroughly than I was. All I had on my side was a burning desire and some knowledge of who Riley was, and what the details were of Jack's case from a legal standpoint. So I'd concentrate on my advantages, which were few and, at the moment, seemingly unhelpful.

The first thing I did, which is the first thing I do whenever I am starting on something that makes me feel overwhelmed, was to call Angie. (My apologies, Patrick, but your talents are very specific and impressive, but Angie is my superhero and I've known her pretty much all my life.)

'What do you want to do?' Angie is direct and to-the-point, which was exactly what I needed.

'If I knew that, I'd be doing it already. Riley's out there somewhere with Grenade Gertie and I have to be doing things the cops aren't.' I opened the door of my Hyundai and strapped myself in as I started the engine. Now all I had to do was figure out where I was going. 'What do I know how to do that they don't?'

'You know how to file a lawsuit,' she said. Angie was spit-balling. I'm used to the process so I let her go on without protest. 'You know how to defend people and how to prosecute them. You know about criminal law so you know about specific crimes. Did you ever prosecute an escaped convict?'

'You'd remember if I did,' I told her.

'Yeah, I would. Too bad. That could help now. How about a kidnapper?'

I thought about that. 'As a matter of fact, I did. The case never went to trial so I sort of forgot about it, but there was one guy I was assigned and we made a plea deal. He'd kidnapped his own son.'

'Really?'

'Oh yeah,' I said. 'He got caught in about ten hours, in North Carolina. The majority of abductions are done by people, usually family members, that the victim knows. Divorced dads are one of the more popular categories.'

'Unlikely this was a family member of Riley's,' Angie said.

'Yeah. I would have recognized Aunt Alicia's voice, even if she was wearing a disguise, and she would have recognized me. I can't imagine why a family member would kidnap Riley. It's not like there was a custody battle going on.'

'Are there any legal steps you can take to get the security video from the mall?' Angie asked.

'I mean, I could file a motion of discovery, but my client is the victim and – any way you look at it – that kind of thing would take weeks at least,' I told her. 'We have forty-four hours.'

Angie stopped for a moment. I still hadn't put my car into gear and the parking garage I was looking at from the inside wasn't inspiring any great strategic plans.

'You already know what you have to do first, but you don't want to do it,' Angie said finally.

As usual, she was right on both counts. 'Really?' I said.

'You got a better idea?'

'I called *you* for a better idea.'

Angie actually laughed. 'You called me because you needed to hear me say it. So I'm saying it.'

'Do I *have* to?' Now I sounded like *I* was eleven years old.

'Yup,' my best friend answered.

'All right. I'll call you after.'

'Godspeed,' Angie said.

I don't think she was kidding.

TWENTY-FIVE

'I'm really not in a mood to tell you anything,' said Lieutenant Luciana Valdez.

After the way I'd left it with her at the mall, I was actually surprised that Valdez had allowed me into her cubicle to talk. But I suppose that technically I was a witness to the crime she was investigating and she probably thought she could get more information out of me than I would ever be able to squeeze out of her. And she was probably right, because I wouldn't hold anything back. I wanted Riley to be found and if that meant telling Valdez something that might help (which I couldn't imagine I'd know), so be it.

'Lieutenant, I regret some of the things I said to you. It was unprofessional and disrespectful to you. But I was very emotional, having seen an eleven-year-old client of mine dragged off violently by someone holding a grenade.'

Valdez regarded me for a few seconds. '*Some* of the things you said?'

This was the moment when I could have pointed out that she had been in charge of the operation that was intended to protect Riley through the meeting with Grenade Gertie, and that it, let's say, hadn't gone that well. But I needed Valdez's good graces, so the catharsis that diatribe would have delivered probably was ill-advised.

Probably.

'I sincerely apologize,' I lied. 'Please understand that my anger was directed at the kidnapper and not at you.'

'Uh-huh.' Valdez sat down behind her desk and looked at her phone, which was not ringing itself off her desk as one might expect. 'And what is it you're here for? Are you here as Riley Schoenberg's lawyer to sue the department, or do you have another trick up your sleeve?'

Wow. She must have had some really bad experiences with lawyers, maybe when she was a child.

'Lieutenant, we've had some differences,' I said. 'I regret that.' *It was mostly your fault, but I regret it.* 'But I think right now both of us have shifted our priority list to where getting Riley back safe is definitely at the top. So maybe we can pool our information and help that happen, OK?'

But Valdez wasn't buying it. 'I have the information and you don't,' she said. 'How is that "pooling"?'

We could debate this nonsense all day, except we were now down to forty-three hours and I didn't think proving that I was right constituted the most efficient use of my time. I dived right in without debating the philosophies involved, cop v. lawyer. 'Did the video surveillance in the mall show anything that could help in identifying the kidnapper?'

Now, here's the thing I've learned about cops: The one thing they love almost as much as catching the bad guys is talking about how smart they are when they catch the bad guys. Valdez, being a cop, couldn't resist.

'There wasn't anything definitive,' she said. 'The FBI is running it through their tech because they think they know everything, but I don't think it'll show anything very important. There might be something with voice patterns from the video but that'll take time.'

'How much time?'

She shook her head. 'Hours, hopefully.'

Hours! 'Hopefully?' I said.

'Yeah. Sometimes these things can take up to a week. We're cutting as much red tape as we can.'

The wheels of bureaucracy grind slow, but on the other hand, they are inefficient.

'How did they get past all the cops you must have had at the exits?' I asked.

Valdez wasn't pleased with the suggestion that her operation had failed, but the outcome didn't actually lend itself to any other interpretation. She scowled. 'We don't know yet. All doors were covered. There are tunnels underneath the mall that can lead to uncovered exits, which is leading me to believe that our grenade launcher might be an employee of the company that owns the mall, and we're checking into that. There. I've told you something. Now dazzle me and tell me something you know that I don't.' So she was going to be that way about it.

'The kidnapper was the person who sent the text, but she didn't call Riley and threaten her,' I said.

Valdez stopped and looked at me a moment. 'How do you know that?'

'The caller mentioned me by name. The woman with the grenade didn't know who Sandy was when Riley called me and didn't recognize me when I stepped forward.' I'd remembered why that was significant.

Valdez nodded slowly, taking that in, and looked at me more closely. 'What else do you know?'

'Peter Lucchesi is a business associate of Riley's mother Helene. Riley used to call him "Uncle Pete". Jack Schoenberg told his daughter that he hadn't seen Peter since he'd been in prison, that they were in separate cellblocks that didn't overlap.'

'Yeah,' Valdez said, looking at her computer screen. 'The jailbreak. Fact is, Lucchesi and Schoenberg were in the same cellblock and the guards say they were practically inseparable in the yard.'

'I figured he was lying,' I agreed. 'Riley asked him if Peter was hiding from him, which I took to be her putting on an innocent act for her daddy. But Lucchesi was in for securities fraud. He doesn't seem the violent type who'd overpower a trained corrections officer and break out of jail.'

Valdez shot me a look that had something like scorn in it. 'Where did you hear that Lucchesi was in for securities fraud?' she asked.

'From Jack. That's what he told me and Riley.'

Her lip curled up on one side. 'Peter Lucchesi was in jail for armed robbery. He got hold of a sawed-off shotgun and broke in on his ex-wife one night, demanding money. The state of California frowns on that sort of thing, and guess what: it wasn't his first violent crime. Luckily the ex-wife had a security system that alerted the police. You should do more checking and trust your client less, counselor. He's a born liar.'

'I think he was just trying to shield his daughter,' I said. 'Jack seems to have an image of Riley that's about three years younger and six years more naïve than she really is.'

'Don't believe it. He's as deceitful as they come.'

I was starting to wonder about everything that Jack – and to some extent Riley – had told me. 'Where are you looking for Riley?' I said. Trench had suggested I look somewhere the police weren't searching. Be good to know where that was.

'Everywhere.'

'That doesn't help me, Lieutenant.'

She looked up from the screen to glare at me. 'Since when is helping you in my job description?'

'I'm a citizen of Los Angeles County,' I said. 'Helping me *is* your job description.'

Valdez gave that some thought, either that or she was engrossed in her computer screen. You can decide which for yourself. 'All highways are being monitored electronically. Airports and train stations are on alert, just like bus lines and even car services and Uber. Prison officials are questioning every inmate. Every relative and acquaintance of Jack Schoenberg, Helene Nestor and Peter Lucchesi is being visited. If the person who took your client is involved in that murder case, and I believe she is, a name is going to surface pretty soon. Now go back to your law office and file a brief or something, OK? Just stay out of our way. We have a manhunt to conduct.'

'Person hunt,' I said. But I was already standing with every intention of leaving police headquarters as soon as possible. I knew where I wanted to go next.

'Uh-huh.' Valdez wasn't great at banter.

I stopped at the entrance (it couldn't be called a door) to her cubicle. 'Lisa Conforto and her husband say Jack Schoenberg was at their house the night Helene was shot,' I said. 'Did they tell you that when you were investigating?'

'As a matter of fact, no,' Valdez answered.

'You're welcome,' I said as I left.

TWENTY-SIX

There were already six texts and a voicemail from T'Aisha Kendall on my phone that I hadn't been ignoring but was too busy or frantic to answer, so I called her back once I was in the car and headed to my next stop.

'That book deal just got a whole lot more likely,' she said as soon as she picked up.

'Yeah, and an eleven-year-old girl has been abducted by someone holding a hand grenade,' I answered. 'That's also on the priority list at the moment. Oddly I haven't been able to field phone calls from interested editors yet.'

T'Aisha didn't miss a beat. 'I'm sorry,' she said, and I believed her. 'Reporters try not to get too involved with the subject of the story because we won't be able to report objectively if we do. I saw a jailbreak and a kidnapping and registered an opportunity. I should have been thinking about Riley.'

'Apology accepted,' I said, as soon as Apple Maps was done telling me to make a right turn in seven hundred feet, like I knew how far seven hundred feet might be. Luckily there was a stop sign coming up that moved the process along a bit. 'I can understand how you'd react like that. But I was there when Riley was taken and I'm still quivering over the thought of it. I've got to find her. Can you help me?'

A car ahead of me was driving ten miles under the speed limit. For a driver from New Jersey, this is tantamount to violating all ten commandments at the same time and then spitting on the sidewalk. But today I found myself less in a hurry to get where I was going because I didn't know what I'd do when I got there.

'Help you?' T'Aisha said. 'I don't know where Riley is or I'd be calling the cops right now. I'm happy to help if I can, but how?'

I gave her the address I was headed to in San Marino, which in New Jersey would be height of luxury and in Los Angeles was upper-middle-class. 'Think you can meet me there?' I asked.

'I know the place well. I'll be there in about forty minutes.'

'So you live ten minutes away and you're compensating for traffic?'

'Exactly.'

I was getting the hang of Los Angeles driving after all. 'See you there.' I made the right turn because apparently that had been seven hundred feet. I probably passed T'Aisha's apartment along the way.

The GPS took me through neighborhoods that were very suburban for a place like LA. The houses were pleasant, friendly looking places that weren't actually trying to impress all the other houses with how much money they were worth. As I drove, the price tags in my head went up gradually, but never reached the stratosphere you can so often hit in Southern California without half trying.

By the time I reached my destination, we (the Hyundai and I) were farther up in the hills. The view was lovely without being especially spectacular. Breath would not be taken away, either by altitude or vista. I pulled the car up through the inevitable security gate and around the circular driveway to the front door of the house where Helene Nestor had been shot and killed.

I had, against every instinct in my mind, asked Patrick to call Emily Webster, because she was a real-estate agent and would therefore have the combination to the lockbox on the front door. After strongly considering a simple Google search of realtors in the Los Angeles area and calling any random name, I had decided that the one I'd most like to have rush out on a wild-goose chase when I had absolutely no intention of buying the property was Emily.

I believed I was well justified.

Sure enough, Emily was already at the front door, having unlocked it, and therefore fulfilled the entirety of the function I had summoned her to perform. But she didn't know that, and was therefore going to show me through Helene and Jack's place as if I were a real customer. She was obligated by law to tell me a person had died in the house, so I was wondering what I'd do if she failed to do so, and whether I could have her thrown out of the real-estate business, even as she was awaiting trial for trying to have me murdered.

'Sandra!' She was so ebullient I thought maybe she'd forgotten that (in her mind) I had stolen her man away from her. Maybe she thought I was some other Sandra, like Bullock, Oh, or Day O'Connor. 'It's so nice to see you again!' Then she looked back at the car after I'd gotten out and walked toward her. 'Patrick's not with you today?' I'm certain she looked terribly let down.

'No, I'm scouting this one out on my own,' I said. 'I hope I didn't disappoint you too much.'

You'd think Emily would have been a better liar after all her years of upselling people on already ridiculously priced homes, and then with the violent criminal activity, but I could see all the emotions on her face. She hated my guts, wanted me dead (literally), but saw the possibility for a pretty decent commission in this place, which was probably something of a white elephant on the market. There had, after all, been a rather bloody killing here and a very public investigation and trial. Anyone other than me who had been living in the area at the time would remember the house. In fact, T'Aisha's articles had been accompanied with some detailed pictures of the place.

'Of course not,' Emily pretended. 'Finally we get a chance to talk just girl-to-girl.' Oh, boy; if she thought that was what we were going to do, she was in for even more disappointment.

'Yeah, that's it.' It just slipped out of my mouth. 'So, about the house.' I pointed, like she didn't know which house I had meant.

'Oh, of course. Well, you can see it's in splendid condition.' She said, *splendid*. I'm asking you.

'Certainly.' My only goal was to get inside and look around. If Emily wanted to go home now and leave me to lock up, I'd have been fine with it. So I ignored the *splendid* and gestured toward the door. 'Shall we go in?' If she could say *splendid*, I could say *shall*.

That was the moment when T'Aisha Kendall drove up in a very cute vintage Peugeot and I decided we were going to be friends. But I also realized that television was treating T'Aisha well and she didn't need the book money. She was in this to get the story. She wouldn't last on a judge show for long.

I introduced T'Aisha to Emily and gave my supposed realtor no explanation as to why this unfamiliar woman was touring the house with us. I didn't even mention that T'Aisha had been a newspaper reporter, but I figured that would become evident as we toured the place.

We entered through a foyer that was modest by Hollywood standards. This was not the home of an extravagant fake-fingernail mogul. Helene had not gone overboard, even after she'd made quite the tidy fortune. This was a home *and* a showcase, but mostly a home. The foyer was still furnished, as was the rest of the house. Emily said the previous owners had 'not removed any of the original pieces and might be persuaded to include some of them in the house if the price is right.' Translation: Jack had been planning on a long stay in the penitentiary and hadn't needed furniture, and Helene was busy being dead, probably without use for a very nice side table.

T'Aisha was quiet as we moved through. I couldn't tell whether it was because she was wondering if I was pulling off some strange trick with Emily, or if the memories she had from reporting on Helene's murder were flooding in too fast for her to process. She stared at objects – like the few photographs framed on the walls – as if she were touring a remarkably profound museum exhibit.

'You must see the kitchen,' Emily went on, either oblivious to the vibe in the place (mostly T'Aisha being dumbstruck and me being anxious). The kitchen? I needed to see the music room, where Helene had died or been staged after dying.

But we dutifully followed Emily through a hallway and past a rather darling dining room to the kitchen, clearly her pride and joy.

It was certainly very nice, large enough to envision a cook or two working for the residents of the house, but also manageable enough to picture yourself (not me, but you maybe) cooking there. It had many of the modern conveniences.

'The refrigerator communicates with you and lets you know when you need milk,' Emily said in an excited tone, as if that weren't borderline terrifying. 'And you can turn on the dishwasher, the oven and the air fryer with an app on your phone! Want to see?' She held out her hand, as if there were anything resembling a chance that I would hand her my iPhone. I was still pretty sure she'd sic-ed the hoodie stalker on me in an attempt to frighten me away from Patrick, or possibly to have me assassinated. But right now my attention was on finding Riley. Nothing else.

'No, that's OK,' I said, hand snugly on the mobile phone in my front pocket. 'What's this way?' I knew from blueprints I'd seen in T'Aisha's articles where the most important room in the house was, and since this was a fact-finding mission and not a house tour, I wanted to cut to the chase.

T'Aisha, meanwhile, was examining everything with a very serious look on her face and occasionally nodding to herself. She did not take any photographs. I got the impression she was storing everything away until Emily might vacate the premises and we could talk candidly.

Emily, meanwhile, looked a little alarmed at the idea of heading directly to the music room, but I was already blazing a trail down the hallway to the door I knew would be to my right. 'Wouldn't you like to see the baths?' she said, sounding like Nero trying to distract us from the fact that Rome was burning and unable to find his fiddle. (History buffs: Nero did not actually fiddle while Rome burned. He tried to help put out the fire.)

'Nah, I want to experience the house my way,' I said, just to give her a taste of her own medicine. Although the powder room I passed was probably larger than any bathroom I've ever had in an apartment I was renting.

I reached the door with the narrow transom over it and knew I'd found what I was looking for. And oddly, T'Aisha joined me at the door before Emily got there. We looked at each other: did we dare? How was this going to make us feel?

Just in case we were about to wallow in anxiety and sentiment, Emily walked up, puffing from the exertion, to pour cold water on the moment. Which, if I'm being fair, was probably what it needed, although she didn't know that. She put her hand on the doorknob and stopped to face me.

'Just before we go into this room, which is lovely and can have so many uses, by the way, I do need to tell you something about it,' Emily said. I was secretly hoping she was going to mention that it had an atrium for more natural lighting and built-in bookcases. But no. 'I'm required to mention that someone died in this room and that's one of the reasons the house is available for such a reasonable price.' We hadn't discussed anything resembling price, for the record.

Damn. There went my possibility of getting Emily Webster disbarred, or whatever they do to real-estate agents who don't mention the dead people in the house.

T'Aisha was about to say that we already knew about it, so I had to jump in and see exactly how uncomfortable I could make Emily because, aside from finding Riley, that had become my purpose in life. (Finding Riley was first, in case you were worried.)

'Really!' I said, looking as surprised as I could manage, which probably wasn't much. 'Did someone have a heart attack or something in there?'

Emily was funneling her energy into not making eye contact with me and was succeeding admirably. 'No,' she answered. 'A person died in there of a . . . gunshot wound.'

Let her off the hook? Why would I do that? 'Oh my,' I said. 'Suicide?'

T'Aisha, situated behind Emily, smiled privately. She couldn't have known why I was maltreating Emily so severely, but she could enjoy its entertainment value without explanation.

Emily shifted her weight from one foot to the other and appeared to find the process fascinating, since she was watching her feet as she did so. 'I'm afraid not,' she said after what felt like an hour. 'I don't have all the details because I came to the house quite a while later, but I believe this was the scene of a homicide.' She didn't want to say *murder* because that's scarier than *homicide*. You could say what you wanted about Emily, and I usually did, but she was a professional real-estate broker and, for all I knew, good at her job.

'A homicide!' I said. I watched Emily's face register disappointment, and it wasn't as much fun as I would have expected. Then I reminded myself I had never intended to buy this house, so I wasn't depriving her of any business other than the same business I was depriving her of ten minutes ago. The goal was to get into the room, see if I could learn anything, and then use that information to find Riley.

Oh, like you had a better plan.

'It was over two years ago,' Emily said, as if that made a difference.

So I decided it had. 'All right, then,' I said, sounding a bit like Patrick. 'Let's go in and see what the room is like.'

Before Emily could make a move, I opened the door and swung it into the music room. T'Aisha closed ranks with me so we could walk in ahead of her. I wasn't going to cut Emily *that* much slack.

Like the rest of the house, the music room had not been emptied of its furniture, but whoever the listing agent was (I hadn't checked because I wasn't buying the house) had clearly spent a good deal of time staging the room, as they had all the others. So it was beautifully appointed and looked very inviting. Whatever house Patrick and I bought, I thought to use the same realtor whenever we decided to sell it, when I assumed Emily would be doing hard time.

The music room lived up to its name by having a baby grand piano at its center. The room was big enough that it didn't seem cluttered or even dominated by the instrument, lovely as it was. The walls were hung with acoustic guitars and there was one electric bass, red, on a hook as well. A few amps indicated that some of the guitars might have had pickups to plug in. No visible soundproofing material was on the walls, but I was willing to bet there was some inside the walls. There were upholstered chairs around a small table, and I assumed the one on which Helene had been discovered had been long since removed.

So it came as an even bigger surprise that there was a dead body on the floor, sprawled out on her side as if sleeping, but with enough blood under her that it seemed unlikely she could get comfortable enough for that.

Each of us stopped and gasped. Nobody screamed like in the movies. But nobody moved for a good few seconds, either.

Then we all reached for our cell phones to call 911.

When I felt I could (and T'Aisha was on the phone with emergency services), I took three steps toward the body.

She had been shot, possibly in the back, and it must have been quick and surprising. Her eyes were open. And even though I had only seen her once and had barely gotten a glimpse of anything but her blue eyes, I knew in a second that I'd seen her before.

'That's Grenade Gertie,' I said.

And I was even more worried about Riley than I'd been before.

TWENTY-SEVEN

This time Trench showed up himself.

Well, almost himself. His trusty assistant/partner/Dr Watson Sergeant Roberts was with the lieutenant, which reassured me in a weird way. If Trench and Roberts were there, there was some sense of order in the universe.

Of course, the uniformed officers and EMTs had arrived first, and they'd asked us our questions and taken the video and the pictures. They'd picked up a few items to put into evidence bags, which was something of a trick because I hadn't noticed any loose objects lying around in the room, except for Gertie, who was still staring off in an eternal expression of astonishment. They hadn't gotten around to bagging her up and carting her away yet. But they had managed to get Emily out of the room, which I was grateful for. She was being questioned by the uniformed officers elsewhere in the house.

Do I sound more callous than usual? I was focused on finding Riley and was livid with Gertie for making that more difficult by getting herself homicide-d here in the same room where Helene Nestor had been shot and started this whole insane ball rolling. And there might just have been a component of me narcotizing myself to the event by putting on a layer of hard-boiled dame from a good noir movie. I'm not above that.

Don't judge until you've been in the music room.

'Well, Ms Moss, I admit I'm surprised it has taken this long for me to be at a crime scene in your presence.' That's Trench being 'funny'. 'What did you see and when did you see it?'

'What you're seeing. We walked into the room, saw Gertie on the floor and called you. Just like that.'

Trench raised an eyebrow, which in another person would be a sign of unquenchable curiosity. 'Gertie?'

Had I said that out loud? 'I'm sorry, Lieutenant. I'm sure her name isn't Gertie.'

'Do you know the victim?' Trench was veritably beside himself, which you could tell by . . . you couldn't tell.

'No. I mean, not by name and we only spoke once for about four seconds. This is the woman who held my client Riley Schoenberg hostage with a hand grenade and abducted her from the shopping mall today.' It sounded stupider when I had to say it.

Trench considered me closely. 'You recognize her?'

'Yes. I made it a priority to memorize any features of her face I could see. Those are definitely the eyes of the woman with the grenade.'

The lieutenant nodded almost imperceptibly. 'Well done, Ms Moss. I've already alerted Lieutenant Valdez and she is on her way.' Swell.

'What do you think it means, Lieutenant?' T'Aisha was on the case and holding her phone, which I assumed was in a recording mode.

'I have no comment for the press, Ms Kendall.' Trench knew every reporter in Los Angeles, and even though T'Aisha was no longer affiliated with the *Times*, he would remember her.

'I'm not working for any news outlet at the moment,' she tried.

'It was the "at the moment" that was telling,' Trench said. 'I have no comment. In fact, I would appreciate it if you would give Sergeant Roberts your statement, please.' Roberts magically appeared at T'Aisha's side and gestured for her to accompany him out of the room. They didn't want two of us giving statements at the same time where we could hear each other. Cop procedure. T'Aisha looked a little annoyed but didn't voice her irritation as she let Roberts lead her away.

'You don't consider us suspects in this murder, do you, Lieutenant?' I had to ask because we were being treated like suspects, but that seemed a little ludicrous, since each of us had two witnesses who had seen us not kill Gertie, whoever she was.

'Until I have more facts, Ms Moss,' Trench began.

'Everyone is a suspect. I know. But seriously.'

'Seriously.' He was such a cop.

'You're such a cop,' I said. He did not react at all. Because he was such a cop.

'How did you recognize the victim?' Trench asked. 'What was

it about her eyes that allowed you to make a positive identification?' I wasn't sure if that was a question as a homicide detective working a case or if he was just curious about my powers of perception and how they might compare to his own.

'When she was holding Riley, and it was becoming clear that she was going to get away, I decided to memorize what I could about her face,' I said. 'I couldn't take a picture because that might have set her off. She was wearing a mask over her nose and mouth and I thought she was wearing a wig under a baseball cap, so her hair wasn't going to do me any good and her forehead was covered by the bangs. I concentrated on her eyes. They're blue – you can see that – but they have a greyish tint to them and the pupils are, or were, sort of oddly shaped. A little horizontal instead of perfectly round, and not as clearly delineated. I mean, you sort of picture a person's pupils having a very clear shape, but they didn't. I've never actually studied pupils before, so maybe there's more variation than I might have realized, but hers seemed just a little bit like slits. You can see there.' I gestured toward Gertie, who – as you might have guessed – had not moved at all.

Trench did not seem to think my diatribe on eye pupils was at all strange. He had probably written a monograph on the subject. 'Very astute indeed, Ms Moss. This would seem to be the same woman you saw in the mall. And that leads to a great many questions.'

'Yeah, like if she's dead, who has Riley now? I've tried her cell phone fifteen times and her voice mailbox is full. Can't you guys trace those things with GPS or something?'

'Not without a court order, and not without some information from the carrier and the manufacturer. It can be done but not quickly.' If that was Trench, his voice had changed radically. I turned to see Valdez walking toward us from the door through which I'd entered the music room and started the roller-coaster up at a higher speed. 'How surprising to find you here, Ms Moss. I'm almost certain I told you not to get in the way of the authorities on this case.'

Let me be clear: I didn't hate Lieutenant Valdez. I'm not even sure I disliked her. But her attitude toward me was condescending, something that was not Trench's style. And right now

I wasn't in the mood to be condescended to because, really, when am I ever in that mood?

'Strangely I didn't see any cops here when I arrived, so I'm pretty sure I was out of everybody's *way*, Lieutenant.' I sounded a little more Jersey there than usual since I'd moved out here. But the 'New Jersey accent' you think you know is really from Brooklyn or Staten Island. We don't talk like that.

I answered all the same questions again and still couldn't tell them who'd killed Gertie or what her real name was. As a witness I was something of a dud. And I had what I'm sure the two lieutenants considered an annoying habit of asking questions even while supposedly answering theirs.

'Do you know where Riley is yet?' I asked Valdez.

Valdez resisted the urge to sigh dramatically, but I could tell it took considerable effort. 'No, Sandy. We haven't found her yet. But I think that this homicide might lead us in a direction, so please just answer my questions.'

'I just did. Right after I answered Lieutenant Trench's questions and before that Officer Crawford's questions. What makes you think I know anything more than I've already told you? The body was on the floor when we got here. She's dead and was when I arrived. I recognized her eyes. She kidnapped Riley. Can we move on to the part where that leads us in a direction?'

It struck me again that I'd walked in on a dead body – a *murdered* dead body – and I wasn't feeling anything about that. I should have been a wreck. As a prosecutor you don't hear about the crime until after the police have filed a report. As a defense attorney I'd never actually been there when the body was discovered in the three murder cases I'd handled before.

The thing is, I'd never discovered a body before, and would have expected a more dramatic reaction from myself. Instead my mind was working the angles on how this was going to affect my chances of finding Riley and getting her safe. It was a little surprising; my focus is rarely that singular. But she was a girl and I'd made a promise and it had not gone well.

Guilt? Yeah, you could call it guilt. Thanks for bringing *that* up.

'I agree with you,' Valdez said, and that came as a surprise because she'd never agreed with me before and also because I'd

---

forgotten what she was agreeing with me about. 'You have answered all the questions you can. So you may leave now.' OK. Wait. I may *what?* 'You want me to leave?' You know that was a stalling tactic. It's not like Valdez hadn't been clear.

'Unless you feel you can aid our investigation with some information that you haven't shared yet,' she said.

I looked at Trench. For some reason I didn't want to leave the music room, and I was just starting to understand why. The whole point of this trip, before Gertie had turned up in a heap on the expensive rug, was to scope out the room where Helene had died. I'd been so consumed with Gertie that I'd forgotten about Helene. If I could figure out who might have killed her and determine it wasn't Jack, that would be progress. Because I'd know who the killer was, which would probably be the person now holding Riley. And even in my head that didn't sound good.

'Do I have to go, Lieutenant?' I asked Trench.

He looked at me oddly, which indicated not that he was odd but that he was thinking I was. 'Our investigation needs to progress, Ms Moss,' he said. 'We have no further questions to ask you at this moment. But I assume you will stay available if there is any other way you can contribute, won't you?'

'Yah. Sure.' I stepped a little bit deeper into the room and took it in. That transom over the door, on which Jack had based his absurd defense, was very narrow, but not in the way it had been described to me. It was wider, perhaps two feet or two and a half, across, but the height was about a foot, as advertised. It would have taken a very small person indeed, or a thin dachshund, to squeeze through there. And I doubted you could teach a dachshund to climb a twelve-foot ladder.

'Ms Moss?' Trench said. He wanted me to leave.

'Right. Right.' The doors were tall and wooden and appeared to have suffered no damage, assuming they hadn't been replaced in two years. There were no windows because the room was meant to keep sound inside, but there was ample lighting that was very natural looking, and there was a small skylight that I assumed would not have a major impact on the room's acoustics, being at the top of a fifteen-foot ceiling. It was sealed and would not have been a point of entry or exit for the killer.

'Sandy,' Valdez said, and I wondered when we'd gotten on a first-name basis. 'You need to leave.'

'Of course.' Another look around, during which I actually spun in a 360-degree pattern to make sure I wasn't missing anything. The cops must have thought I'd lost it, or was imitating Julie Andrews at the beginning of *The Sound of Music*. Which would have indicated that I'd lost it. 'I'm going.' I hadn't taken photographs, but the police report from Helene's murder had included enough. I could study them later.

So I did head for the door where T'Aisha was waiting. I didn't especially care where Emily might be.

'Find out anything?' T'Aisha asked me.

'Yeah. I think Helene Nestor was murdered by Spider-Man. You?'

'They don't seem to know anything. But Roberts let slip that they might have a tentative ID on your friend Gertie.'

That stopped me before we hit the front door. 'Who was she?'

'He didn't go that far, just that they think they know. I figure it's got to be someone involved with Jack or Pete, and that she handed Riley off to them, wherever they are.'

That was when my phone buzzed and I looked down to see a text indicating I'd gotten an email from the Los Angeles County superior court. You find out you have an email because they send you a text. Technology is grand. The email read that my request for a hearing to determine whether Jack Schoenberg should get a new trial had been granted.

There's nothing like bureaucracy.

TWENTY-EIGHT

'I can't believe you didn't call me,' Patrick said.

He wasn't being a nag and he wasn't trying to make me feel like I'd messed up. He really couldn't understand why, having found a dead body on the floor of a room where another dead body had been found, and it being the same day my client had been kidnapped right in front of me in a shopping mall food court, I wouldn't have summoned him like Batman and expected him to make everything all right. This is not just ego (although that's always a consideration with an actor), it's Patrick's nature. He wants to save everybody, but especially me.

'There just wasn't time.' I sat down with a bottle of beer in my hand on a barstool that Angie and I used for dinner seating in our apartment. 'Everything happened so fast and besides, Patrick, what were you going to do?'

'I'd be there for you,' he said, maybe a little miffed.

I reached over and patted him on the shoulder. 'You pretty much always are, whether you're there or not,' I said.

Angie, ever cognizant of the fact that she was what she called the 'fifth wheel' in our little group, put her finger in her mouth and mimed vomiting. Angie has a subtlety that few can really appreciate. I gave her a look behind Patrick's back and she smiled in a way I'm certain she thought was impish.

'Of course I am, love,' Patrick said. 'But it must have been awful for you.'

The impact of opening the music room door still hadn't hit me. 'You would think so,' I said. 'I guess it'll affect me at some point, but it hasn't yet. Maybe because it was Grenade Gertie and I was so livid with her.'

'Who do you think killed her?' Angie is always straight to the point.

'If I knew that, I would have told the cops, and they'd be picking up Riley as we speak,' I told her. 'It's got to be whoever got Gertie to kidnap Riley, and everybody's favorite suspects right now are her dad and her "uncle" Pete.'

Angie was drinking a white wine and Patrick had a glass of some concoction he'd made for himself that involved gin. He was on the next barstool, not letting me get too far away, and Angie was sprawled out on the couch, feet up on the coffee table because Angie likes to give the impression that she's relaxed. Cross her and you'll find out how relaxed she really is.

'You sound as if you don't share that opinion,' Patrick said. Sometimes he's just British enough that he sounds like an inspector on an Acorn TV series. Other times, when he's a little more emotional, his Cockney roots come through and he sounds like what I believe they call a football hooligan. That means soccer. Watch *Ted Lasso*; you'll understand. (Angie got me into that one and Patrick is impressed by the acting and the writing.)

'I don't want to have an opinion yet,' I said. 'Trench said I shouldn't try to prove a theory I've made up. I'm trying to gather information and then act on it, not decide who's guilty and then try to prove it.'

Patrick nodded. 'Wise.'

'But if you don't know who you're tracking, how do you go on from here?' Angie, once again, is practical except when she's not. She once bought a pair of shoes with eight-inch heels. She said she liked the way they made her legs look. She didn't care much for the way they made her feet feel. They went back the next day.

I drank some beer, which is a very satisfying drink because it tickles the back of your throat like soda but then it has alcohol in it. A very liberating burp, that. 'I have to think like a generic person until I know who we're talking about,' I said. 'Or, I can stop looking specifically for Riley and try to find Jack and this Pete guy because I know who they are and I know they're on the loose from prison. They have a very clear motivation. But whatever I do, I have to do it fast. It's already been eight hours since Riley was taken, and that only leaves me forty more.'

Angie and Patrick exchanged a look that contained concern for my sanity and sympathy for my plight. They've gotten to know each other well since Angie took the job.

But she had another part-time job, too, and she likes to share.

'Nate is already on the case,' she said. 'He said he'd call when he found something, but he's on the trail of the two jailbreakers.' I took that in. 'OK, that leaves me with Riley. If she were just on the run herself, I'd have some idea of where to look. But she's not making the decisions. So we have to think like a kidnapper and figure out what the motivation for taking her might be.'

We'd also have to think about dinner soon. In fact, we should have thought about dinner an hour ago. But this was not a normal day. I'd bring it up at the next possible opportunity and then Patrick would have Angie order something. That's how the whole 'executive assistant' thing works. Out of nowhere I gestured toward Angie and said to Patrick, 'You need to give this girl a raise.'

Patrick blinked a couple of times. 'OK,' he said. Such is the power of love.

'Speaking of money.' Angie hadn't missed the reference to a higher salary and certainly didn't doubt Patrick's word, but she was on her game now. 'Couldn't they have kidnapped Riley for her money? She's got a bunch.' She was falling back on her greatest hits.

'There would have been a ransom demand by now,' Patrick said. He's played detectives on TV.

'We've been through this,' I said. 'Ransom doesn't make sense. For one thing, Riley's money is in a trust and even she can't get it. I thought the idea was that Jack figured if he could break out of jail this would be a way to get Riley back, but I'm starting to think that doesn't make sense either. If he broke out of jail and got word to Riley, she would have just gone to him. I've seen that girl when the subject of her father comes up; there's no rational thought behind it.'

Angie and Patrick sat for a moment absorbing what I'd said. Usually that results in one or the other of them (or both) trying to show me in the nicest possible terms (if it's Patrick) how I'm wrong. But not this time. They seemed to be trying to figure out a next move if the motive wasn't financial.

Finally Angie broke the silence while I was trying to decide between Thai takeout and Chinese takeout. 'So the idea is that you want to do something the cops aren't already doing,' she began. I didn't interrupt because she was rolling. 'And you believe that the person who killed Helene Nestor probably also killed Grenade Gertie, and likely is the one who ordered Riley's kidnapping.'

I gave her more time but that seemed to be all she had to say. 'That's right,' I said.

Angie put up her index finger like a teacher determined to make a point. 'OK. So it seems to me there's only one way to proceed from here.'

It required a straight line and Patrick has played in comedies so he knows how to supply one. 'What's that?' he asked, and then waited patiently for the kicker.

'We have to solve the murder of Helene Nestor,' Angie said. 'And we have to do it fast.'

We ordered Chinese takeout.

TWENTY-NINE

'I was involved in ImagiNails at the onset, but I left when the company was absorbed.' Jason Kemper was a middle-aged man who was very concerned about his appearance. His hair was stylishly trimmed and only a little gray. His suit, on the other hand, was not at all gray (it was navy) and impeccably tailored. He had a red pocket square that was arranged perfectly. His nails were trimmed and buffed. I could have seen myself in the tops of his shoes if I'd wanted to look, but I'd seen myself before. Jason Kemper looked as if he'd come out of a corporate executive vending machine.

'So you had left the company before Riley was born,' I said. I already knew that, but I wanted it to seem like I was clarifying, like he had things to tell me that I wasn't yet aware of. Guys like this always want to have the upper hand, whether there's a hand or not.

'That's right. I met Riley only in the year before her mother passed away.' People don't like to say *died* or *was murdered*. They like to pretend the dead person is just in the next room changing clothes and will be back in a minute. Whatever floats your boat. 'She seems like a very intelligent and spirited girl.' Yes, those were two words you could use about Riley.

'But you weren't one of the original three investors who ended up owning large parts of the new ImagiNails corporation, is that right?' I asked. Again, I knew the answer ahead of time; what I wanted to see was Kemper's reaction.

And I got that in spades. 'There were *four* original investors!' he almost shouted. Shouting would have been undignified. 'Sorry. I had bought in on the company when it was still based in Helene's one-bedroom apartment. It was a handshake deal we had and I gave her five thousand dollars. I have the endorsed check in my desk at home. I thought we were going to make a kind of history with that company.' His face twisted a little. 'And they did. They were just about to take it public when Helene was killed.'

I was with Kemper in his office at Amalgamated Something (no, that's the real name of the company), an investment firm he'd started and now ran, looking for budding ideas for companies and providing necessary seed money. Apparently the firm had done quite well because it was headquartered in a very chic but serious building on Santa Monica Boulevard and appointed with furniture and décor that would make the analogous items at Seaton, Taylor crawl away in mortification.

Patrick was shooting *Torn*, of course, as the personality Emil Hutton, which was not his main character on the show (that was Newt O'Brian, and don't ask me who made up these names). Emil required him to use a slight German accent, something he did quite well. Angie was not required on set. Ryan Tanner, one of Patrick's not-executive assistants, held down the fort while Angie was assisting Nate, something I'm sure Nate would say she was not doing at all. She was checking in as Nate went back to interview Riley's Aunt Alicia, a job I was glad to cede to the private investigator as long as I didn't have to be there.

'They cut you out of the deal when the millions were coming in,' I said. Show the witness you're on their side even if you're not. They'll tell you more and a lot of it will be true, depending on your perspective.

Kemper, who had been standing to show me how tall he was, sat carefully in his real-leather chair and undid his jacket so the button wouldn't strain. His words came out like a mournful sigh. 'That is exactly what she did.'

'She? Helene removed you from the merger deal herself?' If you want to talk about motives, that would have been a doozy.

'Yes,' Kemper said, trying to convince me he was moved emotionally. 'Just when we were on the precipice of fulfilling all our dreams, she pushed me out and made me watch while she and three other people made massive fortunes.' Yup, motive material.

'That must have been extremely upsetting for you,' I said, fully realizing that Kemper must not have walked away from the deal completely empty-handed. 'I imagine you were very angry.'

There are times I'm not quite as nuanced as I imagine myself to be, and this was one of them. 'You're not suggesting I had anything to do with Helene's murder,' Kemper said through clenched teeth. 'Because that could lead to charges of slander.'

Now, I was aware that the definition of slander isn't remotely like what Kemper was suggesting, but it wasn't a time to shove my law license in his face. That wouldn't get me the kind of responses I was hoping for, so I ignored his ridiculous assertion and instead pretended his hollow threat had landed. 'Oh no, I wasn't suggesting anything of the sort,' I said. I stopped short of batting my eyelashes at him and clutching my hands to my chest in dismay because you can oversell these things. 'I just thought hearing about such a betrayal would naturally make a person angry.' *But yeah, if you want to confess, I can have a cop here in minutes.*

Kemper sat up in his chair as if trying to reach full height without standing up. 'I was terribly hurt, of course, but this is business and one can't take every blow personally,' he said. 'If I collapsed every time I felt like I hadn't been treated well, I would have been finished years ago.'

'So, who were the three original investors who were kept on, and what justification did Helene Nestor give you for squeezing you out?' There was no need to sugarcoat it; in fact, that might have been less effective as an interrogation tactic.

He looked off into the distance, as if trying to see the past from where he sat. Instead he was actually seeing the oak door to his office, which I had made sure would remain open, and the sumptuous quarters of his secretary, whose office was nicer than mine. 'There were the four of us, initially,' he said, as if I hadn't absorbed that the first time. 'Dan Peters, Christina Manolo, Ken Warshofsky and me. But Helene had a way of playing one against the other, I think for her own entertainment mostly, and I ended up being the odd man out. I guess I didn't play as well as the others.'

It had gone by so fast I'd almost missed it. 'Ken Warshofsky?' I asked. 'The Ken Warshofsky who's married to Lisa Conforto?'

Kemper looked at me for the first time with a wry smile. 'How many Ken Warshofskys do you know?' he asked.

*　　*　　*

'OK,' Angie said over my Bluetooth. 'So Lisa's husband Ken is a multimillionaire and was in on ImagiNails from the beginning?'

'If we're going to believe our buddy Jason Kemper,' I answered, glancing at the GPS to see how far the right turn coming up might be. Nine hundred feet. In case you were wondering. 'And I'm not sure we are. What have you and Nate found out?'

'Nate's police scanner has been busy,' Angie said, while I moved into the right lane to make the turn. Yes, I used my turn signal. No, that didn't stop some idiot in a BMW from speeding up so he wouldn't suffer the indignity of being behind me. 'Apparently there's a stolen car whose license plates have been spotted north of here and cops are closing in. Might be our two fugitives from justice because the car was boosted right near the state prison in Lancaster.'

I turned the car and made a face at the guy in the BMW because that's how classy I am. 'Are we looking at a low-speed chase here? If Riley's with them, I don't want anything too dramatic to be going on.'

'CNN hasn't picked up on it yet,' Angie told me. 'Nate and I are headed in that direction but they've got quite the head start on us.'

'Yeah, at least eighteen hours,' I told her. 'You don't have a prayer of catching them.'

'Nah. They must have crashed for the night. They're only in San Luis Obispo or thereabouts. Wherever they're going, they don't appear to be in a terrific hurry to get there.'

'Or maybe it's not them.'

'That's another possibility,' Angie admitted.

'Should I head up that way? I'm on my way to see T'Aisha. We're going to go over her articles and then maybe see our old buddies Lisa and Ken again, once I figure out what I want to say to them.'

I will never be able to drive in California without GPS. Even if I'd moved here twenty years ago, I'd probably have ended up lost in the desert somewhere. Of course, I was in high school then, so maybe a move to LA would have been foolish, desert or not.

'I don't think so,' Angie answered. 'We're way ahead of you and we'll keep you informed. If there's anything seriously interesting you can always drive up, but Patrick's going to be done shooting early today, so he can join you if you need backup.'

I thought about the possibility of Patrick acting as my backup in any truly difficult situation and, I'll admit it, I cringed a little. 'I don't think that'll be necessary,' I said. 'I'll have T'Aisha if I need help.'

Angie signed off and I drove to the Frances Howard Goldwyn (wife of Sam) Hollywood Library, where T'Aisha had told me she'd be doing some research for the judge show. It's a building that looks almost like it was built with very large bland Lego bricks. It's all tan blocks of stone and kind of random in configuration. Inside, I found it was a nice modern-style building and had the kind of quiet but friendly atmosphere you want in a library.

I found T'Aisha in the legal section (of course), looking up precedents on the local Minneapolis statutes for the adoption of exotic animals. I didn't ask. There was no one else in sight of us, but we spoke in subdued voices because it's a library and that's what you do.

I hadn't lugged in my folder of T'Aisha's reporting on Jack's murder trial, but I had my iPad and that housed all the relevant information without even trying. I opened the file to a piece she'd written during the trial when Judge DeForge had ruled on Cagney Weldon (IV)'s motion to admit Jack's statement about the transom and how it could prove he hadn't killed his wife.

'This is basic trial procedure,' I said to her. 'Are you familiar with the concept of significant error of law?'

Somehow T'Aisha didn't sound like she was bragging when she said, 'I have a law degree from USC. I get the idea.'

I stared at her for a moment. 'Why aren't you practicing law?'

She smiled. Maybe she *had* been bragging a little and it produced the desired effect. 'That was never the idea. I knew I wanted to be a reporter; I also had a degree in journalism. I wanted to write about the courts and so I needed to know about how the system works.'

'I aspire to be as impressive as you are,' I said.

T'Aisha waved a hand to dismiss my statement. 'Don't sell yourself short. You successfully defended two celebrities – three if you count Robert Reeves – on murder charges. That's not nothing.'

Before we started waving our diplomas at each other, I got back to the issue at hand. 'Still, when DeForge denied the motion to admit the defense, you must have known he was making a significant error.'

'Sure,' T'Aisha said. 'But I'm not there to defend the accused any more than I'm there to prosecute the case. I just report on what happened. That's what happened. I figured there'd be an appeal but Weldon never filed. Later I heard that Schoenberg was telling everybody he was guilty, and I figured that was why there was no appeal, but by then I had my current job and I wasn't reporting on the courts anymore.'

I made a mental note to ask her why she stopped doing what she clearly loved to do, but right now I had to find Riley and I wasn't hearing anything about the stolen car from Angie. 'You clearly did a couple of in-depth interviews with Jack Schoenberg during the trial.'

T'Aisha's eyes closed a fraction. 'If you're asking me whether Jack and I had something going on . . .'

'No, I'm not. That never occurred to me.' Now I was wondering about it, though. That was something of a leap. 'I'm trying to find Riley and I'm betting on the probability that Jack is the one who arranged to have her kidnapped so they could run from the law together or something. I want to know if – in the course of reporting on an eight-week trial – you got to know your subject well enough to make an educated guess on where he might be running to.'

She sat back on the wooden chair and thought about that. 'It's been a couple of years,' she said.

'I know. If you want to read through your work to refresh your memory . . .' I turned the iPad around to face her and, to my surprise, she took it and opened a couple of files. She looked them over quickly, using her finger to scan the pages as she went. I wondered if she was searching for a specific passage.

'Jack talked about Riley like you would talk about your hero,' she said as she leafed through the articles. 'He loved her like a father loves a daughter, but he also really admired her, looked up to her almost like a role model. She was only eight or nine when Helene was shot but Jack already thought of Riley as someone he would want to emulate. It was kind of weird.'

'What are you looking for?' I asked her.

'A good man, a more fulfilling job that pays the same and a really great pedicure,' T'Aisha said. 'But in these articles, I'm searching for the one that I did right before the verdict, when the jury was out for those four days.' That is a pretty long period of time for a jury to deliberate, although this was a murder trial and those decisions almost always take longer. I wondered if there was a juror or two holding out on the guilty verdict and trying to persuade the larger majority. But we never actually find those things out, unless some juror decides to talk to the press after the trial is over, and in Jack's case that had not happened.

'I know where that article is,' I said, and maneuvered the tablet back around so I could call it up. Once I had, I turned the screen back toward T'Aisha. 'I read it but I didn't get any ideas about where to look for Riley,' I told her.

'No, but if you give me a second, I'll find my notes,' she answered. The laptop she'd been using for her television research was sitting right at her elbow and T'Aisha was, predictably, a virtuoso of the keyboard. She clacked away for a minute or two and then stopped and looked at the screen. 'Yes. Here.' She gestured at the screen so I stood and walked around her chair to get a good vantage point.

The notes were in paragraphs and typed up cleanly, without the hideous cross-through marks and obvious edits that mine would have shown. They looked like an essay that had been carefully prepared. This woman was dangerously organized. She pointed at one section.

'See here, where I wrote that Jack was going on about how he and Riley would have to adapt now that Helene was no longer alive,' she started. 'He said something about going to the country and living more simply.'

'You know their house,' I said. 'For a woman with tens of millions of dollars, Helene wasn't exactly living like a woman with tens of millions of dollars. It's a very nice house, one I'd consider really upscale, but I've seen mansions and that's not one of them.'

T'Aisha held up her hands at the waist to concede the point.

'But Jack was talking about living a *lot* more simply,' she said. 'I'm wondering if they had like a cabin somewhere, near skiing or just in the woods. Nobody in the family was a hunter, as far as I know, but something like that.'

I picked up my phone and texted Jon. *See if you can find a list of properties the Schoenbergs own, not business but family.* I didn't have to wait for a reply; I knew Jon would be on it and have an answer quickly. The man is a legal research machine.

'You didn't ask at the time?' I said.

T'Aisha gave me a slightly annoyed look. 'I was a newspaper reporter covering a murder trial,' she said. 'You wanted me to check in and see if the defendant, who appeared to be punching his ticket to a long vacation in state prison, had any leisure properties? What relevance did that have to what I was writing about?' OK, so she had a point. This being smarter than me was starting to get on my nerves a little.

'Fair enough. Was there anywhere else, assuming there is a cabin or a ski chalet or something, that Jack might think to go? Relatives I haven't heard about yet, or friends he might try to convince to hide him and Riley?'

'And Pete Lucchesi, don't forget him. I talked to him in jail too because he was Jack's friend.'

'I didn't forget about him, but I figured they must have split up after they broke out of jail,' I said. 'Make it harder to track them both.'

'Don't count on it. Pete is, like, Jack's BFF. They go back to grammar school. My best guess is that Pete is the mastermind behind the jailbreak.'

The wheels were spinning in my head. People's roles were shifting around and my efforts to find my eleven-year-old client were traveling in six different directions at once. 'What about killing Helene?' I asked. 'Could Pete have had a hand in that too?'

T'Aisha moved her jaw from side to side like she was chewing something over. 'I've never thought about it before because he was already locked up when Helene died,' she said, 'but you know I wouldn't put it past him to have arranged the whole thing.'

Seven different directions.

THIRTY

Things started to happen very fast.

Jon texted back and said he'd email me a list of the properties that Helene Schoenberg had owned and were not yet sold. Jack didn't own any properties outright but had been willed some. Parts of Helene's estate, apparently, were still in probate two years after she'd died. With a worth of all those millions, that wasn't unheard of but it was, let's say, a little draggy on the part of the lawyers. I'm not an estate attorney so I'm not taking shots at the competition.

Angie called as I was leaving T'Aisha to finish her television research, which she looked as interested in doing as if someone had asked her to babysit a python that hadn't been fed in a week. But she seemed to remember her needs for shelter and food and dived back into the judge show job.

Emily Webster had left me three messages on my voicemail asking if I wanted to see the Schoenberg house again once the police lines were taken down. I'm not sure if I didn't have the heart to tell her I wasn't shopping for a house there, or if I had just had enough of Emily Webster, but either way I didn't call her back. Patrick could do that if he had the stomach for it.

'What's with the stolen car?' I asked Angie. I was driving back to my office because at the moment I couldn't think of anywhere else to look for Riley. Once I was back there and could research all the properties in Jon's email, I might set out for parts unknown to find my client and try to persuade her father to go back to jail so I could get him a new trial.

Law is a complicated business.

'That seems to have been a wild-goose chase,' Angie told me. 'The cops finally decided it was safe to approach the car and pull it over. They found two renegade weed dealers who had boosted the car because – get ready for this – they thought it would make them less visible to the cops.'

'Two weed dealers? Have they not heard it's legal in California now?'

'Apparently that's what makes them renegades. Anyway, there was no sign of Riley or Jack in the car and the two pea brains who were driving it had never heard of either one of them. They're arrested for grand theft auto, but if you saw this car you'd agree it was maybe average theft auto.'

I exhaled slowly. Driving in Los Angeles has always been more stressful to me than driving back home. New Jersey aspires to have horrible traffic problems but LA has really perfected the whole thing. Not really getting the layout of the streets (aside from a couple of the highways) doesn't help matters. 'So you and Nate are nowhere now,' I said.

'Nah. We'd have to drive an hour to get to nowhere.'

'OK. Tell Nate . . .'

'Wait. I'll put you on speaker.'

I wished she wouldn't do that. 'Angie . . .'

'What's going on, Moss?' Nate.

'Maybe we need to concentrate more on Uncle Pete,' I told him. 'And we might end up looking for a cabin in the woods later.'

Not a pause, not a moment to digest that. 'Uh-huh. You know the whole cabin-in-the-woods thing rarely works out well, don't you?'

'Wasn't my choice. But I don't know if we're doing that yet. What have you been up to besides driving for hours to find out a stolen car *didn't* have the two guys we're looking for?'

Can you hear a scowl? I thought I heard a scowl. 'Nobody saw the kidnapper and the girl leave the mall, which is weird even if you think there's this network of underground tunnels that I don't necessarily believe exists. So our best bet is to think that somewhere along the way, in one of the few areas that isn't subject to video surveillance, she made the girl stop to disguise herself. I don't have access to the video yet and we don't want to take the time to watch the next hour from every single angle possible to the eye, so we're going to let the cops analyze that stuff.'

Sometimes with Nate – like when you only have maybe twenty-nine hours left to find a missing girl – it's a better plan to apply pressure rather than to give him a pat on the back. He's a big boy; he can take it. 'I didn't ask you what you *haven't* been doing,' I said.

You can also hear someone speak through clenched teeth. I was getting through to Nate and now the question was whether that would lead to productive answers. I knew Nate so I bet that it would. 'I have a friend working in the state prison at Lancaster,' he said. 'From what I understand, everyone's favorite pal Uncle Pete was the mastermind behind the prison break. It's not clear if Schoenberg was even aware of the plan before the day they broke out. Apparently he's not the brightest bulb in the chandelier.'

'Any indication that getting this woman, whoever she was, to kidnap Riley was part of the escape plan?' I asked.

'I also checked in with some pals at the LAPD who prefer not to be named.' I was about two miles from my office and in enough traffic that it could take half an hour to get there, so I waited for Nate to deliver his information at his pace. 'We have an ID on the woman who got herself shot at Helene Nestor's house.'

I had a sharp intake of breath, which probably gratified Nate to no end. Even Angie, on the other end of the phone, went, 'What?!?'

Nate was clearly enjoying his moment and didn't acknowledge our reactions. 'Her name was Nathalie – with an H – Morrison, and she was the sister of an old girlfriend of Pete Lucchesi.'

He let that sink in and Angie got there first. 'They killed his girlfriend's sister?' she said.

But even if I wasn't speaking first, I was thinking ahead. 'Nate, we've got to find Nathalie's sister. What's her name?'

'Now it's Rosalind Morrison Bailey,' Nate said. 'She lives in Van Nuys and has three kids. We're on our way to see her right now.'

As I inched my way toward my office I heard Angie say, 'We are?'

'Good work, Nate,' I said. 'I'm going to make a quick diversion now.' I must have sighed for two reasons: first, I'd been so close to my office and second, the last place I wanted to go was where I had decided I had to go. Because this was about family.

'Where you going?' Angie asked.

'To see Aunt Alicia.'

'Oy,' Angie said.

'Yup.'

THIRTY-ONE

The last person I expected to find at my unannounced visit to Alicia Jennings's swanky apartment was Lisa Conforto. Well, no. The last person I would have expected to find there was probably either Riley or LeVar Burton, but either way it was a surprise that Lisa was there.

They were seated in the same immaculate living room where I'd talked to Alicia when Riley was here getting ready for school, and the sight of the place did make a lump catch in my throat. Alicia, decked out in a completely unwrinkled suit and with her hair and nails done perfectly, did not seem to be having the same kind of emotional reaction to recent events.

'I didn't expect to be hearing from you, Ms Moss,' Alicia began. 'I rather thought that Jack's legal defense would have been put on hold once he decided to force his way violently out of prison. Doesn't that tell you anything?'

'It tells me mostly that Riley is in a great deal of danger, and you don't seem to be terribly concerned about it, Ms Jennings.' The claws might just as well come out; I wasn't going to get anywhere being nice to Alicia. Then I turned toward Lisa. 'And I didn't expect to see you here, Lisa. What's the connection? Is this about your husband's stake in ImagiNails?' No more kid gloves for anybody. I was going to find Riley and I didn't care who I had to insult to do so. I'm from New Jersey. I gave up worrying about who I insulted around the time I got my driver's license.

Sure enough Lisa sputtered a bit; she wasn't aware that I knew about Ken's investment in Helene's company and how Jason Kemper had been edged out of the huge haul when it was sold years before.

Lisa recovered nicely and stood up to offer me her hand; I fist-bumped her, which she clearly found confusing. 'I'm here to offer moral support to Alicia,' she said. 'This is a very difficult time for all of us, with Riley missing.'

'Funny how you didn't mention that Ken had been one of the original four investors in ImagiNails,' I said, ignoring her obvious lie. 'So I'm wondering what else there is that you haven't told me.' I turned toward Alicia. 'Both of you. So I'm going to put it to both of you and I want answers that are true this time: What do you know about Riley's kidnapping and where she is now?'

Alicia looked at me the way a queen looks at a cockroach, or someone who wants her to pay taxes. 'I don't know what you're talking about,' she said. 'Of course we don't know where Riley is. Why would you ask me such a question?'

Her tacit disapproval was enough to keep my mood determined. 'Don't try to play the concerned aunt, Alicia. It was obvious in a five-minute conversation that you couldn't care less about Riley. So I'm wondering if that might have led you to have her kidnapped.' That didn't make a lick of sense no matter how you looked at it, but my goal was not so much to prove my case as to keep Alicia pissed off to the point that she might say something rash and actually divulge useful information.

But she barely moved, not wanting to damage the tableau she was inhabiting on the sofa. 'You're delusional,' she said in a tone that might have indicated she was ordering another Cosmo to go with her salad. 'You feel guilty because Riley was taken under your watch and so you're trying to blame me. Well, keep the guilt. It *was* your fault and you *should* feel terrible about it.'

Patrick had shown me an episode of a soap opera he'd once worked on in the UK early in his career, so I was fairly well acquainted with the kind of performance Alicia was giving. Lisa, on the other hand, looked positively stricken and hadn't spoken since I'd suggested she and Alicia were hiding something. Maybe she was trying to determine how she'd cover her own lie by omission, not telling me Ken was a part-owner of ImagiNails.

You go after the weak link if you want to break the chain. I focused on Lisa. 'Come on,' I said to her, 'you're obviously dying to tell me everything you've left out of this story. Let it out. You'll feel better afterward, I promise you.'

Lisa's eyes were a little wide and, if there were headlights handy, I'd be expecting her to develop a small tail and try to help Bambi make it safely and quickly to the woods. 'I don't know anything,' she managed.

'Sure you do. You were trying to get your story straight with the ice queen here, but I don't know how far you'd gotten when I arrived.'

Alicia opened her mouth but didn't speak. I think the 'ice queen' thing got to her. Good. Maybe I could play both ends of this situation. Lisa, meanwhile, was doing her best to look like an innocent babe but she was neither.

She stood across from me looking at Alicia, whose legs were still admirably crossed. If she hadn't been in a different outfit, I would have thought she hadn't moved since the morning I'd come to pick up Riley. Lisa, by contrast, looked gangly and clumsy. She was going to be the best source of a lead. And I was starting not to care how I got that lead. Riley's clock was ticking and there weren't that many hours left.

'I mean, I don't know anything about where Riley is,' Lisa said, trying to cover for the last statement, which was probably just as false but hadn't gotten her the reaction she'd desired (which was likely for me to go away and stop bothering everyone). 'The fact that Ken was on the board of ImagiNails just didn't come up when we met you.'

Alicia's eyebrows flickered up. 'You met her?' she said.

'What's the matter?' I pressed on. 'Some uncertainty in the ranks? Come on, Lisa. If I don't hear some helpful stuff from you telling me what's going on and where we should look for Riley, I'm going to assume that's because you had something to do with her abduction and I will tell that to the police and the FBI.'

'The . . . no!' Lisa looked like she might cry, but sit? Never. 'Look. I don't know where Riley is and that's the truth. I didn't tell you everything about the other stuff because you were trying to get Jack a new trial and—'

'Lisa,' Alicia said in a flat tone. Quietly.

Lisa immediately put her hand to her mouth, the way you see children do when they've said too much because they think that's supposed to be the gesture. But there ain't no getting those words back into your mouth and I knew a compromised witness when I saw one.

'Tell me, Lisa. It can only help you and Riley.' I didn't know how it was going to help Lisa to rat other people and perhaps herself out, but to be honest I wasn't thinking too hard about that at the moment. 'I get that Ken has a lot of money in the company but getting Riley back is more important than that, isn't it?' Again, this was blind shooting. I had no idea what I was talking about but thought I could be vague enough to hit something that might be useful.

'Of course it is,' Lisa said, possibly to herself.

'So tell me what you know.'

Alicia looked like she might just explode from watching the scene taking place in her living room. 'Don't you dare!' she hissed.

And Lisa, god bless her, turned on Alicia with something like fire in her eyes. OK, it was only a match flame, but that can start something bigger, can't it? 'It's Riley's life we have to worry about,' she said. 'Maybe you don't care but I do.'

Alicia, getting back to pretending this was all casual, waved a hand at the irrelevance she'd heard. 'Riley isn't in any danger,' she said.

I pivoted and faced her. 'How do you know that?' I demanded. 'Nobody's heard from Riley in a full day and her father has broken out of jail. She was taken out of a public place with a hand grenade right next to her head. So you tell me, Alicia, how do you know her life isn't being threatened right at this moment?'

'Because the little bitch is a con artist.' Alicia's face did not contort and her mouth did not sneer. She might just as well have been discussing pork belly futures, and if someone could explain to me what those are and why they're important . . . never mind. I probably don't want to know. 'She has you believing she's this innocent little girl who's been left all alone in the world, but she's a millionaire who has been treating me like a servant for two years. I'm sure she knows perfectly well that her father the escaped convict killed her mother, but she wants to put one over on everybody and get him freed. Well, that's not going to happen now, is it?' And then she allowed herself the slightest evil grin. It was quite effective.

I didn't have the proper response lined up in my repertoire but Lisa, of all people, put her hands on her hips like a testy schoolmarm who'd just been told that the kids didn't have to learn this silly grammar stuff because they were needed out in the fields for harvest time. 'What exactly did you do?' she demanded of Alicia. 'Did you send that woman out to kidnap Riley?'

Alicia put her head back and laughed in what appeared to be genuine surprise. 'Why on earth would I do *that*?' she said. 'I can't get rid of that little brat. Why would I ever ask someone to steal her when she's living with me to begin with?'

I took two steps toward her, still posed on the sofa like she was having her portrait painted. 'You didn't want her brought back. You wanted her gone. Didn't you, Alicia?' In my estimation that was an extremely unlikely scenario, but I was still trying to get under Alicia's skin and force her to say something that could help me against her will. 'Did you get Nathalie Morrison to send Riley texts posing as her mom and then set up a meeting so she could take that girl somewhere and kill her?'

And that, for reasons I didn't immediately understand, made Alicia flinch. 'Nathalie?' she said hoarsely. 'That was Nathalie at the mall?'

Lisa leaned on the chair in front of her to steady herself. 'Nathalie's caught up in all this?' She was talking to herself, not to either of us.

I figured if that was the sensitive spot it was the place to press. 'Not anymore,' I said. 'She's dead. Someone shot her in the very same room where Helene Nestor died.'

They both reacted with shock and I didn't think it was feigned. Lisa sat down on the chair she'd been using for support and Alicia actually moved on the sofa. She didn't stand up, but then I didn't want her to do anything that was contrary to her religion. She put her feet on the floor in front of her and rested her head in her hands.

I said the most obvious thing possible. 'So you knew her.'

Alicia pushed her head up and looked at me with fury in her eyes. 'Of course I knew my own best friend,' she said. She added quietly, 'I just saw her last week.'

THIRTY-TWO

' 'm not sure I understand all of it,' I told Patrick on the phone from my car, 'but as far as I can tell Alicia knew Nathalie from high school. Nathalie was married at one point to a guy named Ricky Jennings, whom she divorced four years ago. But she had fixed up her brother-in-law's – that's Jack Schoenberg because he married her sister – friend Pete Lucchesi with Rosalind Morrison, whom she knew from college. Note that she *didn't* fix Pete up with her best friend because she knew what kind of guy he was. Pete and Rosalind didn't work out but he started seeing Rosalind's sister Nathalie, which might have been why it didn't work out, and now Nathalie's dead, having acted as Grenade Gertie to kidnap Riley. Is this all coming across clearly?'

'I can hear you just fine and so can everyone else here,' Patrick said.

Oh, Patrick. 'Everyone else?' I repeated because I was hoping I'd heard him wrong.

'Yes. I told you, I'm in the makeup trailer. I have you on speaker and we can all hear what you're saying. It's fascinating, but does it help you find Riley?'

'That poor girl,' I heard a woman say.

'That's Leslie,' Patrick explained. 'She's doing my face.'

'Great,' I said.

'Hello, Sandy, you lucky girl.'

'Yeah, hi, Leslie. Let me talk to Patrick a moment.' Now I was wondering why I'd called him at all, but the fact is that talking over a case with Patrick adds a perspective I could never achieve on my own and sometimes that illuminates things.

'Oh yeah, of course, dear.' Leslie sounded as if she was in her sixties and liked to call people *dear*.

'So where are you with finding Riley?' Patrick reiterated.

'Not that much closer. Alicia and Lisa, who know each other through Helene and Lisa's husband Ken, the smart investor, were so stunned by the news about Nathalie that pumping them for more just wasn't going to yield anything. Lisa did say she'd heard Jack talk about a country house or a cabin or something where maybe he'd go when he wanted to decompress, but she didn't know where it was. I already have Jon looking through real-estate records to nail that down.'

'So where are you heading now?' Patrick asked.

'Back to my office. I want to check on the backgrounds of the other original investors in ImagiNails and see if there are any common threads. If I can figure out why Helene cut Jason Kemper out of the deal, maybe I can figure out what the motive to murder her was, assuming Jason didn't do it himself.'

'That sounds like a good plan,' another woman said from Patrick's side.

'That's Nancy,' Patrick explained. 'She's doing my hair.'

'Imagine,' I said a little wearily, which I'm sure Patrick caught but the others (however many of them there were) didn't. 'I have to get myself presentable and out the door in the morning all by myself.'

'You poor kid,' Leslie said.

'Thanks, Leslie.' I felt like we were becoming friends.

'What about Ken?' Patrick asked. 'He seems like a random element but he's the glue holding all this together.'

Ken? 'The glue?' I asked Patrick. 'What do you mean?'

'We had cases like this on *Legality*,' he answered.

'Oh, I loved that show,' Nancy said. 'Why did it get cancelled?'

'Because I left,' Patrick told her. 'But Sandy, Ken is the key point. It's the person who stands to one side and doesn't get all the attention you have to think about. Ken's got all this money as an investor in ImagiNails.'

'Those things don't work nearly as well as they say,' Leslie jumped in. 'I used them on *Heroines* and they broke every twenty minutes; I had to use something else.'

'Thanks, Leslie,' I said. That was some makeup trailer. Or maybe it was a typical one.

Patrick did his best to stay on topic. 'So Ken makes this fortune, but he doesn't leave his job. Why not? He didn't have to work as an accountant anymore, but he just kept going into the office. He's the reason Jason Kemper didn't get a share and that gives Jason motive to kill Helene Nestor. And Ken is married to Lisa Conforto, who admits she and her husband saw and talked to Jack Schoenberg the night Helene was shot. Ken is a tie in that direction and to Alicia Jennings.'

That was where he lost me. 'How to Alicia?' I asked. 'Alicia indirectly fixed up Nathalie Morrison with Pete Lucchesi. How does Ken enter into that equation?'

'Yeah,' Nancy said. 'How?'

'His connection isn't about Nathalie Morrison,' Patrick said. He can make it sound so plausible. He's a really good actor. Someday he might get a chance to show it. 'Ken is connected to Lisa.'

'He's *married* to Lisa,' Leslie corrected him. Leslie was serious about this stuff.

'Yes. And when you arrived at Alicia's apartment, who did you find there, Sandy?' Throwing in my name at the end there was strictly to inform the makeup and hair ladies that they were not being asked the question.

'Lisa,' I answered dutifully. Ms Carbone from sixth grade would have been thrilled.

'Precisely,' Patrick said. 'And she knew all about Peter Lucchesi and Nathalie, didn't she? You have to wonder why. And standing in the middle of all this is . . .'

'Ken.' Leslie and Nancy said it together.

'That last one is kind of circumstantial,' I noted.

I could hear Patrick's smile. 'Well you know, I'm not a *real* lawyer. But I think Ken deserves a closer examination, don't you?'

'I do and thank you for the help.' I meant it. Patrick had succeeded in clarifying my thinking, even if it wasn't in the way he believed. He was right about Ken, though.

'What help?' A new female voice had entered the conversation unnoticed.

'Who's that?' I asked.

'That's Betsy,' Patrick said. 'Betsy, this is Sandy. Sandy, Betsy.' It sounded like the name of a bad beach doll for little children.

'Hi, Sandy.'

'Hi, Betsy. Patrick already has hair and makeup. What are you there for?'

Patrick sounded similarly puzzled. 'Yeah, Betsy. What *are* you doing here?'

Her voice was amused, like a mother correcting a son who had spelled *gorilla* wrong. 'You're playing Maurice today,' she told Patrick, referring to one of his personas on *Torn*.

'Ah,' he said. 'Mustache.' Don't even get me started on the idea that a man with a neurological mental health disorder would be able to grow a mustache spontaneously when one of his 'personalities' decided to dominate.

I said goodbye to the gang in the makeup trailer just as my phone rang and I could turn off to a less traffic-jammed street. Bluetooth told me the caller was Jon.

'What's up?' I asked. I'm a woman of few salutations. If you can't beat 'em, join 'em.

'I've got an address on Jack Schoenberg's fishing cabin,' Jon answered. 'How far do you want to drive?'

Having just escaped from a parking lot scenario on the LA streets, and so close to my office, an honest answer would have been, 'Not at all.' But Riley had been taken and I needed to find her. 'How far do I have to?'

'A couple hours, probably. Not that bad.' Not bad for *him*.

And that was when I looked in my rearview mirror and noticed a navy-blue SUV, a Chevrolet Equinox (where do they come up with these names?) if I wasn't mistaken, driven by – you guessed it – a person in a gray hoodie, black face mask, and sunglasses. It followed me for three blocks and then turned off without even looking in my direction.

I didn't even call Trench this time.

THIRTY-THREE

'I don't see why I had to drive,' Nate Garrigan said.

'You're the man,' Angie told him. 'Men drive.'

'I thought you girls were all liberated now.' Nate doesn't really believe it's still 1978. He just likes to act that way.

I'd called Angie immediately when I got the address for Jack Schoenberg's cabin. It was located not in but near the city of Visalia, which I had never heard of before. That wasn't a surprise. Nate knew where it was but he had no idea about cabins there. It is not on the coast and as for fishing, as Jon had suggested, there were no significant lakes or rivers very close to the cabin, although the Kaweah River flowed close enough to Visalia, which was the seat of Tulare County. (Riding as opposed to driving had made a Google search easier to do.) Nate's GPS was also suggesting that the road leading up to Jack's cabin was not a hundred per cent paved.

'You know the roads,' I told Nate. 'You have lived here much longer than Angie or me and you own this monster SUV that can probably get us to the cabin, where my little Hyundai would have ended up with a broken axle trying it. *That's* why you have to drive us.'

I left out the part where I had considered that Nate always has a handgun somewhere on his person or safely stored in his car. Angie had recently been seen carrying such a weapon, but I was hoping she didn't have her gun with her today. That would be all I needed.

After all, we had no idea what kind of reception we'd be receiving, if and when we found Jack, Uncle Pete and – with any luck at all – Riley in that cabin. And if my hoodied doppelgänger was in the area, the last thing I wanted to do was lead them to Riley. Because it had finally occurred to me that maybe what all this shadowing had been about was someone hoping I would lead them to my client.

'Anyway, we talked to Nathalie's sister Rosalind,' Angie said.

'She confirmed everything you said. She dated Pete Lucchesi, who immediately started cheating on her with her own sister. She dumped Pete and he stayed with Nathalie almost until he got thrown in jail for trying to rob his ex-wife. This whole thing is an episode of *Dr Phil*.'

I've never seen that show but I had a general idea of what Angie meant. 'It was just the beginning,' I said.

Visalia was north and east of Los Angeles, a little more than the two hours Jon had suggested if we're being technical. But the cabin wasn't in Visalia exactly; it was hard to tell from online maps precisely where it might be located, and Jon said the deed to the property had three municipalities listed, leading one to believe that it was situated on some serious borders. It was probably hell getting the place assessed accurately for taxes.

'How are we going to play this?' Angie asked.

'Play it?' I was thinking about the dark sunglasses and general lack of facial expression. Maybe I should have Nate drop me off and get a Lyft home to keep from being the bearer of bad people.

'When we get there,' Angie went on. 'Are we just going to bust in on whoever's there, or knock, or what?'

It was a good question. For all the imagining I'd done about rescuing Riley from . . . her father? . . . I had not really pictured how Nate, Angie and I were going to manage that. I'd always jumped to the grateful hug I'd get from my client, and not so much any possible resistance that might come from the people who'd gone to such trouble to secrete her away after breaking out of jail.

Luckily Nate was an ex-cop. 'We're going to scope out the cabin first,' he said. 'And by "we", I mean me. Check the windows, see if I can assess what's going on inside. Then I can make some kind of judgment on the best course of action, which can either be trying to sneak in through an unguarded entrance or kicking in the front door.'

Angie gave me a look I didn't understand because I didn't want to. But deep in my heart I did. Denial is a wonderful thing.

'Well, here's your chance,' she told Nate. 'I think that's the cabin.'

She pointed as if it were necessary. There was only the one

structure at the end of this dirt . . . let's call it a *road*. But if this
was a cabin, you could sign me up to live in the woods.

It was an adorable little house behind an actual white picket
fence, painted in a colorful but tasteful mustard tone with green
shutters. It had a spacious front porch with several white rockers
and a glider on it. There was a garage next to it that could easily
hold four cars, closed so we had no idea if there were vehicles
parked there. The lawn was manicured and green. It could
probably make a fortune as an Airbnb.

'That's a fishing cabin?' Nate said as he parked fifty yards
away and turned off the engine.

'There's a swimming pool in back,' Angie told him. 'Maybe
they fish there.'

Nate turned around in the driver's seat to give her a serious
look. 'I know you,' he said. 'When I told you I was going to
check the place out alone, I meant it. You're not coming.'

'I understand,' Angie said.

'Do you?'

'I do. Are we married now?'

Nate waved a hand at her out of annoyance and nodded at
me because he knew I wasn't going to jump out and storm the
place. Then he opened his door and got out of the SUV, but not
before picking his gun up from the glove compartment and
clipping it to his belt. Once he was standing outside the car, he
covered it with his windbreaker. He took great pains to close the
door quietly.

Angie and I sat silently watching Nate crouch and trot toward
the cabin. Just before he reached the gate, which apparently
was not locked or electrified, Angie looked at me and said,
'OK.' Then she opened the back door on her side and got out of
the car.

I stared at her through my open window. 'Are you nuts?'

'Come on. You don't want to miss out on rescuing Riley.' She
gestured for me to follow her. 'It's fine. I've got my gun.' And
then she showed it to me because in Angie World that would
make me think things were better.

'That's not fine,' I said. And I swear to you, I got out of the
SUV and followed her because I was terrified of what would
happen if I let her go into the cabin by herself.

Unlike Nate, Angie started running toward the building holding the handgun, which admittedly was a small one, in her right hand, pointed at the ground. Because that was either what they taught her in training when she bought the thing, or something she saw in a cop movie; you never knew for sure.

I followed, keeping a discreet distance, which I told myself was a hangover impulse from social distancing. I was lying to myself, but what else is new? It wasn't an especially hot or humid day but by the time we reached the quaint little gate I was sweating by the quart.

Angie reached for the latch. 'What do we do when we're close?' I asked. Because now, in this weird twist on existence, Angie was the one in charge of what course of action I should take in a potentially dangerous situation. I had not seen this coming in Westfield High School.

'Just do what I do,' she said, and that didn't make me feel even a little bit better.

She opened the gate and we went through it. I was careful to latch it behind us because clearly the owners of the property would have wanted us to do so. Angie gestured with the gun, which really terrified me, to tell me to go to the right as she went off to the left. 'Look in the windows but don't let them see you,' she said.

'They're not one-way windows,' I pointed out, but she was already scampering to the left and out of earshot. I wasn't speaking very loudly anyway, largely because I was wishing I was somewhere else. Anywhere else. Back in Nate's SUV. But I couldn't do that because my best friend would call me chicken and here I was back in sixth grade again with somewhat higher stakes.

Angie ran up onto the gorgeous front porch, and I hoped the floorboards were as well cared for as the grounds so she wouldn't give away her presence. There was nothing for me to do but run to the right side of the house. Actually, there were plenty of things to do other than that, but they weren't going to help me find Riley so that's what I did. I was certain with every step that I was making some noise or gesture that would get me noticed by the people inside, mostly Pete Lucchesi, whom I had mentally cast as the villain of the piece, and would be severely disappointed if he'd split with Jack Schoenberg and taken off for parts unknown.

That would mean Jack broke out of prison of his own will and had arranged to have his daughter abducted to reunite with him, and it would probably lead to the conclusion that he'd killed Nathalie Morrison, and *that* would lead to the conclusion that Jack had in fact killed his wife and Riley's mother.

Of course such a conclusion would clear my legal calendar, but that would be at best a Pyrrhic victory.

Everything was so beautifully maintained that there was very little behind which I could conceal myself. Luckily, Jack seemed to have a preference for evergreen trees, so there were a few medium-sized firs on my side and I made it a priority to get to one near a window.

I managed that successfully, but discovered once I was behind the tree that I was too short to see inside the cabin. Now I knew why Angie had climbed up onto the porch, which I'd considered reckless. Now I was on the ground a good seven feet too low, which might not have been reckless but was definitely point-less. For all I knew there was a rager going on in the cabin with fifty people partying their hearts out. But there was no music playing so I decided that was unlikely.

Now I had to make my way back to the front steps and creep up to the porch, or I could venture climbing up from here. But keep in mind this had started out as a workday (and devolved rapidly), so I was wearing a business suit and heels. Climbing was not built into my outfit.

The front steps, then.

I couldn't hear Nate or Angie anywhere, and I didn't know if that was good or bad. I didn't hear anything coming from inside the house, either, but that could just have meant they'd installed upscale soundproofing like . . . in the music room. Best not to think about that now. I moved at what felt like a snail's pace but must have been running, because when I reached the foot of the stairs I was breathing hard.

It took the better part of a minute to get my respiration under control. Was it effort, adrenaline or nerves? I finally decided it didn't matter and looked up at the porch. And that didn't make me feel better.

As you might expect, the front steps led directly to the front door. Angie had drifted off to the left side of the wraparound porch and was still not visible from my vantage point. I didn't know which direction Nate had chosen or if he'd gone right in through the door and was currently being held hostage or having a beer with the guys. But what I could see was that the front door had a window for its top half and that would make me visible to anyone in the front room unless I was especially careful.

I climbed the five steps with no creaky boards. Nice job, whoever the groundskeeper might be. I kept my head low while walking up the stairs and planned to drop down to my knees when I reached the porch level.

But I didn't have the chance. As soon as I set foot on the front porch, the house's door swung open and whatever breath I'd recovered left me in a gasp. Standing there was a man with a gun, and I had a very serious moment of regretting that I hadn't called Patrick to say goodbye.

Until I saw that the man with the gun was Nate.

'For crissakes!' he yelled when he saw me. 'I told you to stay in the car, Sandy! I could have shot you!'

'Glad you didn't,' I managed finally.

From behind Nate and to the left I heard a scream. 'Hold it right there, pal!'

Nate didn't look back but did roll his eyes. 'It's me, Angie.'

'Oh.' She walked out from behind him and looked down at me. 'What are you doing on the floor?' she asked.

'Admiring the craftsmanship.' I held out a hand and Angie helped pull me up.

'Well, since you were both so curious you couldn't wait for me to make it safe, why don't you come in and see for yourselves?' Nate said.

THIRTY-FOUR

N ate held the door open while Angie and I walked inside Jack Schoenberg's cabin.

I don't know about you, but my mental image of a cabin runs more to the Abraham Lincoln/Daniel Boone style place, all logs, dirt floors, disgusting animal heads mounted on the walls and a crackling fireplace whether it was cold outside or not. (I guess in my mental cabin it's always cold outside.) But this was absolutely not like that.

We could have been inside a very cozy suburban house, admittedly one that had some money behind it for décor and upkeep. There were a couple of fishing rods mounted above the fireplace, but this was hardly the domain of an outdoorsman (or outdoorswoman, or outdoorsanybodyelse) taking time off from the daily grind. There was a state-of-the-art flat-screen TV hanging on the wall in the main room where people on the large leather sofa and three leather easy chairs could watch it. The supposedly rustic wooden floor was well polished and did not offer so much as a creak when walked upon. It had an area rug on it that was trying terribly hard to be casual but had probably cost $6,000.

There were bookshelves, stuffed with novels and non-fiction, that looked like they were regularly dusted but probably hadn't been touched in years, given how evenly they were arranged. There was one rack of games ranging from chess to Chutes and Ladders that had probably been there for Riley since she was two years old.

The kitchen was modern and high-end, with a separate refrigerator and freezer, either of which was big enough to be the living room in my apartment. The countertops were granite. The cabinets were a cream color and immaculate. The bedrooms were cozy and inviting. I had to consciously stop myself from taking a nap while the others searched the house.

What this place lacked was people. There were none here.

'So it was a wild-goose chase,' Angie said when we reconvened in the kitchen. 'They never came here.'

Nate had the refrigerator door open, which I thought was a little weird. Was he going to drink some of Jack Schoenberg's beer? 'I wouldn't say that,' he said. 'There's perishables in here. Milk. Eggs. Butter. Bread. There's part of a head of lettuce and some cheese. Some of it's gone. People have been here, and not long ago.'

Angie straightened up and touched the gun she'd stuck in her jacket pocket. 'You think they're out and they'll be back?'

'Nah. They were here but then they moved on to somewhere else. Before the two of you ran all over the driveway, you could see there were no fresh tire marks in the dirt. They've been gone since before it rained, and that was this morning in this area.'

'We didn't get any rain,' I noted.

'California's a big place.' Nate started opening cabinet doors, finding nothing interesting, and closing them again. He was a very polite break-and-enter type of guy.

I walked into the living room again and sat down. The leather armchair was very welcoming. I resisted the impulse to lean back into it and take a few hours off. Angie wandered in from the kitchen, where Nate was still taking notes on what brand of aluminum foil Jack's staff had purchased for him. Or had they?

'They would have had to go to the market to get supplies,' I said aloud. 'But Jack and Pete, if he's with them, would probably still be in prison jumpsuits and wouldn't want to be seen. Who do you trust to buy your eggs if you can't go to the store?'

'Anybody.' Angie sat down in the armchair next to me. She didn't seem as inclined to take up residence in it and call it a day. 'It's eggs.'

'Why not stay here if they think it's safe?' I went on, not acknowledging that the eggs weren't the point. 'Are they on their way somewhere else?'

Nate walked in and stood under the mounted television, which was fine because I wasn't much in the mood anyway. 'It could be,' he said. 'But that would have to mean they either have another place where they think they can stay longer, or . . .'

He did that thing where a person stares off into the distance to indicate they're thinking of something. Patrick would call it bad acting.

Angie and I refused to play straight man, largely because I was trying to come up with a scenario where Jack and Riley might be coming back and I could rescue her from whatever. And Angie was probably thinking about doing sit-ups because that was what she usually did this time of day. So that left Nate to break his own trance and just finish the damn sentence.

'Or maybe they're on their way to pick something up,' he said after he gave in to our haughty attitude.

OK, I'll admit it; that piqued my interest. 'Pick something up? Like what?'

Honest to goodness, I think if Nate smoked a pipe, he would have pulled it out of his inside pocket. He told me once he used to smoke cigars, which didn't surprise me at all, but gave them up when there was a shadow on his chest x-ray that turned out to be scar tissue from a bout of viral pneumonia. 'Think about it,' he said, wishing there were leather patches on his elbows so he could look more academic. 'Jack just busted out of prison and he's got nothing except a stolen car and probably Riley. They need food, shelter, gas for the car. But he can't use cash because he doesn't have any, and he can't access any credit cards, which he also doesn't have, or bank accounts because he's a fugitive. There was to be a stash somewhere, or something valuable they can sell to finance this little vacation. They can't get across the Canadian or Mexican border without passports. In short, they can't make it past today without cashing in some-where. My guess is they're on their way to a source of some funding. Maybe a person they know who has money and will give it to them.'

'Based on what I know about Jack, he probably would know all the supermarkets in his neighborhood and be lost anywhere else,' I said. 'But I've done some looking into Pete Lucchesi and he could do anything.' I'd talked to a few people who knew Pete before he was jailed, and to both Lisa and Alicia, as well as what Rosalind Morrison Bailey, Nathalie's sister, had told Nate and Angie. Pete Lucchesi was a dangerous man from all accounts.

He was in jail for trying to rob his ex-wife, who had since

moved to France (of all places), so they probably weren't heading there. But he'd done so carrying a sawed-off shotgun and he had previously been involved in several bar brawls, one of which consisted of him stabbing a man in the stomach. The man survived and somehow Pete had escaped prosecution, which is no small feat.

'Anything doesn't help us much,' Nate said. Nate is rarely more insufferable than when he makes sense, but I had to admit he had the right to be smug right now.

'They were headed in this direction,' I said. 'Does it make sense to track them further north and maybe east?'

Angie, back from whatever reverie she'd been experiencing, shook her head. 'We have no trail,' she said. 'They came here for a safe haven and then they left again. Nate's probably right that they're after something. For all we know they went back to LA. We can't possibly know which direction to drive. We should probably go home and hope the cops find something soon.'

There couldn't have been a plan I would have hated more than that unless Angie had suggested skydiving naked into a volcano so we could find Riley. My head felt heavy and I was putting active effort into my attempts not to cry. 'We won't be doing *anything*?' I said, probably to myself.

Nate, usually the very source of things to try in an investigation, sat down on the arm of the chair Angie was using. 'We all need to take a breath,' he said quietly (in a most un-Nate-like tone, like I was on a ledge and he was trying to talk me inside). 'This kind of thing is intense and draining. If we don't let our brains recharge, we'll never find Riley.'

And that opened the gate to thoughts of never finding Riley. *Don't cry don't cry don't cry.*

'I want Patrick,' I said. I don't know why I said that, except that it was true. It wasn't exactly relevant to the conversation, but it was the overwhelming feeling in my brain and my body at the moment and I guess I figured that deserved expression. So I expressed it.

Angie nodded. 'Yeah. Let's go to Patrick.'

So we did.

THIRTY-FIVE

B y the time we got to Patrick's house in three cars (we'd picked up mine and Angie's at Nate's place and decided we'd all go to Patrick's for something resembling a dinner), I had regained my composure. But I still held Patrick close to me for an extended moment once he opened the door.

I didn't have a key to this place; I hadn't asked for one. It seemed like you should have to phone ahead to enter the edifice anyway.

Patrick, having been alerted by phone, had actually prepared a dinner himself in his massive kitchen. Coq au vin, carrots and something called colcannon, which seemed to consist of mashed potatoes and cabbage. I wasn't especially hungry but I was impressed.

'I didn't even know you could cook,' I said to him after tasting the chicken, which was really very good.

'That's the beauty of a relationship,' Patrick told me. He was watching me with a certain concern in his eyes. Angie must have taken him aside and told him how close I'd come to breaking down. 'You keep learning new things about each other.' It came out 'each uvver', because Patrick knows I find his 'lower class' accent endearing.

'Where's colcannon from, Patrick?' Nate was behaving like someone who wasn't Nate.

'It's an Irish dish and there are as many recipes as there are Irish cooks,' Patrick said. 'There's a bit of Ireland in my background, as well as some Scots and maybe a little Welsh. The Dunwoodys got around.' He chuckled to himself.

'It's very good. Thank you for making dinner, Patrick.' Angie too was impersonating a polite person. It was weird.

They were taking care of me.

But the elephant was in the room and I had to be the one to point it out because apparently you don't want an elephant in your room. I imagine they tend to be somewhat destructive around breakables.

'I appreciate what you're all doing but we need to figure out how to find Riley,' I said. 'We've got less than twenty-four hours left.'

Angie, freed of the need to be polite, put down her napkin, but not before eating a carrot. 'That's a false construct,' she said. 'It's not like Riley immediately disappears from the earth after forty-eight hours. People get found all the time.'

'It's a statistical fact,' I said, holding onto my morbid sense of urgency. 'If the search goes on longer than forty-eight hours, the odds of finding the missing person go down dramatically.'

Nate burped, which he does on a regular basis. 'Up,' he said.

'What?'

'The odds go up. Low odds are more likely to happen than high odds. If something is a two-to-one bet you have a one-in-two chance of winning. But if it's fifty-to-one . . .' Nate stopped talking, possibly because he had just actually heard himself.

I hadn't eaten much and I felt bad about that. It was the first time Patrick had ever cooked for me, and the food was quite good, but my stomach was in turmoil. So naturally it was Patrick who woke me up.

'Have you tried calling Lieutenant Valdez for an update?' he asked. 'With all the law enforcement personnel searching out there, I think we have a decent chance some progress has been made.'

Oy. Valdez. 'I'll call Lieutenant Trench,' I said. 'I don't think I could stand Valdez right now.' I didn't thank Patrick for giving me at least something to do in this situation but I did appreciate it. I'd tell him later.

Trench answered on the first ring. More efficient that way, you know. 'Ms Moss.'

'Lieutenant, I know it's inappropriate for me to call, but—'

Trench cut me off. 'We have some progress on the murder of Nathalie Morrison,' he said. 'I realize you don't have a client yet, but I am certain that once we arrest someone for the crime you will be the first in line to represent that person, so I will convey the information for your future file.' The man would kill at a standup open mic night for cops.

What he was offering wasn't what I was hoping for, but I had decided that whoever killed Nathalie Morrison (and probably Helene Nestor) was also the person who was currently holding Riley hostage, so this could be useful. 'Thank you, Lieutenant,' I said, despite the fact that all he'd done so far was mock me mercilessly in the driest way possible.

'First of all, we recovered the supposed grenade that Ms Morrison was using to threaten your client,' Trench said. 'It was a replica with no explosive charge and was completely harmless.'

'Great.' So Riley had been kidnapped and Nathalie Morrison killed over a fake grenade.

'Also, ballistics on the bullet discovered in Ms Morrison and the two others we found in walls in that room matched those on the gun that killed Helene Nestor,' he went on. 'That is curious in that we had confiscated that weapon from Mr Schoenberg's sock drawer the night his wife was murdered, and it had not been surrendered to anyone since then.'

'I don't know a ton about California gun laws, but I am willing to bet that they don't let you keep your gun when you're in prison,' I said to Trench. 'How did they manage to get the exact same gun back again after it was entered into evidence in Jack's trial?'

Trench hesitated and I could guess why; he hates to admit that the LAPD sometimes makes mistakes, which is perhaps his one fatal flaw. There isn't a police organization on this planet that doesn't screw up at least occasionally. I've seen some that do it as a matter of habit.

'It seems the weapon was not properly secured and stored as it should have been after the trial,' he said through what must have been a clenched jaw. 'Instead, after one hundred eighty days it was returned to the owner, which is the exact opposite of what should have happened. There appears to have been some kind of mix-up with the forms. The firearm should have been destroyed but—'

Alarms were sounding in my head. 'Hang on. Back up. Because of a paper snafu the gun was returned to a man who had been sentenced to life in prison for shooting his wife? With that gun?'

'Ms Moss.' Trench's tone was admonishing, of all things. 'Of course the gun was not returned to Jack Schoenberg. In such cases – when the weapon is disposed of at trial and no longer evidential, but when the owner is not at fault and entitled to its return . . .'

'Which was not the case in this instance,' I said.

'I believe we have established that. No, the error here sent the weapon to the gun owner's next of kin. It was a serious mistake and we now see that very weapon being used in a second homicide, perhaps by the same shooter.'

But I had stopped listening before that last sentence. 'The next of kin. You're telling me they sent the gun that killed Helene Nestor to her daughter Riley?'

'I'm afraid so, Ms Moss.'

I spent the night with Patrick because while Angie is a great ally and a wonderful friend, she's not great at comfort. Her style runs more into the active planning style, and she tends to become overenthusiastic about things. She quite often regards a situation and immediately begins talking about taking revenge, which is somehow charming in a weird way because it shows her loyalty, but also deeply disturbing because generally speaking she's not kidding.

Also Patrick and I would be living together soon . . . somewhere, and it's not like this was the first night I'd spent in his house. But it was the one in which I was in the worst mood.

'I don't care what anybody says, the clock is ticking and Riley's life is hanging in the balance,' I said aloud. Patrick wasn't even in the room. He was setting the alarm system and checking once again on his collection of film memorabilia. I did not resent the huge amount of collectibles the way Patrick's late wife Patsy had. I thought it was very endearing that he liked to preserve the history of the art form in which he worked. But it was a *lot* of stuff and it took up a great deal of room. We could talk about what to do when we found the right house.

Of course, as far as I knew, Patrick thought I was convinced we *had* found the right house and was holding back because he wanted me to be happy.

That was definitely not my most pressing problem at the moment. So I was rehearsing what I'd say to Patrick when he came in. Hey, *he* rehearsed before he made an important speech. The fact that someone else had written it for him and he was pretending to be a fictional character didn't enter into my thought process right now.

'Riley had the gun,' I said to Imaginary Patrick. 'The cops sent it back to her because, well, they screwed up. So she had it in her possession. Does that mean she shot Nathalie Morrison after they got back to Riley's old house? If Riley had the gun on her, why didn't she use it when Nathalie put a fake grenade to her throat? *Why* did Nathalie put a fake grenade to Riley's throat?'

Patrick still didn't come into the bedroom. I was wondering if he'd gotten lost in the labyrinthine corridors out in that series of mazes he called home. But it gave me more time to cross-examine myself. 'Who put her up to it? Pete? Why would she do that for her ex-boyfriend, who probably didn't treat her very well (given past behavior as related by witnesses)? Was he going to give her a lot of money? If so, where was he going to get it? Couldn't be from Jack as ransom for Riley. For that matter it couldn't be from Riley, because she was living on a trust and had a modest allowance until she turns eighteen.'

I was a willing witness, but a largely useless one. I didn't know the answer to any of the questions, and as an attorney I shouldn't have been asking questions to which I didn't know the answers. I was failing myself on both ends.

'The real question, as it is in all criminal matters, is who stands to benefit? Who was going to be better off, financially or otherwise, if Helene Nestor died? Because it seems to me that Nathalie Morrison was killed just to cover the tracks of the kidnapper(s).' And yes, I did say those parentheses around the 's'. It's who I am and there's nothing you can do about it.

I wasn't even looking in the mirror. When actors talk to themselves they look in the mirror to see how it's going to come across on film or in a theater. I didn't have that worry. I wasn't even sure what it was I was rehearsing for. I just needed to hear myself think out loud.

'The thing is, nobody benefits from kidnapping Riley. The only motive is for Jack to see his daughter again. Everybody who got their money from the merger of ImagiNails has gotten it already, except Jason Kemper. I don't see how he'd benefit from taking Riley and not demanding ransom. Is it just plain old revenge?'

It did occur to me that this whole line of questioning, hypothetical as it was, had not been getting me anywhere in my search for Riley. Helene Nestor's murder and that of Nathalie Morrison, although awful things to have happened, were only factoring into my thinking in connection to the search for my client. And I was unlikely to get any information from myself that I didn't already know, no matter what hypnotists will tell you. Besides, there was no hypnotist handy at the moment.

'The real question is not one of motive.' Now apparently I was summing up for the jury. I didn't know why, or on what charge, or who might have been on trial. I'd had dreams like this. Just go with it, Sandy. 'It's not about why they did what they did. It's not even about who killed Helene or Nathalie. All that can be determined later. The real point is where Riley is right now and whether she's OK. And there are just too many places to look. I'm willing to bet the police have covered most of them already and not found her. So what's left for me to do? Sit here in this fortress of a house and wait for . . .'

Patrick walked into the bedroom and looked at me standing next to the bed and looking like I was delivering an oration to someone I couldn't actually see. No doubt this caused him some consternation. It was one of those moments when he didn't even think to pretend otherwise, which for an actor is rare.

'Sandra?' he said. When he's being especially careful with me, he uses my full name, but with the accent it sounds like 'Sondra', which is actually kind of hot. Just not at the moment. 'Are you OK?'

'Patrick,' I said. I held my arms open and he walked into them. I closed them around him. I think he believed he was comforting me, but we were actually celebrating and Patrick didn't know it. 'I know how to get Riley back.'

He loosened his embrace and put his hands on my upper arms. 'I don't understand,' he said. 'What do we have to do?' I loved it that he said *we*.

'We're going to get the kidnappers to bring her to us.'

THIRTY-SIX

'What do you think?' I asked Angie. 'Is this going to be convincing?'

'Read it again.'

We were sitting in the football-field-size kitchen in Patrick's house, at a table in what Patrick called his 'cozy breakfast area', which could encompass both the living room and kitchen of my apartment. I know you're aware; the place was big. Angie was drinking a black coffee that Patrick, before he'd left for his early morning call on the set of *Torn*, had prepared with the caveat that I contact Angie before embarking on 'your rather daft plan.' He had hoped Angie would talk some sense into me. Instead, she had embraced the idea close to her bosom and was nurturing it with me.

I held up my iPhone and read the prepared text to be sent to Riley's mobile: *Don't worry. We've located you and alerted LAPD. They'll be there shortly. If you need me I'm at Patrick's house.* Then I typed in the address. 'What do you think?' I said again.

'It needs a little something,' she answered after a moment. 'Make it more urgent.'

I read the text over again. 'I said I'm sending the cops right now. How much more urgent do you need it?'

'Say, "Get your butt to Patrick's house and here are the directions!" and then we'll talk,' Angie said.

'It's possible that would be a tad too obvious, don't you think?'

Angie took another sip of her coffee, which was her third of the morning. If I had that much coffee this early, I'd be caroming off the walls, assuming I could run that far. 'What makes you think Riley's even getting her texts?' she asked. 'She hasn't been answering any of your voicemails or anything.'

'I'm *counting* on the phone being confiscated and checked,' I explained. 'If the kidnappers read that, they'll get out of wherever they are and come here to exact their revenge.'

She stood up and started pacing. 'I'm starting not to like this plan so much.'

'I'm gonna send it,' I said, but my finger hovered over the button.

'Should we tell the cops what you're doing?' Angie asked, making sure that it was clear *I* was doing this and she wasn't. 'Maybe get some extra security around this place?'

I moved my finger away. 'The whole idea of using this house instead of our apartment is that there are security cameras everywhere and an alarm system that goes off pretty much every time a bird poops out in the yard.'

'Great. Make it easier for them to find the bodies later.'

I sat there and thought about it for a moment. I didn't want any more coffee. Suddenly being more alert didn't seem like that great an idea. Angie's eyebrows were closing the distance between themselves and her nose and that meant she thought the situation was serious. 'I haven't sent the text yet,' I said.

'But you're gonna and we both know it.'

That was true enough. I took in a breath and got up to walk around a little, get the blood flowing in my body. Then again, probably not the best time to be thinking about my blood, either. I walked to the window and looked out on the little wooded area next to Patrick's house.

Standing there, leaning against a tree and looking as casual as one can look while still being a deadly threat, was the person in the hoodie (gray today), black face mask and sunglasses. Just leaning. Maybe they saw me looking at them; maybe not. Didn't matter. They were just going to lean against that tree and . . . how the hell did they get past the security gate?

'Ang, do you have the number for the service that sent Judy the bodyguard?' I asked as lightly as I could pretend to be.

Immediately Angie was at my side, but I didn't take my eyes off the hoodied visitor. So I could be sure that when Angie looked, she'd see them too. 'Is that who I think it is?' she asked.

'Yah.'

'I'm on it.' Angie pulled out her phone, the work one she had from Patrick, and started calling. But it was obvious from the time she mentioned Judy's name that something was up. She put the phone on mute and looked at me. 'Judy's already working.'

'Ask for Carolyn.' Carolyn Townsend, who had filled in for Judy when she couldn't be present in the past, was an ex-cop and almost as inscrutable as Judy. Almost. I didn't trust her quite as much but she'd do in a pinch, and this was for sure a pinch.

Angie asked about Carolyn and must have been given the same answer, because she looked at me and shook her head. 'Take anybody we can get,' I said, 'but not a man.' I'm not usually sexist, but there was something about having an unknown guy watching my life all the time that didn't appeal. I'm quirky that way.

There followed a few minutes of haggling and then Angie reported that someone would be at the house shortly. I didn't ask how long a shortly was, but when I looked out again the person in the hoodie was gone. Keeping an eye on this human was beyond my capacity for concentration.

But finding Riley was never far from my conscious thoughts. The unsent text was just sitting there on my screen, taunting me. 'I'm going to send it,' I told Angie.

'Now? You don't want to wait for Sheila?'

I looked at her. 'Sheila?'

'People are allowed to be named Sheila.'

'No I don't want to wait for Sheila.' Sure. Sheila. Whatever works. 'We only have about four hours left. We can't waste any of that time.'

'You're taking this forty-eight-hour thing way too literally. It's not like Riley suddenly evaporates if we don't find her in the next four hours.'

I found myself biting my lower lip. 'We don't know that she hasn't evaporated already. I'm sending it. Let's get the ball rolling.' And before Angie could come up with a cogent argument that would have dissuaded me, I pushed the button and heard the *whoosh* sound that meant the text was probably already in Riley's phone. Now we'd see who read it and how they responded.

That was going to involve a lot of looking at security screens. Luckily Patrick had given me the codes to the house's system, and I called it up on my laptop to access all the cameras. There were a *lot* of cameras.

We watched for a while, waiting for Sheila, who was taking

her sweet time reporting in, and finally Angie said, 'This is, like, the worst reality show ever.'

She was right. There was no one in the house except the two of us, and there was no pleasure in watching security camera footage of us watching security camera footage. Everywhere else in the building and on the grounds there was blank space, which was disquieting in and of itself. Where was the person in the hoodie?

'We both saw them,' I said.

'Who, them?'

'The person in the hoodie and the sunglasses.'

'There was only one of them.'

'Yeah, but I don't know what gender they are and I'm trying to be polite.'

Angie regarded me for a long moment. 'To a person who's been stalking you?'

'Politeness knows no bounds,' I said.

'Wait.' Angie's voice took on an urgency that did not make me relax. 'There.' She pointed at the screen.

'Where?'

'Front door camera.'

I diverted my attention and that didn't make me relax either. The figure in the hoodie and sunglasses was walking, very erect and purposefully, for Patrick's front door. 'This is bold,' Angie said.

'And out of character. The one time we were in the same room it was an elevator, and I got the impression they were uncomfortable with that.'

But the sound of the doorbell ringing put an end to that discussion. We looked at each other.

'Do we answer it?' I asked.

'Gee, I dunno. Would it be *impolite* to ignore it?' I love Angie dearly, but . . .

'The hell with it. I'm tired of waiting for something to happen.' I got up from the table we'd been using as a viewing station and started the extended trek to the front door. Luckily I had dropped bread crumbs along the way so I could find my way back easily enough.

The doorbell rang again. I reminded myself that if it was

Dracula outside in a hoodie, the trick was not to invite him in.

I stood in front of the door and collected myself. Behind me of course were Angie's footsteps, and I would have bet everything I owned that she was holding her gun. It was the first time since she had gotten the handgun that I was glad to have her holding it.

Angie motioned with her hands – one holding the gun, which as it turned out did *not* make me feel better – to stand to either side of the door. The idea that she was telling me the hoodie stalker might also be carrying a firearm had occurred to me before, but now it was real.

We looked at each other another moment, as if to ask whether we were actually going to do this, and I wondered where the hell Sheila was already but there was no turning back. I nodded and reached for the doorknob.

In my mind (in addition to the running playlist of music that I am constantly racing with, but that's another story) I counted down: three, two, one . . .

I unlocked the door and opened it in one motion.

Standing there was the hoodied figure, tall and now I could see definitely female, but a particular kind of female. The kind that spends a lot of time in the gym to get strong.

I tried to growl. 'OK, waddaya want?' I can't possibly convey in prose how utterly pathetic that sounded. If Robert De Niro had a daughter with Mindy Kaling (first of all, eww . . .) then maybe you'd have an idea.

The sunglasses had to look down at me. 'Just to let you know I'm here, ma'am.'

Wait. I knew that voice! '*Judy?*'

Angie: 'Judy! *You're* the stalker in the hoodie?'

Sure enough, the sunglasses came off and there was the woman who had served as my bodyguard twice before. 'Yes, ma'am. I understand you called my office looking for me, so I told them not to send Sheila and that I'd handle it from here.'

Well, this certainly required a good deal of explanation, but at this moment I did not feel comfortable standing in an open doorway, even if it had turned out that my stalker was actually on our side. 'Come on in,' I said. 'I'm glad to see you.'

Angie put the gun back in her purse. 'Yeah.' Her eloquence is unlimited.

Judy was clearly already on the job, even as she walked into Patrick's arena-sized front room. She was scanning the area for possible hiding places for bad guys and angles at the windows. Judy was the very definition of a pro, something we had been lacking in a big way.

I filled her in on the situation, much of which she had already been told in a briefing. She listened attentively, even if her glance was rarely directed at me or Angie. She was a security officer and had no sense of humor as far as I could tell. Everything was information for the job, and now it appeared *I* was the job.

'So why were you following me around and not letting me know about it?' I said when I'd finished the multi-generational saga about Riley and the two murders and the completely fool-hardy thing I'd done a little while back in trying to goad the kidnappers into revealing themselves.

'That was the assignment,' Judy said. She had refused to sit down, which made Angie and me feel like we couldn't stand either, so the three of us were in a room full of expensive, comfortable furniture on our feet talking to each other and probably, in Judy's mind, making ourselves easier targets from outside. 'I was told to keep you in my sights at all times because of possible danger to your safety.'

'Who hired you?' Angie asked. I thought it seemed a logical question, but Judy's face indicated it was a gross breach of her confidences.

'I have been specifically instructed not to divulge that inform-ation,' she said. There was no point in pushing the question; if Judy said she wasn't going to tell you something, you could pretty much assume that you'd never find it out for as long as you lived.

'But I know you,' I said. 'I mean, I get that you're pretty much covering your whole face and you've worn more clothing than you needed to, but you're too good at what you do for me to have spotted you tailing me all those times, including getting on the same elevator with Jon and me. What was that about, Judy?'

'I was told that you should see me on occasion but that I

should not make my identity known to you,' she answered. 'I believe the idea was to remind you that you should stay vigilant.'

That was so goofy it had to be a Patrick special. 'Did Mr McNabb put you up to this, Judy?' I asked. Angie covered her mouth, not to conceal a laugh, which was the first thing I had suspected. No, she was considering the idea that Patrick might pull off a plan like this and not tell her and she was appalled.

'I'm not at liberty to divulge that information,' Judy said. Judy is the very epitome of consistency. You can set your watch by Judy, if you still wear a watch.

My mind was reeling and I wasn't even thinking about the imminent arrival of violent, possibly murderous, kidnappers at the moment. Luckily Angie was.

'Do you think we went too far with the text to the kidnappers, Judy?' she asked. 'What do you think was the right way to proceed?'

'It's always best to let the law enforcement professionals handle a situation like this one,' she answered. Judy is, after all, an ex-cop.

'OK, but we didn't,' Angie said. 'We have our reasons for that but it's too late now. We sent that text.' I appreciated her using the *we* there, since I had the reasons and I'd sent the text. 'Was that a terrible mistake?'

'I believe we'll find out if you get a response to that message,' Judy said.

Sure enough, that's when my phone buzzed and there was our response.

Nice try.

There was a collective intake of breath – except from Judy, who I'm not sure needs oxygen the way we humans do – and then I sat down. The hell with being judged. Riley was still out there.

'I would say that the text message does not appear to have helped very much,' Judy said.

THIRTY-SEVEN

I felt like I was running in place. The forty-eight-hour deadline (and I didn't like the sound of that word at all) was approaching fast and, if anything, I was farther from finding Riley than I'd been when I started looking again this morning. We'd (OK, I'd) alerted the kidnappers to our location and managed to mistake Judy for a deranged stalker when she could have been helping me the whole time. Except I hadn't known she was involved because Patrick – it had to be Patrick – had given her strict instructions not to make herself recognizable. And she'd done an admirable job, as she always does.

We wandered back into the kitchen because that's where I always do my best thinking. 'Have we done irreparable damage?' I asked Judy.

'I'm not investigating the case,' she noted. 'I'm here to see to your security.'

'Yeah, but you used to be a police officer and you know about this stuff. What's your opinion?' I got a bagel, or what aspires to be one in California, out of the freezer and put it in the microwave to defrost. Finding a missing person is always easier with a bagel.

'As I said, I believe the best chance to recover a missing person is to allow the law enforcement agencies to conduct their investigations,' Judy told me. Judy wouldn't eat a bagel while on duty if it would save her life. I have never seen Judy eat. It's possible she doesn't but is capable of taking in nourishment through sunlight or something. 'I can contact someone in the department to find out about any progress if you like.'

What the hell; it was better than me calling Valdez. 'Please do,' I said.

Judy moved as far away from me as she dared, which was maybe fifteen feet, and pulled her phone out of the pocket of her hoodie, which no longer seemed threatening at all. I looked over at Angie. 'Do you think that's what we should do? Just sit around and wait for someone else to find Riley?'

Angie's eyebrows arched over the bridge of her nose. 'You know I'm not great at sitting around. Do you think we should taunt the kidnappers some more and hope they make a mistake?'

I shook my head. 'We're the ones who have made all the mistakes. Goading them isn't going to help with so little time left.'

Angie grunted. 'Will you stop with the forty-eight-hour thing, please? It's an arbitrary deadline you've set for yourself. If it takes forty-nine hours to find Riley, is that a failure?'

Why *was* I fixated on the number? Because I'd had it drummed into my head enough times or because I thought it was a legitimate statistic? 'It just feels like Riley is safe until then and after the deadline passes she's not. I can't explain it better than that.'

The microwave beeped and I took out the now-too-hot bagel, which was really a Kaiser roll with a hole in the middle. I'd have to ask my mother to FedEx me some bagels from home. Really, it's the only thing I miss. I reached into the fridge to get some cream cheese because at least that's the same everywhere.

'If this were a mystery movie, you would gather all the suspects together in a room and sweat it out until someone confessed,' Angie suggested.

I was about to cite one of the six million reasons that wouldn't work in this case, not the least of which was that this wasn't a mystery movie where everything is written out before anyone does anything and they all know who did it ahead of time. But Judy, putting her phone back into her pocket, approached me rapidly, closing the gap so she could feel like she was doing her appointed job once more.

'My contact is not involved directly with the search, but says word around the department is that they have tried all the most probable places for the two men to have fled and been unsuccessful to this point. But the general belief is that they have not left Southern California and are most likely in the Los Angeles area,' she said. Sometimes Judy talks like an LAPD spokesperson. The rest of the time she doesn't talk at all.

'What are they doing now?' Angie asked.

'Going to areas considered less probable and looking into the possibility that the car they stole has crossed state lines into Arizona.'

That was not promising. If the cops were going to go by the book, I'd skip straight to the movie. 'We're going to gather all the suspects in one place and sweat them out until someone confesses,' I announced.

Angie stared at me. Judy just looked. She might have been thinking that I was the biggest buffoon on the planet, but you couldn't drag it out of her with hot lights and bad music playing at full volume for three days. 'Who are we bringing in for questioning, Inspector?' Angie asked.

'All of them. Everyone who might have had a hand in Helene's murder, the prison break and the abduction. We don't have time to waste.'

'That's true. And this is LA, so that means traffic is horrendous no matter where they are. By the time you've got all those people to come here and sit down, your crazy forty-eight hours will have passed.'

I probably smiled a smug pain-in-the-ass smile. 'Oh Angela,' I said. 'Get out of the twentieth century.'

With help from T'Aisha, who knew everyone involved in Helene's murder and had their contact information, it took only about half an hour to set up the weirdest Zoom meeting in my experience. I was staring into my laptop screen with Angie to my left and Judy to the right, both out of camera range.

On the screen was a true rogue's gallery of suspects: Lisa Conforto and her husband Ken Warshofsky were oddly in separate rooms. From the backgrounds I guessed that Ken was at his desk at ImagiNails and Lisa was in her bedroom. Alicia Nestor Jennings had not moved off that stupid sofa and although I couldn't see her legs, I was certain they were crossed perfectly. Jason Kemper might have been anywhere. Well, anywhere indoors. But his virtual backdrop was very good; it was only because I'd been to his office that I knew he didn't really have a full-sized American flag mounted on the wall. I wondered if Jason wanted to run for office.

Of the people I thought might have killed Helene Nestor, only Jack Schoenberg and Peter Lucchesi had not responded to the invitation. I guessed they had other things they needed to be doing that day, like evading every cop in a 200-mile radius, not to mention the FBI. That'd take up a lot of your time, I supposed. I had them all muted because – as the host of the event – I had that ability, and quite frankly they'd all been talking at once when I let them into the session, mostly complaining about having their day interrupted by some lawyer who wanted god knows what when they were very busy important people who didn't need to sit still for this kind of inquisition. What kind of inquisition they *did* need to sit still for was a topic I had chosen not to explore.

Once everyone was present and without sound, I unmuted my own microphone, gave first Judy and then Angie one last look to bolster my diminishing confidence in this scheme, and cleared my throat. That didn't seem to have any effect on the people in the conference, so I just dived right in.

'I suppose you're all wondering why I called you here today,' I said. Why not? How often do you get a chance like this? 'As you're all no doubt aware, Riley Schoenberg is missing and her abduction seems almost certainly connected to the murder of her mother. I've asked you all to attend this meeting – and thank you all for coming – because I think we might be able to help find Riley if we have some very frank conversations about Helene's murder.'

That seemed straightforward enough, but there was a good deal of eye-rolling going on in front of me, particularly from Alicia, who no doubt had some much more urgent sitting on her couch to do. I pressed on without unmuting anybody.

'I'm going to talk to each of you separately because crosstalk is only going to make this conversation last much longer and keep you all away from your busy schedules.' Let them think you have their interests at heart, even when you definitely don't. 'So let me start with you, Jason. Some of the others might not know you well, but allow me to explain that Jason Kemper was a business associate of Helene's, one of the first investors in ImagiNails, and now runs a private investment firm. Is that a fair introduction, Jason?'

Before he could even answer, a chat message from Alicia appeared: *We all know Jack killed Helene. Why are we even doing this?*

I chose to ignore her because I knew she wouldn't leave for fear that the others would talk about her behind her back.

'That is fairly accurate,' Jason said, no doubt having either missed or ignored Alicia's message entirely. 'But you failed to mention that I should have been one of the four people who profited from ImagiNails' merger, but wasn't because Helene chose to exclude me from that deal.'

He has motive, Lisa added in chat. Being muted in a Zoom meeting wasn't going to stop this crowd.

'You've never explained to me exactly how she did that,' I told Jason. I decided on the spot I wouldn't respond to any chat messages but let the group see them if possible. Let them stew on it. 'Could Helene simply decide who would and would not be included in the deal?'

'Pretty much, yes,' Jason said. 'It was a very informal company at that point, operating basically out of a storefront. We had board meetings that were the five of us and a couple of pizzas. So when Helene, who was the sole owner of the company, no matter how much the rest of us had invested, decided to cut me out and keep the others, she could do it.'

'Why?' I asked. I had asked him this in less direct terms once before and not gotten a satisfactory answer. 'Why did Helene single you out among the four investors?'

It was Ken, who spoke only when it was absolutely necessary and sanctioned by his wife, who broke in on chat. *I know why she did that.*

'OK, hang on. I'm going to mute you for a while, Jason and talk to Ken.' It was a way of manipulating the conversation without acknowledging that I was doing so based on the chat or I'd have a four-person melee going on in my chat box. 'Ken, you were one of the investors who was not excluded from the merger deal. Do you have any idea why Jason was not brought in with the rest?'

I might have been wrong about Ken being in his office because from the background noise it seemed much more likely he was in his car. Who uses a Zoom background in a car? 'I was there when Helene told us she was doing it,' he answered. 'She said that Jason wasn't to be trusted because he had reservations about the product.'

The product? 'He didn't believe in the fake fingernails?' I said. When I'm surprised my bluntness is more, you know, blunt.

'Jason kept saying there was a flaw in the formula, that the nails didn't really grow on people's fingers or that they would prove to be dangerous if we didn't go back to the drawing board.'

From Jason on chat: *I never said any such thing.*

'Yes you did, Jason,' Ken continued. I made an executive decision and unmuted Jason so they could argue this one independent of the others. 'Helene knew you were going to go to the press with it and so she cut you out of the merger. It came up again before the IPO was going to happen and everybody knew it was you.'

'It's not true,' Jason protested. 'I didn't even have a voice in the actual formula of the product. I came on after Helene had invented it herself.'

'I work with that end of the company,' Ken told him. 'I have emails dating back to then showing you threatening to go to the *LA Times*. I mean, print? Really?'

I've never been good at texting while doing something else. Other people can text while walking, text while eating, text while playing piano, for all I know. I have to be doing just that and nothing else, so it was a serious effort for me to get my phone off the table in front of me, place it under the table and therefore out of sight from those watching me on Zoom, and text T'Aisha Kendall: *Did you know of any questions from Jason Kemper about the formula of ImagiNails?*

'It never happened,' Jason insisted. He was just going to keep repeating himself so I muted him again. Then I muted Ken too because how much can you take?

'Lisa,' I said, hitting the button to make her audible, 'you said the night Helene was killed that Jack came to see you and Ken, is that right?'

Lisa looked a little startled that I'd spoken to her. She looked around, as if trying to find the source of that odd voice, but then looked directly – and somewhat eerily – into her webcam. 'Yes. Well, Jack came to see me but Ken was there because he's my husband.' And the way she said it made me wonder if they really were married. I texted Jon to look for a record of marriage between the two. If you're going to text under the table, go to town I say.

'Jack wanted to talk about some new business venture he was planning?' You have to prod them sometimes or they won't say anything interesting.

'That's right. Jack wanted to supply movie sets with biodegradable utensils and things for their craft services departments. He thought it would bring him income so he wouldn't have to rely on Helene so much anymore.'

This was like questioning a witness in court, I decided. 'So then Jack had plans to start a new business and he wasn't just livid with Helene that night,' I said.

'He was ticked off at her because she'd kind of insulted him, but no, he wasn't livid,' Lisa said.

'And did Ken talk to Jack about the business angle?' I asked.

Ken was shaking his head but – like Lisa – I felt it was best not to let him speak. 'No,' she said. 'He was more interested in the ingredients of the hors d'oeuvres he was serving that night. Like the oven temperature he'd set was too high and he had boiled the vinegar or something. I never understand when he talks about those things.' Ken rolled his eyes. Wives.

I wasn't exactly Perry-Mason-ing this interrogation. None of my witnesses had confessed to killing Helene, and so far I hadn't gotten one inch closer to finding Riley. So that left me with Alicia.

A text from T'Aisha made me surreptitiously – I thought – look down at my phone. *NTYMI, there were rumblings about the ImagiNails formula, but not from Kemper. Pretty much from Helene herself. Not corroborated after she died.* I left the phone on my lap to keep this multitasking conversation alive.

NTYMI? I sent back

Now that you mention it. I just wasn't made for these times.

After muting everyone else and unmuting her I asked Alicia, since she knew both Jack and Pete, where she thought they might have taken Riley.

'I don't know and frankly I don't care,' she said. Lauren Bacall on her best day couldn't have topped Alicia's nonchalance.

Jason, of all people, wrote *bitch* in the chat space. But he sent it just to me so I wasn't sure which of us he was discussing.

In my lap the phone vibrated, and I looked down to see a text from Jon. *No marriage license for Warshofsky and Conforto.* That was interesting. I didn't know if it was relevant, but any information gained could always turn out to be helpful.

'Everybody's very impressed with how much you don't care, but right now I'm asking for an opinion,' I said. 'An eleven-year-old girl's life might be on the line and your indifference just isn't playing too well. So answer my question: Where would Pete and/or Jack take Riley to hide? And let's keep in mind that I've been to Jack's supposed fishing cabin and they're not there.'

'Oh, fine,' Alicia said. My trying to save her niece's life was such an inconvenience. 'I'd have bet they'd go back to the old house. It's never been sold.'

The cops would look there first. Advice in chat from Ken. *And they probably still have people watching the house because somebody just got shot there. Again.* In chat Ken was downright snippy. It's funny how people's inhibitions are dissolved online, but don't get me started about Twitter.

'It's true.' I'd given up all pretense about not watching the chat because it was clear everyone else was. Watching. 'I don't see how they could occupy their old house now.'

'Not *that* house.' Alicia was so weary of dealing with the unwashed. Like me. 'The original one, the one that they lived in when Helene was just starting the business. In Chatsworth.'

Even on the chat there was a stunned silence. Angie, next to me, said under her breath, 'Chatsworth?' Apparently that was a surprise. I didn't know Chatsworth from Venice. The one in Italy.

'What house in Chatsworth?' I said, because somebody had to.

'When Helene was starting out,' she said again, because clearly everyone else on this meeting was too deficient mentally to grasp the concept. 'She got out of the apartment once she had a fairly steady income from the nails thing and bought a little house – well, it was really a trailer if the truth be known – in Chatsworth.'

'And it was never sold, even after all the millions were part of the picture?' I asked. Why keep a trailer when you had a perfect little home where you could get shot and still maintain some sense of family?

'Yeah. I don't know if it slipped through the cracks or what, but the place was never even put on the market. I asked Helene about it once and she made some noises about it being where she first lived with Jack so it was sentimental or something. Now I have another meeting I have to get on so I'm going to leave now. Good luck finding the kid.' And she was gone before I could protest.

I didn't even care if anyone saw me texting during the meeting now. I was back to Jon and Nate at the same time. *Helene Nestor owns a trailer in Chatsworth. Find it.*

On it. That was Jon.

You know, I have actual work. Nate. That meant he'd be on the task in a moment.

I looked over at Angie once I'd closed the meeting. 'Well that led to a whole lot of nothing,' she said.

'Not at all,' I told her. 'I know where Riley is and I know who killed Helene Nestor.'

THIRTY-EIGHT

'Chatsworth isn't exactly Bel Air,' Patrick said. 'But it's not the ends of the earth, either. There are sections that are less upscale, and if Helene and her husband were living in a converted trailer, it's quite likely that is the type of neighborhood we're going to enter.'

The Zoom meeting had broken up within seconds of Alicia bailing out and had left me with a number of questions, which Nate, Jon and T'Aisha were busy answering now. Angie had gone off to meet Nate so we could try to coordinate at the Chatsworth house, but it would take time to get to Nate's and then start out. I wasn't willing to wait.

I had no doubt that Alicia, who had wanted to help the least, had provided us with the right direction to find Riley. Jack would appreciate the sentimentality of going back to the house he'd first shared with his late wife. Pete, if he was calling the shots, would be more enamored of the property's total anonymity while he was trying to get funding together to get out of Los Angeles and probably the country. He'd need fake driver's licenses, passports and cash. In fact, he'd need the cash to get the fake driver's licenses and passports.

'I get that it's not the lap of luxury,' I told him. 'But the very least we can do is get there.' The traffic on Route 405 ('the 405' to natives and those who have successfully assimilated) was even worse than a normal Los Angeles rush hour. Which is to say we weren't moving at all. My best guess was that someone was herding a rout of exotic snails (look it up) across the highway, and everyone else just had to wait until they'd made it safely to the other side.

Judy, in the back seat and constantly on the alert, said, 'I believe it would have made more sense and been more practical to have alerted Lieutenant Valdez or Lieutenant Trench to your theories, ma'am.' Judy would sooner have her fingernails pulled out with a rusty pair of pliers than call me Sandy.

'You're right to call them theories, Judy, and that's exactly why I'm not calling either of the lieutenants,' I said. Literally, we were going nowhere. We could have plugged in Patrick's Tesla right here on the highway and had no anxiety about having to leave too soon to completely charge it. Luckily right now he was driving his hybrid Lexus (he'd returned the Rolls) because he knew the roads and I didn't. Of course, knowing the roads is only an advantage if you're actually traveling somewhere, and not posing for a picture of Los Angeles traffic that will one day grace a museum exhibit on how we ignored climate change until it was too late. 'They'd tell me I was just guessing and keep doing whatever it is they're doing now. If they knew about the Chatsworth house I'd be surprised. It didn't even show up in a list of Helene's real-estate holdings, because guess whose name it's listed under.'

'Riley's,' Patrick and Judy said together.

'OK, so you know how to not help me feel smart, but you're right. And the cops or the FBI or MI6 or whoever is searching for Riley isn't going to think to look for real-estate properties owned by an eleven-year-old girl. We have to get there first and find Riley and we only have ninety-three minutes left.'

I just knew I had to get there in the next . . . ninety-*two* minutes now, and we had not progressed as much as an inch. The 405 (there, you got me to say it) is notorious even among Los Angeles highways, and it was living up to its horrendous reputation today of all days.

This wasn't even rush hour.

'How far is the house from here?' I asked Judy, who would undoubtedly know without having to check on any piece of technology.

'Five-point-one miles,' she said. Perhaps Judy *is* a piece of technology. It would explain so much.

I did some quick math in my head, which is rarely a winning strategy for me. 'I'm gonna walk it,' I said.

'What?' Patrick turned around from the driver's seat because why not?

'I'll walk it. I'll get there faster that way.' I unbuckled the harness I was wearing (to save me from zero-mile-per-hour collisions) and reached for the door handle.

'Sandy!' Patrick shouted. 'You have no idea where you're going and you're on a five-lane highway.'

I turned back and kissed him on the cheek. 'I have the GPS on my phone and I'm in absolutely no danger of being run over. It's a used car lot out there.'

Judy unbuckled her harness as well. 'If you're going, I'm going with you, ma'am.' There was no arguing with Judy. So I didn't argue with Judy.

'I'm worried about you, love.' Patrick hates not being the hero because he's so used to it. He's a hero at least once a week on television. More often if you binge him on Hulu. 'You don't know what you'll be facing once you get to the house. Those people might be more dangerous than you think.'

'At least one of them has already killed two women and kidnapped a preteen,' I pointed out. 'I'm fairly sure they're dangerous, but I'll have Judy with me and the element of surprise.'

'The element of surprise,' Patrick grumbled.

I tried to smile reassuringly, but I'm no actress. 'Look at the bright side, Patrick. If they kill me you won't have to buy the teal house, and I know you don't want to.' I had no intention of making him buy the teal house, but it was an exit line. Not a great exit line, but the best I had in the moment.

'Did Angie tell you something?' Now Patrick didn't know whether to be terrified or just pissed off at Angie.

'You didn't tell me you hired Judy,' I pointed out. My exit line was getting farther and farther from my exit. I opened the door.

'I *didn't* hire Judy!' he shouted as I climbed out of the car. And Patrick doesn't lie to me. That was a stumper.

But it was too late to argue, and the exit line's expiration date had passed, so I was off to the shoulder of the highway with Judy in tow, as she prefers to be. She can see me and any possible danger that way. It was a comment on my life in Los Angeles that I was actually accustomed to Judy's method of doing her job.

We crossed three lanes of what would be traffic if it had been moving, but was instead something of a modern automotive frieze. A few drivers actually honked their horns at us, as if we were in some way impeding their progress. I did not offer a

Garden State one-finger salute but that was largely because I was focused on the task at hand.

Walking a little over five miles to Riley.

I led the way because of Judy's rule about being behind me. That meant I had to keep my phone's GPS on the target address, and when you're walking that thing can never seem to understand the concept of which direction in which to walk. Or I can't. One of the two.

After three minutes of watching me circle around trying to determine a direction, Judy said, 'To the left, ma'am,' and from then on she was my GPS. Saved the battery on my phone. That's what I told myself. That and she was watching for people following us, which I considered unlikely seeing as how I hadn't even known I'd be walking this way until five minutes ago. Of course, until a few hours ago I'd thought that Judy was the threat, so it was possible my judgment was somewhat faulty.

We trudged on. Judy, excellent bodyguard that she was, did not quite meet that level of excellence as a conversationalist. Mostly what I heard from her was, 'Right here, ma'am,' or 'Another two hundred yards, ma'am.' I wasn't expecting an Aaron Sorkin walk-and-talk, but this was the bare bones of discussion.

One highlight was when I asked her how much time we had left and Judy answered, 'That's impossible to say without knowing the situation at our destination, ma'am,' which led to me being silent for twenty minutes. She knew what I meant. Damn her for being, you know, accurate.

But Judy's opposite-of-sparkling conversational skills left me time to think about the Chatsworth house and what I might expect when we reached it, even as my feet were already starting to bark. There were many possibilities, some more likely than others. I felt that anticipating a dangerous situation on arrival was probably the best strategy, because I could adjust to anything less stressful, but it would be hard to go from *Maybe we'll all sit around and sing folk songs*, to *They've got guns!*

I was unarmed, and when I decided I'd let Judy off the silent list, I asked her if she had a weapon. She indicated that she did, and did not acknowledge the emotional torment she clearly must have been experiencing when I was snubbing her. Hopefully it had taught her a lesson. About what I'm not sure.

Before we'd left Patrick's house, I'd studied charts and drone pictures (Zillow is so accommodating) of the area. The converted trailer we were looking for, Number 38 on the block, was not on the corner. There were similar dwellings on either side and more across the street and behind. It wouldn't be easy to sneak up on whoever was inside.

My best guess was that there would be Riley, being guarded perhaps, and three other people at least in the house. The place wasn't large by any stretch of the imagination, so we should expect a concentration of kidnappers in the front room as soon as we made our way in. What was the best way to approach, I wondered. Ringing the doorbell would just give the captors time to sneak Riley out the one other door, which led to what could laughingly be called a backyard. It would also give someone the opportunity to shoot me through the door at the first signal, if they were serious about not letting anyone inside. I assumed that – if possible – they would have installed some kind of video surveillance system to at least keep an eye on the front door.

We hit a stretch that was unpaved and overgrown and that puzzled me. I looked back at Judy. 'GPS is sending us through here?'

'No, ma'am. I believe this shortcut can save us three minutes.'

'Good thinking, Judy.'

But I'm a suburban Jersey girl, and not used to walking around in brush up to my waist. Thank goodness I'd changed into jeans and sneakers before we'd left. I was having some unsettling thoughts, though.

'Are there snakes in this brush, Judy?'

She just kept walking behind me. 'I imagine there might be, ma'am, but I would say most of them are not poisonous.'

'*Most?*'

The thing about walking is that it doesn't really divert the attention. You just do it until you get where you're going and your mind can wander. Mine was wandering toward the trailer and coming up with multiple ways things could go sideways if I made one wrong choice. After having made a reckless promise to Riley and seeing it go bad in the worst way, I was not wildly confident about my decision-making skills.

I couldn't stop thinking about how she'd said, 'You promised,' before she left. It was the least Riley thing she'd said to me, and the most eleven-year-old girl thing. It made my stomach clench every time I went over it in my head, so in order to torture myself I did that on continuous loop for a while.

'How much farther, Judy?'

'One-point-four miles, ma'am.'

Back on pavement, something for which my ankles, which had been anticipating snake traffic, were eternally grateful, we serpentined our way around blocks in what I could tell from the sun was a generally western direction (hey, I had been a Girl Scout). I kept checking my phone to see the time. It's amazing how quickly time goes by when you don't think you have very much of it left.

Twenty-six minutes.

I'll admit it: my feet were hurting pretty severely, even in Nikes. Just Do It my butt. You get over here and walk five-point-one miles, Just Do It. It ain't easy, especially when you can feel urgency in your throat.

We did pass a sign that read, Welcome to Chatsworth, and you can't get a much clearer indicator than that as to where you might be. We proceeded on and I noticed that the residences in this section of town were decidedly not converted trailers. They were on a par with at least the teal house, if not some of the more upscale places that Patrick and I had visited.

'Distance?' I called to Judy.

'Zero-point-three miles, ma'am.'

Sure enough this was a town and not the middle of nowhere. Jack Schoenberg's fishing cabin might as well have been in another country, or on another planet.

It wasn't the most densely populated neighborhood of Los Angeles that I'd seen but it certainly wasn't the least, either. As we trudged on (actually, I trudged and Judy came within inches of marching), the larger, more luxurious and better-appointed houses faded into our rearview mirror – if we'd had one – and we found ourselves in an area that stacked its houses side by side with a thin driveway between each. People had decorated each one to lend it some unique personality, but it was clear they'd all been mobile at one time or another.

'Stop please, ma'am.' I know, you thought that was me talking but no, Judy was giving me a new instruction, and as always I obeyed her without question. She was right. We were getting close and we needed to have a plan in place. 'I believe the yellow structure in the center of the block is our target.' Judy is ex-military and doesn't really understand us civilians.

Patrick texted me: *Almost at the exit.*

We never would have made it in time.

Before Judy could start issuing orders, I told her what I'd been thinking about for at least three-point-six miles. 'I'm going to go in through the front door,' I said. 'They have no reason to expect me but they also have no reason to fear me. I'm unarmed and not at all imposing. I'll try to negotiate Riley's release. If I have to I will promise not to call the police and give away their location. But if I can't, I'm still getting her out of there any way I can and that's where you come in.'

She looked a little surprised – no, she looked shocked – that I was telling her how to handle this situation. So I kept going rather than listen to a list of reasons I was wrong.

'You can enter through the back door. They definitely won't be expecting you and they'll be dealing with me in the front room. You can break down the door if necessary, and you are, in fact, armed.'

'Yes I am,' Judy said.

'Then the priority is simple: we get Riley out of the house. Patrick will be coming in his car but we can't wait for him. Can you see if Jack and Pete have a car in the driveway?'

Judy took a small pair of binoculars out of a pocket in her cargo pants and aimed them in the direction of the house. 'It's not a perfect angle but I believe there is a vehicle there. It seems odd they would park it where it can be seen.'

That was a good point, but maybe Pete (I'd decided Pete was the ringleader) had managed to get them license plates that wouldn't immediately cause a stir in a passing police cruiser, or they had just figured no one was looking for them in Chatsworth.

'You're right,' I said. 'But I'll ask your advice: Do you think it makes more sense to try and steal their car once we have Riley outside, or to disable it so they can't follow us?'

Judy considered that but not for very long. We had nine minutes left. 'Disabling their vehicle would be faster than trying to start it with people, perhaps armed people, on our tail,' she said.

'That's what we'll do then. Um . . . how do you do that?'

Judy just looked down at me, as she should. 'Leave it to me.'

'Does the plan work for you, Judy?' I asked. I wasn't going to change it, but I always like to have the entire legal team sign onto the plan for a trial and this was undoubtedly going to be a trial.

'It does, ma'am.' She managed to disguise her natural inclination to sound surprised that I would have come up with something that might work.

'Let's go, then.'

We walked as directly as possible, but without looking like we had urgent business, to the trailer home. It had a concrete foundation, as many such buildings do, and wasn't going anywhere without major excavation being done. It was indeed yellow and had not been especially well maintained, which I thought was surprising. Helene had owned the place until she died, just as she'd owned Jack's cabin, which looked downright pristine. This was in need of a paint job, and the one step up to the front door, also in concrete, was cracked. There was no welcome mat. I was OK with that because I was assuming we would not be welcomed.

Judy had clearly decided we should not speak this close to the house, so she gestured to me that she was going toward the driveway and therefore the car to sabotage it in some way. She held up three fingers, indicating I should wait three minutes before announcing myself to the occupants of the place. I nodded. Judy headed off to the driveway, which thankfully was made of asphalt and not gravel. No footsteps would be heard inside the house.

We had six minutes.

I actually counted to 180 without keeping a death stare on the driveway. I let Judy do her thing and didn't ask questions or appear to be monitoring. Sure enough, when I hit my target number for three minutes, I looked in that direction and Judy was nowhere to be seen.

Phase One complete.

I took a breath, tried to quell my rising tension, and strolled as casually as a mass of taut nerves can to the front door. Once there I adjusted my phone to silent mode (the last thing I needed was for it to ring when I was trying to be undetected) and hesitated. There was a small cracked plastic button for a doorbell. Should I ring it and let them look out the window to see who was there, so they could prepare for me? The idea was to distract them from the back, where Judy would be making her entrance shortly. Maybe I needed to make a bigger noise.

That was it. I'd kick the door in. It wasn't what I'd told Judy I'd do, but it would serve the purpose better. I leaned back and positioned my right leg to push the door in just like they do in the movies.

I knew from those observations to kick with the heel of my shoe and not the toe. Even in Nikes. I had only three minutes left and that was cutting it close enough. I reached back with all my strength and slammed the sole of my right foot into the door.

Nothing happened. Except my ankle hurt and there was a dull thud sound.

It took a few seconds to absorb that information. Luckily the ankle wasn't sprained or anything because I was going to have to try again. I flexed it a little bit, got the feeling back and braced myself for another shot. Again I rubbed my hands together, planted my left foot for support and swung that right leg back to gain momentum. And BANG! it went against the door one more time.

Again, nothing. Doors are built better than I'd thought. Or I wasn't built as well as I'd anticipated.

But I figured third time's the charm, and geared myself up for the last assault. This one would do it for sure. The hands were rubbed, the leg was planted and the sole of the foot headed for the door.

And it opened on its own.

There stood a man in his forties with a flat-top cut, a pair of jeans and a T-shirt that indicated he'd spent a good deal of time in the prison gym. Because he was the only guy I wouldn't recognize in this house, and that made him Pete Lucchesi, recently escaped convict.

'What do you want?' he demanded. He was blocking the doorway but I could see inside. There was a card table in the living room with no cards on it, just drinking glasses, mostly empty. I could see a man behind it, but he was sitting in shadow and his face was obscured.

There was no sign of Riley, but I knew she was here.

I didn't think there was any point in playing a game I'd probably lose. 'I'm here for Riley,' I said. 'Let me take her home and I won't give you any trouble.'

Lucchesi broke into a wide grin. 'You won't give me any trouble, huh? Who the hell are you?'

From behind Lucchesi came a voice I recognized, and Jack Schoenberg walked out from a back room (bedroom?). 'That's the lawyer Riley hired to get me out of prison,' he said. 'Sandy something.'

'Sandra Moss,' I said. 'And I'm here to get my client.' I looked at Lucchesi. 'So if you'll just stand to one side or bring her here, I'll be leaving.' They stood there and looked at me, Lucchesi with the menacing grin and Jack just looking tired. 'Now.'

Lucchesi actually barked out a laugh. Jack looked worriedly at the hallway behind him and that's how I knew where Riley was. But with Lucchesi blocking the door and the third man in the room still in shadows (so I had to assume the worst that he was armed and ready to kill me), I was stymied.

I pulled my phone out of my pocket and held it to my right side, away from the door and out of reach for Lucchesi. 'I can call the police now,' I said. 'I have Lieutenant Trench in my contacts. Or you can let me in, we can talk about Riley, and I won't have to call the lieutenant at all. Your choice.'

'Go home, lady,' Lucchesi said. 'If you'd wanted to call the cops you would have called them by now. You don't want to know what'll happen to you if you come in this house.' I felt like correcting him that it should be 'come *into* this house,' but that didn't seem like the most important thing at the moment.

I had to take a chance and play my hole card. 'You going to shoot me like you shot Nathalie Morrison?' I asked him. Then I shouted in at the man in the shadows, 'Or is that your department, Ken? Like you shot Helene Nestor?'

Sure enough, Ken Warshofsky stood up from the table and into the light, only from the shoulders up. But he didn't look like the milquetoast husband that Lisa Conforto had tried to present when Nate and I were at her house. His face was pure malice and it was directed at me. He didn't look at Lucchesi, but it was clear to whom he was directing his words.

'Let her in,' he said.

Lucchesi looked displeased but stepped aside from the doorway and I stepped inside. I'd gotten what I wanted, but suddenly it didn't feel like a victory.

Lucchesi locked the door behind me.

THIRTY-NINE

The room was exactly as depressing as you'd imagine. I've seen trailers that were elegant and beautiful (Patrick's trailer at *Torn* could have been a wonderful home for a family of four), but this wasn't one of them.

Its furniture was done in early thrift shop, with undertones of we-found-it-at-the-curb. The card table had a book holding up one leg. *For Whom the Minivan Rolls.* I'd never heard of the author.

Lucchesi turned back toward me and scowled. Ken Warshofsky, looking taller than he had the last time I'd seen him, was now holding a handgun. I saw no reason to act the way he wanted me to act.

'No hors d'oeuvres today, Ken? You're not being a great host.'

He gritted his teeth. 'I didn't kill Helene, Sandy,' he said. 'You know I was at the house with Lisa that night.'

Jack Schoenberg did a take at that but didn't say anything. He was watching Lucchesi the way a dog watches an owner who mistreats it. His wariness was driven by fear.

'No you weren't,' I told Ken. 'See, the idea was supposed to be that Lisa was pretending to be Jack's alibi for the evening, and nobody believed it. But she was really covering for you. Remember? You said you had to make guacamole because the oven was broken that night, but then Lisa said you were concerned that something in the oven had been turned out badly that night. She was lying because she didn't want anyone to know you weren't home when Helene was shot. She knew you'd gone to Helene's house and killed her.'

Jack looked at Ken with rage in his eyes. 'You son of a bitch,' he said in a growl.

'That's ridiculous,' Ken spat out. 'You're going to claim I murdered Helene because my wife got a detail about some snacks wrong?'

'She's not your wife, Ken,' I said in the calmest tone possible.

'There's no record of a marriage license between you and Lisa. Jack came over that night to talk to Lisa about his business idea, but you weren't there. You were confronting Helene about some chemical problem she'd discovered with the formula for ImagiNails. She knew they broke too easily and she told you. Because you're the chemical expert, aren't you?'

'I'm not a—'

'Yeah, you are. You understand the chemistry of cooking and you yourself said you work with the people on that end of the business. We looked it up, and guess what? You have an actual PhD in chemistry from Stanford, of all places. So you knew about the problems with ImagiNails, and Helene was about to go public with it, wasn't she? That'd make your stock pretty much worthless, so you destroyed whatever evidence there was and you killed her.'

Jack Schoenberg, with blood in his eyes, lunged at Ken with an unrecognizable sound emanating from his throat. But Ken reacted with the butt of his gun to Jack's head and Jack went down hard. He was still breathing but badly stunned.

At exactly that moment, just as I'd expected, Judy walked in from the back room. She had Riley with her. What I hadn't anticipated was that Riley would be holding Judy's gun and pointing it at her back.

Maybe Riley really was a pistol after all.

Judy, contrary to every reaction I'd ever seen her have to anything, was sobbing and stiff-legged as she walked into the room, holding her hands in the air like a cornered criminal in a cartoon show.

'Mr Warshofsky killed my mom?' Riley said. Little-girl voice. Like she was asking what flavors of ice cream were available.

'Don't believe what that woman tells you, Riley,' Ken said, still looking at the small patch of blood on the back of Jack's head, even as Jack managed to get to his knees. 'She's a pathological liar. Do you know what that means?'

Riley looked at him while shepherding Judy into the room. 'I know what a liar is,' she said.

I finally regained the power of speech. 'Riley,' I said.

'Don't be surprised, Sandy,' she answered. The temperature

in the room went down three degrees. 'I hired you to get my dad out of jail, but he did it himself and then he came for me.'

'He could have sent you word about where he was,' I told her. 'He didn't have to send a woman to kidnap you and then kill her. But that was Ken, wasn't it, Ken?'

'I don't know what you're talking about,' Ken said unconvincingly.

'Yeah, you do. You also made the phone call to Riley saying you were going to kill her and me, didn't you? That was a class act, Ken, threatening a little girl. What was the matter; there were no puppies to kick?' Ken just scowled at me.

'Who's this?' Lucchesi was more interested in Judy than in the drama playing out on and near the floor.

'She's a guard or something,' Riley said. 'She came with Sandy the lawyer. She was supposed to rescue me.' Riley chuckled at the thought of needing to be rescued. 'She thinks I want to go home to Aunt Alicia.'

'And you just want to be here with your daddy, don't you?' Lucchesi apparently thought Riley was four years old.

'Of course.' She'd learned the catchphrase from Alicia. Riley looked absurd holding a gun on Judy, who was a good foot taller than she was, but Judy was not resisting, just looking at the floor with shame and barely controlling her tears. 'That's what I always wanted, isn't it, Sandy?'

I shook my head. 'Not like this.'

Riley's voice was hard. 'You don't get to choose how,' she said.

It just wasn't adding up for me. Riley wasn't acting like Riley and Judy *really* wasn't acting like Judy, but I couldn't put it together in my mind. Had I been that wrong about my client all this time? Should I have stayed out of this whole business? I was convinced that Ken Warshofsky had killed Helene and probably Nathalie Morrison, but kidnapping Riley appeared to have been a massive hoax, and now Riley, at eleven, was committing crimes that would put her in custody of some sort for a very long time.

Assuming Judy and I survived to testify against her.

Lucchesi must have been reading my mind. 'Now we have to decide what to do with these two,' he said. 'I wasn't planning on leaving more bodies behind. We still need to get that money, Ken, and so far you're not paying up.'

'I've done my bit,' Ken said. 'Pay your own way into Mexico if you want.'

'Mexico, hell,' Lucchesi told him. 'I'm going somewhere without an extradition treaty. Taiwan. Morocco. Vietnam. With a little cash, a man can live there like a king. So cough up the cash, Ken. Jack and I are fugitives from justice and we have the goods on you. Do the right thing.'

Jack managed to get himself upright. He stood and glared at Ken but didn't make a move toward him, probably for fear of another blow to the head. He turned and faced Riley. 'Don't get yourself into this kind of trouble, baby,' he said. 'That's not what I want for you.'

'You know better than anybody, Dad,' she said. 'You don't ever get what you want.'

'Don't wimp out on me, Jack,' Lucchesi said. 'I didn't force you into a jailbreak so you could just go right back. And we got your girl here for you, like you wanted. You should have some gratitude.'

'Sandy could have gotten me out in court and I could have stayed out,' Jack told him. 'You put a gun to my head and told me to walk into a world where the cops would always be on my tail. Not the same thing.'

I was trying to make eye contact with Judy, but the gun held at her back was drawing most of my attention, and Judy was looking hard at her feet, in particular the right one. I wondered if she'd injured herself in a struggle with . . . Riley? How did that make sense?

'Shoot them both,' Ken said to Lucchesi. 'If Jack is going to be a drag, you might want to shoot him, too.'

Lucchesi turned hard toward me and suddenly there was a gun in his hand. 'I'll kill the two women but you're going to have to shoot Jack,' he told Ken. Now they were negotiating over who got to shoot whom.

That was it for me. I was *not* going to just go along and be a good girl, Ms Carbone's class be damned. 'Hey!' I shouted. Maybe someone outside could hear me. 'You're not going to just shoot us! We have rights!' I had no idea what rights I was talking about in a room with two or possibly three violent criminals, but enough defendants had said it to me and I figured I could borrow their line. 'I'll put you both in prison for the rest of your lives. Watch me.'

'That one's annoying,' Ken said. 'Tell you what, Pete. I'll shoot her myself.'

'Like you shot Helene and Nathalie?' I said.

Ken actually rolled his eyes. 'Yes, for the record. Exactly as I shot Helene and Nathalie.'

He turned his body toward me, handgun aimed at my midsection, as I mentally apologized to Patrick for wanting a smaller house. But as Ken did that, Lucchesi, perhaps just registering the idea that he'd have to deal with Judy, started to turn back. Judy reached down to scratch her right shin.

'Dad!' Riley yelled, and when Jack faced her, she tossed the gun she'd been holding on Judy to her father, who caught it while looking surprised. I did a drop-and-roll on the floor to give Ken less of a target, but I got my bearings quickly enough to see Judy pull a small handgun from her boot and aim it at Lucchesi.

'I'd advise you not to try it,' she said, sounding very much like Judy again.

'Same with you, Ken,' Jack said. 'If you shoot Sandy, you're not making it out of this house alive. If you don't, you have a chance.'

'You wouldn't,' Ken said.

Jack shot a hole in the floor about three inches from Ken's foot. Ken, impressed, dropped the gun he'd been holding. 'That's gonna get someone to call the cops. Hands behind your head, Ken,' Jack said. 'Riley, there's some rope in a drawer in the kitchen. Bring it with a sharp knife.'

Judy continued to hold the gun on Lucchesi, who had similarly disarmed himself. Judy pushed the gun away from him with her foot. 'That was nicely played, Riley,' she said.

From the kitchen, Riley said, 'Thank you, ma'am.'

'I'm going to need years of therapy,' I said to no one in particular.

I heard a car door slam outside the house and in moments Patrick had opened the front door and looked inside.

'Well,' he said. 'I see I've arrived just in time.'

FORTY

I knew it was a major crime scene when both lieutenants, Trench and Valdez, arrived on the scene in separate cars. Trench had Sergeant Roberts in tow as ever and Valdez had come alone. It is a fact that everything is more difficult for women in police work.

Uniformed officers had long since carted Lucchesi and Ken outside but left Jack for the detectives. There was an armed uniformed cop outside the trailer, and one in the back just in case the escaped convict decided to escape again.

'Ms Moss, you never disappoint,' Trench said after all the statements had been stated and the weird, twisted story had been told from every possible perspective. 'I always know as soon as you become involved in a case that it will end in some highly improbable fashion.'

'So happy to have entertained you, Lieutenant,' I answered. 'It was worth almost getting shot dead just for that.'

Patrick was not letting me out of his sight, and his arm around my shoulders was actually comforting, now that I was digesting exactly how close I'd come to being killed by someone named Ken Warshofsky.

'But we have no evidence to prove the charges.' Valdez, as ever, was doing her best impression of a wet blanket. 'Lucchesi can say Jack was the mastermind behind the jailbreak and that he had nothing to do with killing Helene Nestor. And Warshofsky can say he was defending himself against you and your bodyguard, who came to steal Jack's daughter away after they'd rescued her from Nathalie Morrison. They'll walk.'

I took my iPhone out of my pocket and turned the sound back on, then I went into voice memos and hit the playback button. Immediately Lucchesi could be heard: *Don't wimp out on me, Jack. I didn't force you into a jailbreak so you could just go right back. You should have some gratitude.*

I went forward a little to when Ken was being condescending:

Yes, for the record. Exactly as I shot Helene and Nathalie. OK, it took three tries, but I finally got to that line.

'Never underestimate Ms Moss, Lieutenant,' Trench told Valdez. 'It is a losing proposition.' Coming from Trench, that was tantamount to a marriage proposal. I basked in it for a moment.

'But you underestimated the danger,' I told him. 'You said not to worry about . . .' I looked over at the bodyguard in her hoodie and her sunglasses (which were hanging from her collar at the moment). 'You, Lieutenant.'

'Me?' Valdez said.

'No.' I looked at Trench. 'You hired Judy because you were concerned about me dealing with the case after the phoned-in death threat. You told her to make sure I was aware there was danger so I'd be vigilant. And you made sure it was Judy so that – what? – I would feel more foolish when I found out?'

'You have a very active fantasy life, Ms Moss,' Trench said. But there was a two per cent rise at each corner of his mouth, which was the Trench version of hysterical laughter.

I turned to look at Judy for confirmation, but her face was in an impassive contest with Trench's and it was winning. It didn't matter; I knew what I knew.

'I don't understand,' Patrick said. 'How did Ken Warshofsky climb through that tiny transom to shoot Helene and then get out again? He's far too large to fit through that box, I'd think.' No doubt he was already thinking of pitching the idea in the *Torn* writers' room.

'That wasn't Mr Warshofsky.' Riley's voice was very much like that of an eleven-year-old again, and one who had been through a lot. 'That was me. But my mom was already, you know, when I went in. I heard a loud bang from my bedroom and I came down but the music room door was locked. So I climbed up on the furniture in the hall and went through the window. I don't remember a lot after that, but I was lying on the floor next to my mom until my dad was holding me and took me out of the room. I never said anything at the trial because I thought it would make it sound like he was guilty.'

'I had the opposite worry.' Jack shook his head, which was still buried chin-to-chest. 'Riley doesn't remember because she was in shock, but when I heard her in there I banged on the door and she let me in. It was awful, but I had to think of Riley. I thought the police might suspect that Riley had some involvement, probably not voluntary, so I tried to cover up any signs she'd been there. I carried her out so she wouldn't make any marks and made up a person who would have climbed through the transom, but the judge threw it out at trial. I figured he would but by then I'd already been arrested and charged.'

'So how did Ken get into the room and lock it on the way out?' Patrick asked.

'Ken and I had lunch that day and I drove him home from the restaurant,' Jack said. 'I didn't need the key to the music room that day, so I'm guessing he stole it from the keyring lying in the console after I'd gotten my car back from the valet, and he put it in my sock drawer with the gun after he shot Helene. Helene had the gun that day; she said she was worried about her safety. He must have taken it off of her. If I had known it was him . . .' He sagged quietly into one of the kitchen chairs and just sat there, staring at nothing in particular.

'And how did Ms Morrison, Pete Lucchesi's ex, get involved?' Valdez asked Jack. She clearly had very little regard for his emotional state.

But surprisingly that seemed to help him focus on the present and the question being asked. 'I'm not sure because Pete had clearly gotten to her before he put the gun in my ear and made me go with him. But he told me later that she was carrying a torch for him and would do anything he asked because she wanted to get back together. He got her a cell phone that somehow he managed to register in Helene's name, and told her to text Riley that creepy message to get her somewhere they could grab her. Then he sent her to the mall to get Riley in an attempt to keep me in line. He figured if Riley was there I wouldn't turn myself in and get him caught too. Ken decided to kill Nathalie when she dropped Riley off at the house. Said she was a loose end.' Jack shook his head. 'Thank goodness Riley wasn't in the room when he did that.'

Riley gave me a look that indicated her father's account might not have been accurate. Pete Lucchesi could have told him anything.

'Prison records indicate that Ms Morrison visited Lucchesi a week before the escape,' Valdez said. 'We have information that she brought the gun and bribed a guard to get it to Pete. The guard is, well, cooperating with the investigation now, and said Morrison had stolen it from Alicia Jennings's apartment on a visit. That could have been when they planned what was going to happen, but Morrison didn't know she'd end up dead.' No kidding, Valdez.

'Lieutenant,' I said, looking directly at Trench, 'do you need me for anything else right now?'

Trench looked at me, then at Riley. 'No, I believe we are done for the time being, Ms Moss.'

'Then may Riley and I go outside until it's time for us all to leave?'

There was no objection, although Patrick probably wanted to stay by my side, but he understood. He hung back and I took Riley out through the back door so she wouldn't see the several police vehicles and the ambulance (that had been called just in case) out front.

There were exactly two lawn chairs on the sparse piece of grass behind the trailer, so we used them. I looked Riley in the eye. 'Throwing someone a gun is unbelievably dangerous,' I said.

'It worked, didn't it?'

There's no point in arguing with some eleven-year-olds. 'You OK?' I asked.

'No. But I will be. Do you think this will help my dad get a new trial?' She was never anything but focused. I should have remembered that when she and Judy were playing out their odd psychodrama.

I smiled at her in a way I hoped was reassuring. 'I seriously doubt he'll need one,' I said.

FORTY-ONE

'Your Honor, the prosecution moves to dismiss all charges.' Deputy District Attorney Albert Fleischer was staring down at his file and not at the judge, because prosecutors hate to admit they made mistakes and sincerely believe that whoever they charged is definitely guilty of the crime. This was causing Fleischer pain, the kind of pain I could remember from my days doing his job. I understood but didn't sympathize. A better prosecutor would have seen the holes in the case.

'Given the video footage of the jailbreak, it is clear the defendant was not a willing participant, and we have the recorded confession of another man to the crime of which Mr Schoenberg was convicted,' Judge Henry Drummond said. 'I see no reason not to dismiss. So this case is dismissed, with apologies to Mr Schoenberg. He is remanded to his own custody.' He hit his gavel on the surface in front of him and that was that.

Riley hugged her dad. She was sitting next to him in an actual dress and Jack was wearing a suit that was not orange and had a tie. These were sides of my two clients I'd never seen before.

Jack also had insisted on paying my firm's usual fees, since – as he pointed out – Riley had hired me pro bono to represent his interests in getting a new trial in the killing of his wife, which had turned out to be unnecessary. I'd offered up token protest but taken the money and told Holly about it so she wouldn't think I was Queen of the Pushovers.

T'Aisha Kendall's book contract was already signed and it promised to be a doozy, to the point that she'd already quit the judge show to work on it full time. She'd offered me a finder's fee but I had declined. T'Aisha had a literary agent who would be taking a percentage of everything she made, and I had a steady job that served my needs. Win-win.

We all stood up and headed for the exit, Jack smiling sadly and Riley holding his hand just like a real eleven-year-old girl.

OK, so most girls that age don't necessarily hold their fathers' hands, but how many of them had just dodged a life sentence?

'You know I really thought I was being kidnapped, right?' she said to me when we hit the hallway. 'I wasn't in on the plan.'

'You *were* really being kidnapped,' I told her. 'I'm just glad it ended up OK eventually. But you did give me a scare. I didn't think anybody could get a gun off of Judy.'

'Nobody could,' Riley said and then she laughed. 'Unless Judy wanted her to. It was my idea, though. Judy said it would be hard to hold even two guns on two men by herself. So I wanted to throw the gun to Dad.' Sixth graders. I ask you.

Ken Warshofsky was awaiting trial for two murders and a slew of other charges. He had not approached me about representing him, and I would not have agreed if he had. Lieutenant Trench would have to find other ways to amuse himself. Charges were also filed against Pete Lucchesi and Harvey Manning, the former guard at state prison who had supplied an inmate with a firearm.

Patrick, who had been waiting outside the courtroom because he needed to be in a place where he could answer his phone for business, and uncharacteristically didn't want to disrupt the proceedings, had ambled over. 'From what I hear you were very convincing as a criminal,' he said. 'You might want to look into acting, Riley.' She beamed. Maybe she'd be OK after all.

We took our leave of the two Schoenbergs and headed to the courtroom garage where Patrick's Lexus was waiting. We had one more house to go look at now that the teal place was off our radar. I thought we'd come close to convincing Emily Webster to leave the real-estate business, but she was made of tougher stuff than that and had agreed to show us the one house I'd asked about.

Patrick likes to roll around my cases in his mind because he's interested in what I do, but also because I think at some point he's going to want to produce a film or TV series based on at least one of them. I can tell when he's mulling because he stops talking, which is a rarity. And that's what he was doing in the car on the way to the house.

He also doesn't bother to segue on these occasions. 'The connections are somewhat confusing,' he said out of nowhere, but I was ready for it.

'Which connections? Between Ken Warshofsky and Pete Lucchesi?'

'That is the most obvious one, yes.'

I love it when Patrick drives because I don't have to pretend I'm trying to learn the streets of the city in which I live. He just drives and I notice landmarks that I will unquestionably forget within an hour. 'Well, Pete and Ken both worked at ImagiNails at one point. They had a common point of intersection at Jack Schoenberg.'

'I'm aware Pete knew Jack from his days at the firm and Jack knew Ken from the supposed marriage to Lisa Conforto. By the way, why did they pretend to be married?'

'Lisa has stopped covering for everybody, but she did tell me, once Trench and Valdez weren't around, that Ken had offered her some of his ImagiNails stock if she'd provide an alibi for the night Helene was shot. Jack really did show up at her house that night to discuss this biodegradable craft services business plan of his, but Ken wasn't there. Jack didn't know to say that Ken wasn't there because nobody was asking about Ken.'

'Why hasn't Lisa been charged, then?'

'She gave me a dollar so she's my client and I can't divulge that kind of information,' I told him. Lisa wasn't bright and had covered up a murder, so I'd gone through some soul-searching about it, but putting her in jail wasn't going to protect the public from anything. You make decisions.

'Did Ken shoot Helene in the music room?'

'As it turns out, no.' Ken wasn't exactly unloading his conscience, especially now that his lawyer had arrived to tell him to shut up, but what Riley had told Trench about how the room looked when she climbed into it and then erased the image she'd found was enough for the lieutenant to piece it together. He'd also gotten information from Lisa, Jack and – of all people – Alicia, who had known her sister wasn't in her house that night. 'The overwhelming odds are that Ken confronted Helene at a board meeting and Helene told him she was going to stop production and the IPO on ImagiNails until the formula could fully deliver what the company had promised.

'The meeting was at a restaurant on Wilshire and all the board members remember Ken and Helene walking out together.' I knew this from Trench. Valdez still didn't want to talk to me much but she wasn't a bad cop. She was just hard to warm up to. 'Nobody thought anything about it afterward, because Helene was found in her house and the gun was in her husband's bureau. But it's probable he killed Helene in the parking lot and drove her to the house in the trunk of his car.'

'Can't they check the car for blood and evidence?' Patrick asked. 'Even after all this time there might be traces.'

'Ken donated the car to a charity a week later. They sold it to a company that clears vehicles and it's probably in Montana right now. I'm sure Valdez is putting in a search for it so she can use anything they find at the next trial. Ken's trial.'

Patrick pulled the car over to the side and parked it, which was odd because we were still about a hundred yards from the front door. 'I want to explain about the teal house,' he said. 'We haven't had the time.'

'You don't have to explain,' I told him, despite wanting that explanation very badly. I had believed I'd fallen in love with the teal house, which I liked because it wasn't a mansion, and Patrick had apparently hated it from the beginning. 'We agreed that if one of us didn't like a place, we wouldn't buy it.'

He bit his lower lip. 'Sandy, you remember that my father left us when I was young.'

'Yes, and he remarried and had your sister Cynthia.'

Patrick nodded. 'When he left, my mother was distraught and not thinking clearly. She fell in with a man she thought she loved and we moved in with him. But the relationship bordered on abusive. Through my bedroom wall I could hear the arguing and my mother crying. I hated that place, and we were only there three months before my mother ended it and we moved out.'

I looked at him for a long moment. 'I'm so sorry for you, Patrick.' I reached out my hand and touched his face and he smiled sadly.

'The walls in that bedroom were painted exactly the same shade of teal as that house,' Patrick said. 'I still have a reaction to it that I didn't realize until I saw it. I wanted to like it because you did, but the memories would have been destructive, I think.'

It took me a moment to absorb what he was telling me. 'We could have painted the house another color,' I said.

'Yes, we could. But we'd already started calling it the teal house, and the memory of it would have stayed in my mind.'

Actors are nuts.

Still, I got where he was coming from. 'It's fine,' I said. 'Let's go see this place because there aren't any bad memories here, right?'

Patrick laughed. 'Of course not.' He started the car again.

'Besides, who paints a boy's bedroom that shade of teal?'

'I know!' Patrick was smiling. That had been hard for him but I was glad he'd shared it with me.

We pulled up to the house I'd toured with T'Aisha and Emily Webster once before. Patrick stopped at the entrance and gave it a good look. 'You sure you're interested in this place?' he asked. 'Two women died here, and you discovered one of them.' Because apparently he thought I might have forgotten.

'One woman died here. The other was brought in after. And yes, I can separate the case from the house. I think it's a really good fit for both of us, but you know the drill.'

He smiled. 'Yes. If I don't like it I have to say so.'

'Yes, you do.'

He kissed me very tenderly. 'I promise,' he said.

FORTY-TWO

'I'm not moving out for a couple of months. There's no reason to pack.'

Angie stood in the living room of what was still our apartment but would (relatively) soon be just hers, arms crossed on her chest and a pile of flattened-out carboard boxes at her feet. A large pile.

'Patrick said you bought the house, the one with the dead lady in it,' she said.

I let out a breath. 'First of all, the dead lady hasn't been there for weeks and the place has been professionally sanitized by a crime scene cleaning service. And I'm having the doors removed from the music room. But the real point is that's the right house for Patrick and me. And the real *real* point is that it'll take at least eight weeks until the papers are ready to be signed and all the searches and deeds and whatever have been taken care of, *plus* painting and repairs and moving in the furniture, so I'm not moving out so quick, Ang.'

She looked at me a moment. 'Searches and deeds and whatever?'

'I'm not a real-estate lawyer.'

'Well, I'm keeping the boxes here. You can fill them up when you want to.' She sat down on the sofa, which was not coming with me to the new house, and looked a little sad. 'You're not going to live here anymore, Sandy.'

I sat next to her. 'I know. But I'll still see you all the time. And you'll still be working with Patrick.'

Angie's eyes widened. 'I know! He keeps promoting me. Now I'm the management executive for Dunwoody Productions.'

I had known before she did, but played along. 'What does that mean, exactly?' I asked.

'How would I know? And because you told him to give me a raise, he *doubled my salary* so I can afford to keep this place.'

'It wasn't because of me. It's because you're really good at what you do.' I gave Angie a hug. 'This wasn't what I was expecting when I moved out here.'

She laughed. 'It wasn't what I was expecting when I came out to keep you alive for a couple of weeks.'

My phone rang at that point so I looked down at it. 'I've got to take this one,' I said. Angie nodded. I got up and walked into my bedroom. Not that Angie wasn't welcome to say hello, but this was always a special conversation for me. She could join in later if she wanted.

'I read about that whole kidnapping thing online. Are you sure you're all right?'

I nodded because this was a FaceTime call and he was looking right at me. 'I'm fine, Dad. You can see I'm fine. How about you? Are you taking your meds?'

My father chuckled. 'I'm not having another heart attack, Sandy. Yes, I'm taking my meds, I'm exercising and I'm watching what I eat. Believe it or not, in the past twenty-five years it's gotten to be something of a habit.'

'Good.' Say what you want, a girl can look out for her father if she has to. Ask Riley.

'I'm even having sex every once in a while.' My father treats me uncomfortably like a friend on occasion, just because he knows it gets to me. 'Great for the cardiovascular system.'

'Dad!' See?

Another light laugh. 'Just wanted to see if I could still shock you, sweetie.'

'Lana's still with you?' I asked. I mean, the comment about sex sort of opened that door for me to discuss my dad's girlfriend of the past seven years.

'Yeah, she hasn't caught on to me yet. How about you and Patrick?'

I told him about the house and asked if he'd come out to see it once we'd settled in. My father said he would, but sounded hesitant.

'Don't worry,' I said. 'I won't invite Mom at the same time you're going to be here.'

'Don't dis your mother, Sandy.' He was still my dad. 'It just gets awkward, you know.'

'I know.' Divorces are never easy, and even if my parents'

wasn't as acrimonious as a lot I'd worked on since I'd joined Seaton, Taylor, it was not without some hurt feelings on both sides, no doubt well earned. Unlike some divorcing couples, they had mercifully kept me out of it. The fact that I was already in my twenties had helped.

'I'm glad you like it out there,' my father said. 'Sounds like you've carved out quite a life.'

'Go figure,' I said.

CAST OF CHARACTERS

Sandy Moss: a lawyer in Los Angeles transplanted from New Jersey

Angie: Sandy's best friend from Jersey, who came out to LA to visit and stayed

Patrick McNabb: Famous TV actor whom Sandy defended successfully in a murder trial

Detective Lieutenant K.C. Trench: LAPD homicide detective

Nate Garrigan: An investigator sometimes employed by Sandy's law firm

Riley Schoenberg: Sandy's client, eleven years old

Holiday Wentworth: Sandy's immediate superior at the firm

Emily Webster: real-estate agent and Patrick's former fiancée

Jon Irvin: Sandy's associate

Jack Schoenberg: Riley's dad and convicted murderer of her mother

Lisa Conforto: associate of Jack and Helene

Helene Nestor: Riley's deceased mother

Peter Lucchesi: 'Uncle Pete' to Sandy, associate of Jack

Jason Kemper: business associate of Helene's

Lieutenant Luciana Valdez: homicide cop who is not Lieutenant Trench

Judge Lamont DeForge: first trial judge

Judge Henry Drummond: presiding over Jack's case

Aaron Judge: outfielder for the New York Yankees, not appearing in this book

T'Aisha Kendall: *LA Times* reporter

Albert Fleischer: assistant district attorney

Cagney Weldon IV: Jack's former attorney

Ken Warshofsky: Lisa Conforto's 'friend'

Alicia Nestor Jennings: Helene's sister and Riley's aunt

Nathalie Morrison: ex-girlfriend of Pete Lucchesi

Judy: bodyguard from a security service

AUTHOR'S NOTE

At the risk of repeating myself (again!): No work of entertainment is achieved by one person alone. Even an artist at a canvas must find an exhibitor or you won't ever be able to see their work. So despite the fact that a writer sits at a keyboard in a room alone and types the words that seem to fit the story, there exists a team of people who brought this book to your eyes.

I apologize to those who actually read authors' notes religiously (or secularly) but you're about to see many of the same names you've seen here before. First and foremost I am grateful to Josh Getzler and the gang at HG Literary for making sure the good folks at Severn House knew this series could exist and made it happen. Sandy Moss spent a number of years wondering if her story would be told and it was our friends at HG Literary and Severn House (particularly Rachel Slatter, Natasha Bell and Penny Isaac), who not only publish this book but help make sure it's coherent.

These have not been easy times, but I am among the most lucky, and that's largely thanks to Jessica, Josh and Eve, who keep me sane (on a relative basis) and give me three wonderful reasons to keep going. I don't know what I did to deserve you, but I try ever day to justify my place with you.

At the end of the day (although it's only 3:38 in the afternoon) it's the readers who matter, because without you, there would be no reason for Sandy to keep getting herself into and out of trouble. Your trust in me is never taken for granted and your communication (when I hear from you) is always appreciated. (On the other hand, if you hated the book, feel free not to let me know. I don't want to trouble you.)

Thanks to the librarians, the bookstore owners and clerks, the reviewers (most of the reviewers) and everyone who so much as picked this book up and looked at it. Those who designed the cover, printed the words and got the word out, on both sides of the Atlantic, are greatly appreciated.

I promise: You keep reading and I'll keep writing.

E.J. Copperman
Deepest New Jersey
June, 2022

Milton Keynes UK
Ingram Content Group UK Ltd.
UKHW011847240124
436635UK00005B/392